Praise for
Just a Cowboy and His Baby

"I love my cowboys and there are none better than Carolyn Brown's."

—*Fresh Fiction*

"Brown provides an up close and personal look at the rodeo arena, with exciting action scenes written in her vivid, you-feel-like-you're-right-there style."

—*USA Today Happy Ever After*

"Another great read by Carolyn Brown… you feel the sizzle… these two are steaming hot whether they are fighting or giving in."

—*Night Owl Reviews* Reviewer Top Pick, 4.5 Stars

"Brown's writing holds you spellbound as you slip into the world of tantalizing cowboys and love of family, with a lot of fun added in for good measure."

—*Thoughts in Progress*

"I know when I read a book by Carolyn Brown, I'm in for a treat."

—*Long and Short Reviews*

"I can't turn down Carolyn Brown's cowboys. They're as addictive as Janet Evanovich's Ranger."

—*Drey's Library*

"…tty, adrenaline-packed contemporary romance that …n one sitting, unable to put it down."

—*Romance Junkies*

Praise for *One Hot Cowboy Wedding*

"Funny, frank, and full of heart… One more welcome example of Brown's Texas-size talent for storytelling."

—*USA Today Happy Ever After*

"Alive with humor… Another page-turning joy of a book by an engaging author."

—*Fresh Fiction*

"Will make readers laugh along with the large and colorful cast of characters… The couple's relationship is hot as the Texas sun.

—*RT Book Reviews*, 4 Stars

"Sizzling hot and absolutely delectable… Brimming with humor, a sweet talking cowboy, a feisty city girl, steamy passion, romance, and loads of love."

—*Romance Junkies*

"Classic characters, a dash of spice, and a healthy addition of Southern twang. It's a winner."

—*Long and Short Reviews*

"Delightfully fresh and unique… Brown's writing has such a down-home country feel that you will feel like you are right in the heart of Texas."

—*Book Reviews and More by Kath*

Praise for Carolyn Brown's Christmas Cowboy Romances

"Sassy and quirky and peopled with an abundance of engaging characters, this fast-paced holiday romp brims with music, laughter… and plenty of Texas flavor."

—*Library Journal*

"A sweet romance that really stresses the chemistry that builds between two highly likable characters… Readers will enjoy this cozy bright contemporary romance."

—*RT Book Reviews*, 4 Stars

"Carolyn Brown is a master storyteller! A love between two people that will enrapture and capture your heart."

—*Wendy's Minding Spot*

"Sassy contemporary romance… with all the local color and humorous repartee her fans adore."

—*Booklist*

"Full of sizzling chemistry and razor-sharp dialogue."

—*Night Owl Reviews* Reviewer Top Pick, 4.5 Stars

"This book makes me believe in Christmas miracles and long slow kisses under the mistletoe."

—*The Romance Studio*

"Carolyn Brown creates some handsomefied, hunkified, HOT cowboys! A fun, enjoyable four-star-Christmas-to-remember novel."

—*The Romance Reviews*

Also by Carolyn Brown

Lucky in Love

One Lucky Cowboy

Getting Lucky

I Love This Bar

Hell, Yeah

My Give a Damn's Busted

Honky Tonk Christmas

Love Drunk Cowboy

Red's Hot Cowboy

Darn Good Cowboy Christmas

One Hot Cowboy Wedding

Mistletoe Cowboy

Just a Cowboy and His Baby

Women's Fiction

The Blue-Ribbon Jalapeño Society Jubilee

Billion Dollar Cowboy

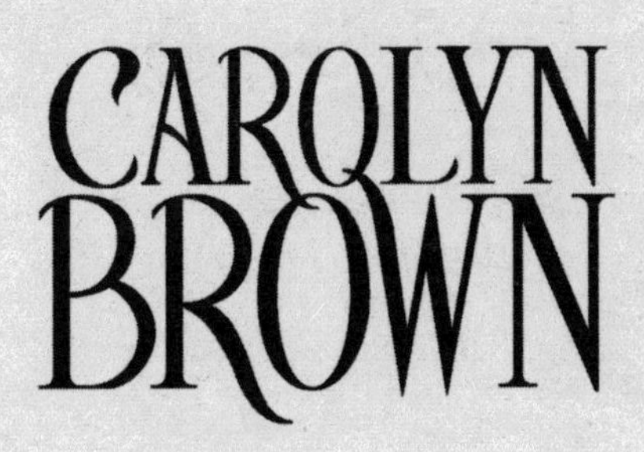

Cover design by Blake Morrow/Shannon Associates

Published by Sourcebooks Casablanca, an imprint of Sourcebooks, Inc.
P.O. Box 4410, Naperville, Illinois 60567-4410
(630) 961-3900
FAX: (630) 961-2168
www.sourcebooks.com

Printed and bound in Canada
WC 10 9 8 7 6 5 4 3 2 1

To Patti G. Russell

DNA makes us sisters; hearts make us friends.

The day our parents brought you home from the hospital, I cried. I thought they'd gone to get me a kitten and all they brought home was another baby. Today I'm really glad that they brought me a sister… don't know how I'd have made it through all the sorrows and joys without you!

Chapter 1

It was just supper, for God's sake; it wasn't an inquisition. They weren't going to take her out in the yard and stone her to death if she ate with the wrong fork. Andy had said they were just like family, and since she was his assistant she should meet them, but she didn't want to get all friendly with the "family." She just wanted to work off her debt and get out of Ambrose, Texas. She'd managed to avoid most of them for a whole week and thought she could do so for months, but oh, no, Andy decided it was time for her to break bread with them that very evening.

Laura sat up straighter in the chair and pushed her glasses up on her nose. She hated going back to glasses after years and years of wearing contacts. She could wear her contacts on special occasions, but not more than a couple of hours. Tonight didn't qualify for that in her opinion.

"We are glad that you came to supper, Laura," Maudie said.

Maudie was tall, thin, with salt-and-pepper hair, and not nearly enough wrinkles to be Colton's grandmother. She'd never be worth a damn in a poker game because Laura could easily read her through her green eyes. She'd popped in and out of the office at least once a day, so Laura had met her, but saying a brief hello and sitting at the supper table with her were two different things.

Laura's smile was strained at best. "Thank you."

Andy clapped his hands once. Conversation stopped and all eyes were on Laura. She sincerely thought about crawling under the table and hiding, but she refused to let anyone intimidate her. Not even the people who lived in a house so big that it took her breath away when she first saw it. It had turrets and wings and tall windows, a deep wraparound porch, and would put Tara from *Gone with the Wind* to absolute shame.

"Introductions!" Andy said with a sweep of his hand. "Maudie is the only one who has met Laura, who has been getting settled into the apartment and the job this week. As you all know, she is my distant cousin so I've known her since we were both kids."

Laura nodded at Maudie even though saying hello from behind a desk and computer was far different than knowing them.

"And," Andy went on, "that feller over there with the platter of steaks in his hand is Rusty. He's the ranch foreman and the person who knows what's going on in any corner of the ranch. The kid beside him is Roxie, our new resident teenager."

Rusty smiled. "I'd begun to think you were just a figment of Andy's imagination or that he'd hired a robot. Welcome to the ranch. If I can help you with anything, you just holler. The apartment suiting you all right?"

"Yes, sir. It's great," she said.

Roxie looked up and Laura's heart went out to her. There was something in her blue eyes that said she wasn't real sure of her place in the world or where she'd fit in if she figured out that she even had a place.

"Hello," Roxie said in a soft Southern drawl.

Laura saw herself at sixteen when someone new came to dinner at Aunt Dotty's ranch. Trying to remember her manners and not talking too much, but being friendly. It was an awkward age at best. Andy had already mentioned that Roxie had just recently come to the ranch on a full-time basis and was more than a little bit shy.

Andy pointed in the opposite direction. "The cowboy at the head of the table that looks like shit is Colton."

"Thanks a lot, Andy, for telling your kin that I don't run my own ranch and that I look like shit. He's a real good best friend, Laura. I want to thank you for taking on the job of working with Andy. It can't be easy as picky as he is about everything," Colton growled.

"I'm pretty much a perfectionist too. It must run in the family," Laura answered.

Andy picked up a basket of hot rolls and passed it to Rusty. "Laura is a whiz kid on computers, so she's kept her nose to the grindstone this week. We're catching up, though, so you'll see more of her from now on. I had to twist her arm to get her to come to supper. She's never been shy before, so I don't know what her problem is."

Roxie caught her eye and smiled. The girl had blond hair pulled up in a ponytail, crystal clear blue eyes, and a flawless complexion. She was so tiny that she looked fragile, but Laura would guess there was a tough interior hiding inside her soul that would surface in a hurry if someone pushed her too hard.

"What's the matter with you, Colton? You look like you've got a hangover. You never pass up hot rolls. Are you sick?" Maudie looked genuinely worried.

Colton passed the green beans on to Rusty. "I think I was drugged last night."

Laura glanced toward the end of the table. She'd seen Colton from her second-story window several times and with his swagger, boots, and hat, she'd thought he was handsome. Sitting at the table with him proved that he went beyond handsome even with the slightly green cast around his mouth and bloodshot eyes. Biceps stretched at his shirt sleeves that had been rolled up to just above his elbows. His dark brown hair was feathered back away from his face in a perfect cut. His light green eyes left no doubt that he had the mother of all hangovers. Before he'd settled into his place at the table, she'd seen the way he filled out those jeans and she could well understand the problems he'd have with the women even if he was just a poor dirt farmer. Add a bank account that would stagger Fort Knox and it was no wonder that the man was the most sought after bachelor in all of northern Texas.

"Good thing I was there," Rusty said seriously.

Colton nodded. "No telling where I'd be today if you hadn't hauled me home, but dammit! I hate needing a babysitter everywhere I go. Why do women act like that?"

"I'm not your babysitter. I'm your bodyguard," Rusty said.

"Money! That's why women act like that. You don't remember one bit of it, do you?" Maudie asked.

"I remember drinking one beer and looking out over the crowd. Then I ordered another one and didn't even finish it," Colton said. "I'm going up to my room. Maybe later I'll make some toast or feel like having a milkshake. Right now my head hurts too bad to even chew. Nice meeting you, Laura. I'm real glad that Andy hired you. Now maybe he'll stop whining like a little girl about how much work he has to do."

Laura looked up from her plate and pushed her glasses up again. "Thank you. It's a pleasure to meet you. Sorry that you don't feel so good."

Maudie looked at Rusty. "Two beers? Really?"

He shrugged. "We hadn't been there thirty minutes so he's probably telling the truth. A tall blonde and a brunette sat down on the bar stools, one on either side of him. She was sneaky about it so I could never prove it, but I do think the blonde put it in his drink while the brunette distracted him."

Maudie shook her head slowly from side to side when Colton was out of the room. "Now they are drugging him? What are we going to do? One of them is bound to kill him if we don't think of something."

Andy laid his fork and knife down and sipped sweet tea. "Money sure brings out the monsters."

Laura knew a little about the money and the monsters, but from the other side of the fence. She wouldn't be sitting at the table with Andy that evening if she didn't, but she did feel sorry for Colton. Andy had told her that the poor man hadn't had a normal life since he'd gotten rich and that things went from bad to worse every day.

Rusty nodded seriously. He was Andy's opposite. Where Andy was medium height, overweight, and barely thirty with a full head of curly blond hair and pale blue eyes, Rusty was tall and lanky, had graying hair, and brown eyes set in a face with a ready smile and enough wrinkles to testify to lots of experience.

"I barely got him in the house and on the sofa in the den. I pulled his boots off and threw a cover over him.

That the way you found him this morning, Maudie?" Rusty asked.

She shook her head. "He was in his room, passed out on top of his covers. I tried to wake him for breakfast, but it didn't work. Must've been something powerful that the woman dosed him with. He's strong as a bull."

Laura had been hired to help Andy in the office, not to sit at the table and hear all about the family's problems. So the rich cowboy had major issues with the women wanting to lasso him. She had problems with a sister who wouldn't or couldn't fight her addiction to gambling. Everyone had their own sad tale of woe, but she didn't have the time or energy to get involved in Colton's.

"He'll live. Enough about our family problems. Laura, please join us for any meals that you want. We want you to feel right at home here on the ranch." Maudie looked across the table at her.

"Thank you." Laura squirmed in her seat. She damn sure didn't plan on eating three meals a day in the big house.

"And what did you do before Andy hired you?" Rusty asked.

"I worked at a greenhouse in Amarillo. The owner sold it and the new owners brought in their own staff. So, Roxie, what grade are you in?" Laura deliberately turned the conversation in a different direction.

"I'll be a junior this fall," she said.

"She's in summer school to make up classes she missed when she skipped school," Andy said.

Roxie looked at her plate. The gesture reminded her so much of her sister, Janet, that it shot a pang of homesickness through Laura's heart.

"And what are you going to be when you grow up?" Laura asked.

Roxie raised her eyes. "A fashion designer or an interior decorator."

"That takes college and to go you've got to have good grades in school," Laura said.

"What you ought to do is take lots of computer classes and go to work for the ranch. You're really good with technology," Andy said.

Roxie gave him a shy smile. "That's what Dillon says. Maybe I will change my mind, but right now I just want out of Ambrose. I want to go where nobody knows me."

Laura had felt the same about Claude, Texas, and there had been two summers that she had to do makeup work at school. Not for skipping classes but for being too shy in those days to raise her hand to answer questions. Janet was the one who had to attend summer school for skipping, and Aunt Dotty had given her extra chores as punishment.

They talked about crops, church, and Roxie's class schedule, but Laura only listened with one ear. She wondered what Janet was doing that evening. It had been a whole week since they'd hugged and said their good-byes. It would be a long time before they saw each other or even had phone privileges again. If only she'd had another way to get the money to bail Janet out one more time, but she'd had no other recourse than biting the bullet and going to Andy. She just hoped that Janet was holding up her end of the bargain.

At first she was angry at Andy for laying down such rules. She and Janet were sisters and adults. He didn't have to be such a hard-ass about loaning her the money, but the more she'd thought about it that week, the more she realized that he was a genius. Janet would never stop gambling if she could run to Laura every time she got into trouble.

Andy's rules had been simple. Number one: they could have no contact, not even phone, emails, or texting until the debt was paid in full. Number two: they could not see each other until the debt was paid in full. Number three: Janet had to stay out of casinos, bingo halls, anything that had to do with gambling, and she had to go to Gambler's Anonymous twice a week.

Laura shook the rules from her mind and pushed back her chair. "It's been a pleasure meeting you all. Thank you for supper. I'll be getting back to the office now to finish up the day's work."

"We are glad to have you here on the ranch. Feel free to take any of your meals with us. There's buffet breakfast and lunch and we sit around the table at supper." Maudie waved her away with a flick of her wrist.

"Thank you," Laura said, but she sure did not intend to eat three meals a day with the family. No sir!

"Don't let Andy chain you to the computer in that office," Rusty said.

"I'm sure I'll be out and around more often as soon as we get caught up," Laura said.

She escaped across the foyer and down the hallway to the small office that she shared with Andy Joe. She flopped down into her office chair, leaned back, laid her glasses on her lap, and pressed her thumbs into her temples. Thank God for Andy and his offer to come to her rescue, but she'd be damned if she made that supper thing a nightly affair. A tuna fish sandwich with peace surrounding her was a lot better than all those eyes on her.

"Hey." Andy poked his head into the room.

She sat up so quickly that the room did a couple of spins before she got it all under control. "I was just resting my eyes for a minute."

"It's been a long day, Laura. We'll finish up those reports tomorrow morning. We're trying to figure out some things in the dining room. You missed dessert so I brought you a slice of pecan pie."

"Thank you. Maybe I'll get a run in tonight before I go to bed," she said.

"If you get lost in the big town of Ambrose, call me and I'll come get you. Believe me, Claude is a metropolis compared to Ambrose." He grinned. He turned off the lights and set the pie on the fax machine. "See you tomorrow morning."

She stuck her glasses on top of her head, ate every bite of the pie, and headed back toward the kitchen to put the dirty plate away. She could hear the soft drone of voices floating down the hall and stopped in her tracks when she heard her name. She tiptoed closer to the open dining room door and plastered her body against the wall.

"That's crazy. She'll never do it," Rusty said. "And neither will Colton."

"How do you know? We could at least ask them," Maudie said.

"I vote that we don't ask. We just orchestrate it and see what happens," Andy said.

"I think it's mean," Roxie said.

Laura was amazed that the girl spoke up, but what in

the devil were they talking about. It had to do with her and Colton and something they'd both never go for… but what?

Rusty's deep voice carried better than Roxie's when he said, "She will pitch a fit when she finds out. You might be her cousin, but you'll be in big trouble, Andy. She don't fool me one bit hiding behind those glasses. She's a fighter."

"Yes, she is. She's always had to be, but I can handle it," Andy said.

"It sounds like a good plan, and the only way it will work is if you blindside them with it," Rusty answered.

"I vote we at least give it a try. Raise your hand if you are with me," Andy said.

She couldn't see the vote but rustling said that they had cast their vote and were on their way out of the dining room. She hurried down the foyer and out the back door before she got caught eavesdropping.

"Damn!" she whispered as she climbed the steps to her apartment. They were up to something that involved her and Colton together and she'd sure like to know what it was before it happened.

Her apartment was the upper floor of the old carriage house that now garaged three of the family's pickup trucks. The sun hung above the treetops like it didn't know whether it wanted to set that night or just look at the world a while longer. Laura looked at the clock when she opened the door. If she hurried, she could get in a run before dusk.

In Amarillo, Laura had a schedule that included running three times a week in addition to the exercise she got at the greenhouse. And she didn't eat three huge meals a day. Breakfast was usually yogurt in the middle of the morning, dinner was a salad or a sandwich that she brought from home, and supper was one of those lean frozen dinners that she popped into the microwave.

She changed into her favorite old gray sweat suit, put on her running shoes, and did a few stretches in her room. The night air was pleasant, not too hot for the first week in June, which could be getting close to triple digits hot. She'd started to work for Andy on Saturday morning, the first day of June, and now it was a full week later. The sun dipped behind the tall pecan trees lining the lane as she took off in an easy warm-up trot on the gravel road. By the time she reached the road leading into Ambrose, she had built up a good speed. She didn't see anyone, not until she reached the T in the road and turned north into Ambrose. Then a rusted-out old pickup slowed down behind her. The driver honked, stuck his hand out the window, and waved as he went on by.

Calling Ambrose a town was a far stretch of the imagination. It had a population of less than a hundred people, and the post office had long since been shut down. Now the mail came out of Bells on a rural route. The old school was the color of the formations at the bottom of the Palo Duro Canyon not far from Amarillo and was now a community center. The yard looked unkempt and she visualized a few lantana plants and iris bulbs along with some coleus set back in the corners to perk it up.

She was about to rest a minute on the community center porch when she noticed the church off to her left. It looked far more inviting with its deep shade and freshly mowed yard. Surely God wouldn't mind if she caught her breath before she ran back to the ranch. The roses were lovely, the sweet williams were thick and luxurious, and the hedges had been clipped, and the smell of fresh clipped grass filled the evening air. She sat down on the porch steps, leaned forward, and put her head on her knees.

She'd barely taken three good long breaths when the church doors creaked open. Her first thought was that whoever took care of the yard should spray some oil on the hinges. Then she looked up to see a short man in faded jeans, a red bandana rolled up and tied around his forehead, and a big smile on his face.

"Hello. You lost or out for exercise?" His big booming voice sounded like it should have come from a six-foot cowboy like Colton, not a yard man for the church.

"Exercise," she gasped.

He sat down beside her. "I'm Roger Green, the preacher here at this church. Don't think I've seen you around. Are you new to Ambrose?"

Running in heat must have killed the brain cells that pertained to sight and hearing. The man said he was a preacher? Preachers did not wear sweat rags made from bandanas, and they didn't wear faded jeans and a red knit shirt with a hole in the sleeve.

"I'm Laura Baker. I work at the Circle 6," she said.

"Well, I'm pleased to make your acquaintance. Expect you'll be in church tomorrow morning with the family?"

Laura didn't want to lie and say that she'd be sitting on the family pew the next morning, but she wouldn't make a promise that she had no intention of keeping. "I'm not sure," she hedged as she stood up and stretched.

"Sorry to rush but got to get back to the ranch before it gets dark."

"I'll look forward to seeing all y'all tomorrow." His voice rang out behind her as she sped away.

Church!

Damn!

Did Andy go every single week?

Andy said that since she'd be on a ranch she could wear her jeans and boots. She had brought three or four sundresses for days when jeans and boots were too hot to wear to work, but they weren't church clothing. Aunt Dotty had always insisted that she and Janet be dressed proper on Sunday morning and that meant sleeves, panty hose, and closed-toed shoes.

She was still worrying about what to wear when she turned the corner into the lane and slowed down to a fast trot to the house. She'd barely sat down on the top porch step to cool off when Colton came out of the house and sat down in the swing.

"Looks like you've been running. So what did you think of Ambrose?" he asked.

"What makes you think I ran into town? And I thought you were sick."

"Preacher called. Said he met you and invited you to come to church with us tomorrow morning. And I'm feeling better."

"Damn!" Her most overworked swear word slipped out slicker than boiled okra.

"Does that mean no?"

"It means I didn't bring things for church. I just packed working clothes for the most part."

"You got a dress?"

"Couple of sundresses."

"What's it look like?"

"It's blue and it doesn't have sleeves and it only comes to my knee."

"Sounds fine to me. Wear it and you'll look great or wear jeans and boots," Colton said.

She looked over at him. "You must be feeling better."

"I am, but the thought of heavy food gags me. I'm thinking a snow cone might taste good. You want one?"

He was just being nice, but a rainbow snow cone did sound wonderful. "How far is it to get one?"

"Seven miles over to Bells. They've got a place that makes wonderful snow cones. You look hot and I'm ready to put something in my stomach. You might as well ride over with me."

"Okay," she said slowly. Was this part of what the family was talking about in the dining room? Had they already let him in on the proposition and now it was just a matter of being nice to her so that she'd get on board? There was only one way to find out.

Bells is six miles south of Ambrose on a little two-lane farm road. Colton could easily get there in less than ten minutes, but he poked along at forty-five miles an hour. Laura wore the same jeans and shirt she'd had on at supper. She had changed from boots to running shoes and had rolled the legs of her jeans up to right under her knees. Even with the glasses and the bandana tying all that blond hair back, she was still attractive in a hauntingly cute way. She reminded him of someone but he could not put his finger on it. Maybe it was a woman he'd seen in a bar.

He bit back a groan. Could she be running her own scam on him?

Andy said that she was his cousin and that she needed a job and a loan to get her sister out of gambling debt. She had worked in a greenhouse for eight years but got laid off when it sold; however, she was an expert computer geek just like him. Andy would never lie to him, not in a million years. They'd been friends since day one of kindergarten and Colton would trust Andy with his life. The cousin, not so much! At least not until she proved that she wasn't pulling the wool over his eyes and poor old Andy's!

"Look!" His forefinger grazed her breast when he reached across to point out a big buck and his harem of half a dozen does just over the pasture fence.

Heat shot from the tip of his finger through his entire hand. He slapped it back on the steering wheel. It didn't look like he'd held it over an open campfire, but it damn sure felt like it. He'd been without a woman far too long, but hell's bells, trusting didn't come easy even for a casual relationship.

"Wow!" she mumbled.

She pointed up at a flock of ducks coming in for a landing on a farm pond. "They are so graceful. Janet says I was born with no grace at all."

"Whoever Janet is, don't believe her. You are very graceful," he said.

"Janet is my sister," she said tightly. "Yeah, right! I'm a nerd. I know it. I accept it."

He changed the subject. "So you have a sister, you worked at a greenhouse, and you like snow cones?"

She continued to look up at the last of the ducks floating down from the sky to the pond.

"Yes, to all of the above."

"Let's play the old twenty questions," he said. "I'll ask five and then you can ask five. That way I'll get to know who my best friend in the world has hired and you can get to know your boss."

Her brows knit together and a veil dropped over her clear blue eyes.

"I thought Andy was my boss. And besides, it takes too long to play twenty questions so let's just play five questions."

"He is your immediate supervisor. I'm your boss," Colton said.

Why didn't she want to answer simple questions? What was she hiding anyway?

He looked across the cab of the truck at her. "Hey, it's not bare-thy-soul confession time. Just answer with the first thing that comes to mind. Favorite flower?"

"Daisies."

"See? That wasn't so hard. Favorite food?" he asked.

She smiled and the tension between them eased. "Breakfast. Love pancakes, eggs, gravy, sausage, biscuits, bagels, all of it."

He grinned. "Three more and then it's your turn. Favorite color?"

She asked, "For what? My favorite color is different for painting my living room than it is for what I would buy to wear or what I like in nature."

"Nature, then," he said.

"Emerald green."

"Why?"

"Because three years ago my sister and I drove to Florida and spent two days on the beach and that's what color the water was. It reminds me of peace and eternity."

She sounded as wistful as a child with no money standing in front of the snow cone stand.

"Eternity?" he asked.

"Yes, and that's your fourth question." She nodded. "I sat on the beach and looked out across the water and there was nothing but water and sky. I felt like God lived way out there where the emerald green water met the sky. Your eyes are the color of that water, Colton."

"Is that a compliment?"

"Number five, and yes it is. My turn. I already know that your favorite food is steak, so I don't have to ask that."

"It is not! It's pizza."

She giggled.

He slapped the steering wheel. "That was sneaky."

"I didn't ask, so I still have five, but since I did trick you, you can have one more."

"So what is your sister's name?"

"Janet Elizabeth Baker."

"Is she as pretty as you?"

"That's question six, but I'll answer it. Janet is much prettier than I am. Now it's my turn for real. Do you pout when you don't get what you want?"

He fought the urge to step on the brakes and ask her what kind of question was that anyway. Instead he thought about it and said, "No, I'm not the pouting type."

"Did you have serious relationships before you got rich?"

Mercy! She was skipping the small stuff and getting right into the heart of the matter.

"A couple," he answered softly.

"If you could go back and not buy a ranch but travel and enjoy life with your money, would you?"

He shook his head. "No, I'm doing exactly what I want to do. I wouldn't change any of it, except maybe this problem I've got with women."

"Well, you are sexy and you are a billionaire. That comes with the territory. Now what is it about ranching that you like?"

"All of it! I like plowing and cows and the smell of hay. I like finding a litter of kittens snuggled down in the hay barn. I like new baby calves and all four seasons on the ranch. So you think I'm sexy?"

She pointed. "There is the Bells sign. We are here and that was only four questions so I get another one sometime in the future. Right now I want to eat my first snow cone of the year and think about nothing but how good it tastes. And Colton, I may wear thick glasses, but I'm not blind."

She'd popped those questions off so fast he scarcely had time to think. If they'd been playing poker instead of twenty questions she would have taken him straight to the cleaners.

He pulled up to the drive-by window on the side of the small snow cone stand and studied the list of flavors. "See something that you like?"

"I want a rainbow with cherry, banana, and grape," she said without looking at the menu.

If there was a doubt in his mind that she was about to fleece him and Andy both, it disappeared when she ordered the snow cone.

"How did you know that?" He narrowed his eyes at her.

She leaned across the seat and looked at the chart. "Know what? It's what I always order. Don't they have those flavors?"

"I heard the lady, and for you?" the teenager asked from the other side of the window.

"The same," he said.

"You are kidding, right?" Laura said.

"I swear it's what I always get. Cherry on one side, grape on the other, and a thin strip of banana in the middle."

He was onto her and she wouldn't get away with it. She and her sister had cooked up something and dragged poor old Andy into the middle of it. There was no better way to get suckered into a first-class con than inviting it to come live in the house.

"So where to now?" he asked.

"To the school yard to eat them while we swing," she said.

Yes, sir, that girl had done her homework.

Laura was cute as a bug's ear and as unimposing as a child with those thick glasses and her big blue eyes, but there was no way that it was coincidence that she ate the same flavor snow cone as he did or that she liked to sit on the school yard swings while she did.

He drove to the elementary school and parked in the lot beside the playground, got out of the truck, and was rounding the backside of it when she opened her own door. She slurped up a mouthful of cherry syrup from the side of the cone-shaped paper cup and headed toward the swings.

Her lips and tongue were stained bright red from the cherry syrup. Colton kept stealing glances toward her full mouth after they'd sat down on the swings. Would they be warm and inviting or cold as the snow cone?

"I love rainbow snow cones even better than ice cream, and I really, really love homemade banana ice cream," she said.

"Aha, and I didn't even ask what your favorite dessert is."

"That's not my favorite dessert. It's just something I like."

"I'd ask you the question, but then you'd want to ask one, right?"

She nodded. "Tit for tat."

"So you worked on a ranch, did you?"

"I lived on one until I was eighteen," she answered. "Now I get to ask one. Why are you asking?"

"Just thought that when Andy gets caught up that you might drive a tractor or whatever else needs done. There's always room for extra help during the summer and after this month the computer business slows down a little," he said.

He waited for her reaction, expecting her to stutter and stammer her way around the fact that she didn't know a blessed thing about real ranch work. Sure, Andy said that she'd lived on a ranch with her great-aunt, but that didn't mean she'd done any work there.

"Sure. I'll do whatever needs to be done until I can get Andy paid," she said. "It's just like riding a bicycle. It all comes back to a person. I kind of like getting outside to work." Her tongue was turning purple now that she was working on the grape side.

"I'll talk to Andy. He's been a lifesaver even when the women started hounding me. Guess a billionaire sounds better to gold diggers than a plain old millionaire." Using the straw/spoon combination, he shoveled a bite of pure banana into his mouth. "I just want to go to the feed store without worrying about a paternity suit. He said that he was working on a plan to help me out, but he didn't want to tell me the details just yet. I just hope he's not sending off to Russia to buy me a wife from one of those places you hear about on the Internet."

She smiled. "Is it really that bad?"

"Worse."

She giggled. "What would you do if he did?"

"Fire his sorry ass. That's where I draw the line. You don't buy people and I sure don't want a woman that I didn't pick out or one that I can't understand." He laughed with her.

She looked so danged cute with a purple tongue and cherry red lips.

"Andy wouldn't do that for real anyway. I was just joking," Colton said.

"You must feel better," she said.

She pushed out of the swing and carried her empty paper cone to the trash can. He followed her and together they walked back to his truck. He opened the door for her and she hiked a hip up onto the seat. He reached across her to fasten the seat belt like a gentleman and looked up right into her mesmerizing blue eyes.

He cleared his throat and stepped back quickly. He had doubts about her and he'd be damned if he played into her scam by kissing her.

They were back on the ranch in less than an hour. She bailed out of the truck before he had time to open the door and hurried toward the carriage house, throwing a word of thanks over her shoulder for the snow cone.

The sound of her boot heels on the wooden steps leading up to her tiny apartment made the same sound that they did when she climbed the steps to her apartment in Amarillo. Janet lived there now and hopefully she'd keep the rent paid and the place clean.

Laura had learned to like the rut she'd fallen into the past week. It would work really well until she was ready to leave. No commitments, except to hold up her end of the bargain with Andy. No friendships, except with Andy, and she'd been his friend since they were kids.

She went into the office at eight every morning, ate a sandwich while she worked at noon, and then took an hour break at supper before going back to finish up for the day. Andy said that once they got caught up, she'd have Saturdays and Sundays off each week, but they'd worked all day on Saturday and Sunday afternoon when he got home from church the first weekend. The one redeeming thing about working so many hours was that she could pay off her note to Andy faster with all the overtime.

She flipped a switch just inside the door and wished she had never agreed to go to supper that evening. Less than four hours had already turned her life around.

First there was supper with the family, then meeting the preacher, and going for a snow cone. And she still didn't know what Andy was talking about when he and the rest of the family were discussing her and Colton. She really believed the snow cone trip had been a spur-of-the-moment thing. She was very good at reading people and he couldn't have had an underlying motive or she would have seen it.

A single lamp illuminated the small efficiency apartment. A bank of cabinets covered the south wall of the apartment. A small sink, apartment-sized stove, and under-the-counter dorm-sized refrigerator made it into a kitchen. The queen-sized bed took up a chunk of the remaining area. A rocker/recliner faced a television at the foot of the bed, and a doorway right beside it led into a bathroom.

That is where Laura headed, leaving clothing and running shoes in her wake. She turned on the water in an old cast-iron claw-foot tub and crawled into it as it filled. She leaned on the sloped back and shut her eyes. Had she missed a nuance in Colton's actions? He'd changed slightly when she ordered the rainbow snow cone, but that's what she always got. He'd ordered the same one, so what was the big deal? Then he'd had a strange expression when she wanted to go to the school playground, but again, that was her favorite place to go.

It always reminded her of summertime in Amarillo. When Aunt Dotty finished at the feed store and the grocery store, she would let Janet and Laura have a snow cone—if they'd been good that week. And she'd take them to the school playground to swing while they ate it. That was the highlight of their Saturday afternoons when they were kids.

She worked her toes around the faucet handle and turned off the water without sitting up. Andy said the old tub was still in the apartment because they'd have to take a wall out to remove it. She was glad no one had wanted it gone because it had become her refuge—the place where she escaped to each evening while she tried to convince herself that keeping her promise to Andy was the right thing to do when she wanted to call Janet so badly. Just hearing her voice would be enough, but she'd agreed not to even talk to her.

Knowing that Andy was right didn't make it a bit easier. After all, Janet was her sister and Andy was just a distant cousin. True, without him, she might not have a sister. But she'd always taken care of Janet. Could she really, really practice tough love, as Andy called it, this late in the game?

She leaned back and stared at the ceiling, her thoughts going back to the broken bits of conversation she'd overheard and the snow cone incident. She had moved past that and was thinking about a new computer firewall program when she dozed off, awaking a while later to chill bumps on her bare arms and a kink in her neck. She quickly sat up and pulled the rubber plug, letting the cold water drain as she got out and wrapped a towel around her body. She dried off on the towel and draped it over the side of the tub. She had just finished pulling her favorite tattered old flannel robe over a faded nightshirt when someone knocked on the door.

No one had ever come to visit before. It wasn't fair to get her first visitor when her clothing was strewn from door to bathroom and a wet towel was crumpled on the floor. Lord, she hoped it wasn't Colton.

"Hey, Laura, you in there?" Andy yelled.

She slung open the door. "Come in."

Andy's grin brightened the room. He'd always been a teddy bear—slightly overweight, wearing his jeans below his belly, and addicted to T-shirts from country music concerts. His curly hair never looked like it had been cut, and his round face always looked slightly scruffy but his blue eyes were as honest as an angel's. She'd always known that Andy would do anything for her. That's why she called him when she had no other place to turn.

"Naw," he said. "I just come to invite you to church with me tomorrow morning. Sorry, I didn't think about it last week. Ambrose is just a little bitty place, but we got a pretty nice congregation. It'll get you out and into the community."

"I met the preacher this evening when I was out jogging. I sat down on the church steps to catch my breath. He asked me to come to church tomorrow but I skirted the issue. That's my day to do laundry and catch up on my housework. It takes a lot of work to keep a place this size clean," she said.

He leaned against the doorjamb. "I remember when I first came to the ranch and lived here. Man, it took me all of fifteen minutes every Sunday morning. You can do your laundry tomorrow afternoon after church. The utility room is available in the afternoon as well as the morning."

"We work on Sunday afternoon," she said.

"Not this week. We're going to church and you are going to do laundry and then maybe catch up on some rest. Pick you up at ten thirty. Church starts at eleven. Oh, and Maudie says to ask you to eat with the family from now on," Andy said.

The skin on the back of Laura's neck prickled, kind of like when Janet looked at her with a deer-in-the-headlights stare that said she was in trouble again. She tried to think of an excuse not to go to church but nothing, not one thing, came to mind. Yet, that little voice in the back of her mind kept screaming that Andy had something hiding behind that teddy bear facade. She told herself that she was seeing demons in the shadows because of what she'd heard that evening. Hell, nothing could happen at church. All those righteous people, the preacher, and even God would be there.

"I'll be ready," she said and immediately wished she could cram the words back into her mouth. But truth was, she owed Andy big-time and if he wanted her to go to church, then she'd go.

"That's great. Preacher Roger delivers a good sermon and you'll love the singing. See you in the morning, then."

She stood in the open door and watched him all the way across the yard and into the back door of the house. Was he going to try to fix her up with a preacher? Well, he could just wake up and smell the coffee. She didn't have time for romance. And even if she was looking for a relationship, it wouldn't be with a preacher.

Chapter 2

She slept poorly, dreaming about Janet and waking in a cold sweat. If only she could pick up the phone and call her sister, she'd feel a lot better. But she wouldn't go against Andy's conditions. She knew Janet wouldn't either. Janet had been so afraid of what would happen to her.

Laura wished she hadn't said that she'd go to church, but she told herself again that whatever they were cooking up to protect Colton from the gold diggers in the big bad world had nothing to do with Sunday morning services. Nobody in their right mind would piss off God intentionally, and that's exactly what would happen if they used Him for their own agenda.

She finally slung the covers back at nine thirty and made a cup of instant coffee. It wasn't good but it woke her up enough to whine about having to get dressed up. Thankfully, it was only an hour. Maybe after the laundry was done, she'd treat herself to a long hike around the ranch. A loud clap of thunder made her jump and she spilled coffee over her robe and nightshirt.

"Well, shit!" she said loudly. "So much for a nice hike."

Another rumble brought the first big drops of rain and in ten minutes it was pouring. She threw her robe and nightshirt in the direction of the clothes hamper and opened the closet doors. Standing there in nothing but bikini panties, she flipped through the hangers, finally settling on a cute little pink and white checked sundress with a short-sleeved bolero sweater over it.

Her cell phone rang at ten o'clock and she answered. "Good mornin', Andy. Are we still going to church?"

"Just making sure you are awake. I'll park right at the end of the steps and bring an umbrella up to fetch you," Andy said.

"Who all is going?" she asked.

"All of us. Colton is feeling human again this morning. He's of the opinion that a snow cone will fix anything. And Rusty, Maudie, and Roxie. We sit together every Sunday morning," he said cheerfully. "I'll be there in half an hour. Hope the rain lets up by then."

Those two words, *sit together*, kept running through her mind. She'd been uncomfortable sitting around the dinner table with the whole bunch and now she had to line up with them on a church pew. She sighed as she laid the dress on the bed and went to the bathroom to put on makeup and do something with her shoulder-length blond hair. She was still buckling the strap on her sandal when she heard the sound of Andy Joe's boots coming up the stairs. She hoped the umbrella was big enough to keep the rain from her hair. She'd twisted it up into a loose twist held with a big clamp and used lots of hair spray to keep it there. If it got wet, it would look like yellow strands of yarn plastered together with superglue.

"Well, you sure look beautiful. You still having trouble with your contacts?" Andy asked.

"I know the glasses look dorky, but the doctor said that I can only wear the contacts occasionally now, not every day," she said.

"Not dorky. Well, maybe a little nerdy, but I like your blue eyes and they're hid behind those thick glasses," he said.

"I think the thick lenses make me look like an alien." She smiled.

"Well, there is that, but the rest of you looks beautiful," Andy said.

"Honey, I'll even take a left-handed compliment today. Don't you dare let that umbrella fly away or I'm going right back inside my apartment. I refuse to go to church looking like a drowned kitten." She looped her arm in his and huddled under the umbrella.

"I thought it was a drowned rat," he teased.

"Not with blond hair and fair skin like mine. I'd look more like one of those pitiful little yellow kittens that hasn't got enough sense to find its way in out of the rain," she told him.

He opened the truck door for her and held the umbrella just right so that not a drop of rain fell on her hair. A few did find their way to her glasses and she busied herself cleaning them as he jogged around the front of the truck, got inside, and broke the umbrella down.

"I guess Colton is glad to see the rain." She set her glasses back on her face and pushed them up.

"Not as glad as Rusty. He was fairly well dancing at breakfast this morning. They just planted hundreds of acres of alfalfa and this rain is coming at a perfect time," Andy answered.

"Did you hear from Janet?" She changed the subject.

"I did. She made her meetings, has not been to a casino, hasn't missed a day of work this whole week, and is doing fine. Said to tell you that she's found a new love and it's called the library, where she checks out books by the dozens," Andy answered.

"Is she telling the truth?"

"Hell if I know. If not, she's going to fall right on her own ass this time. She's thirty. It's time to be accountable."

"I miss her, Andy."

"I know you do and I feel horrible that I set down those rules, but it's for the best, Laura. She's got to learn to stop gambling and she won't as long as you keep paying her debts. If Aunt Dotty was still alive she'd skin you for all you've already done," he said.

"That's the truth." Laura managed a weak smile.

The rain had slacked off slightly when they reached the church. He couldn't drive her right up to the door and most of the close parking spots were taken, but he did bring the umbrella around to her side of the truck and got her inside all dry and presentable.

He shook the water from the umbrella and stood it in the corner with dozens of others. A door designating that it was the men's room was on her right. The ladies' room was on her left, and right ahead was the one leading from the foyer into the sanctuary.

That prickly sensation on her neck was back. It had been years since she'd been to church. Not since she graduated from high school and moved into town with her sister, Janet. Aunt Dotty, who'd taken her and Janet in when her mother died, had given them a place to live, taught them how to work hard on a ranch, took them to church every Sunday, and made sure they were fed and clothed. It was her duty to see to it that her blood kin didn't wind up in foster care, she said, but it was not her duty to mollycoddle them just because they were girls.

Andy swung the door open and led the way. People were already seated, but there was a low buzz from folks' whispers as they waited for services to begin. When she walked in behind him, the whole church went as silent as the eye of a tornado. It wasn't until he stood to one side and let her into the pew before him that the buzz started again. She looked up expecting Andy to slide in beside her, but he marched on up the aisle, across the front of the church, and down the side aisle to sit at the far end of the pew next to Rusty.

"Good morning," Colton whispered. His warm breath caressed the soft skin on her exposed neck, causing a shiver to tickle her backbone.

"Good morning." She was amazed that she could speak. Damn that Andy! He'd better enjoy visiting with God for the next hour because he was about to get hit with a devil of a fight after church was over.

Laura felt like a bug under a microscope, one of those that had a straight pin pushed through its body to keep it from crawling away. The old man across the aisle smiled as if he'd found something miraculous under the lens of the scope. The old lady in the pew in front of him had turned to stare at her with a scowl as if she'd like to drag up a cross and hang her on it.

Laura removed a hymnbook from the back of the pew in front of her and studied it. When she'd first moved away from Aunt Dotty's ranch, she'd learned to love to read and every Saturday morning after she finished her half day at the greenhouse, she went to the library. That morning she was reminded of the scariest book she'd ever read, titled *Harvest Home*, and written by Thomas Tryon. It was an older book, written long before cell phones or Internet, but it had scared the bejesus out of Laura because it wasn't fantasy. It could really happen in a small town set off in the middle of nowhere... somewhat like Ambrose, Texas.

The hair on her forearms stood straight up as she looked up at all the people staring at her. Did these people have a harvest ritual and were they thinking about her for the next harvest queen? She shuddered from head to toe just thinking about that book and how the setting was so much like Ambrose.

"Preacher has the air-conditioning turned down. Guess he's going to give us a hot sermon," Colton whispered.

"Shhh." Maudie shot a look his way.

Roxie winked shyly at Laura.

"Let's begin with singing 'Abide with Me' and we'll sing every verse today." The preacher gave out the hymn number and Maudie grabbed the only remaining hymnbook in the pew pocket.

Colton scooted close enough to Laura that she caught a full blast of his shaving lotion which just made her even more nervous. Sharing a hymnbook with a man was a first for Laura. She didn't know about Ambrose, but in the little church where Aunt Dotty took her all those years, it was a big, big thing. If a girl shared a hymnal, it was right up there next to being engaged.

She blushed scarlet. Was that why they all turned around in their seats and stared at her? They wanted to see what kind of woman had the privilege of sharing a hymnbook with the rich and sexy bachelor, Colton Nelson?

Just as the last notes of the hymn settled over the congregation, Preacher Roger cleared his throat and said, "We have a visitor this morning. I understand that Laura Baker has taken on the job as an assistant out on Colton Nelson's ranch. We are glad that you have joined us, Miss Baker, and hope that you make your presence a regular thing."

She smiled up at him, but inwardly she wanted to crawl under the seat, through all the shined cowboy boots and high heels, to the back door where she'd sneak away and walk all the way back to the ranch. She would not be making her presence a regular thing at the Ambrose church, especially if she found out they had a fall harvest festival like Tryon talked about in that book.

"Now if everyone will open your hymnals, we'll sing one more song before I begin my sermon."

As soon as the last note of the hymn faded, Preacher Roger went right into reading the Scripture about the Good Samaritan. To get her mind off Colton's shoulder snuggled up to hers in the packed pew, Laura sent up a silent prayer that Janet hadn't fallen back into the gambling pit.

Janet loved her and she'd proven it too many times to count. It was just that Janet couldn't stay out of trouble, especially at the casinos. She was always looking for the fast buck and always wanted more than her salary as a hairdresser could buy.

Preacher Roger had speechified for the full thirty minutes, but Laura had been off in her own thoughts so she was surprised when he wound down his sermon by saying, "The Ladies Auxiliary has gotten together a potluck reception in the fellowship hall and everyone is invited to stay for food and fellowship. Now Sister Ina Dean, will you please deliver the benediction?"

The elderly woman who had given her the evil eye stood up and bowed her head. "Dear Lord," she started and went on so long that Laura began to worry that all the casseroles would be molding before she finally said, "Amen!" The whole congregation said it a split second after she did, probably because they were starving, and the noise level shot up from zero to ten in two seconds.

"I'm going to the ladies' room. Tell Andy I'll meet him at the truck," Laura whispered to Colton.

"We're all staying for the lunch. It's kind of expected of us since we supplied the meat for the shindig," Colton said. "See those doors right back behind the pulpit? They lead into the reception hall. Just follow your nose and the noise."

Oh yes, sir, that rotten Andy was in hot water so deep that he might never get out of it. She pushed the door open into a room with yellow flowers and bright green vines trailing from floor to ceiling on the wallpaper. The stalls, woodwork, and vanity were all painted pale pink, and small baskets filled with fancy little lacy sachets were placed on the back of the potties. The aroma of roses filled the room from the sachets and threatened to choke her to death. The vines looked as if they could reach out and finish the job that the overpowering fake rose scent started. The room got smaller and smaller and her breath came in short gasps.

She slipped into a stall, put the lid down, and sank down. Putting her head between her knees, she took several long deep breaths. When she straightened up she was still mad enough to eat nails. Andy had to have known about the church lunch and he didn't even bother to tell her. If he had, she would have brought her own truck so she could duck out. Spending Sunday afternoon with that woman who gave her evil looks and then delivered the benediction wasn't her idea of a day of rest.

She was about to push the stall door open when several women rushed inside the tiny room and they all started talking at once. When she heard her name, she slowly sat back down and pulled her feet up so nothing was showing under the door.

"Did you turn around and look at that woman sitting beside Colton Nelson? Roger said her name was Laura something-or-other," a woman's voice said loudly.

"Laura Baker. He said her name was Laura Baker. Did you see those boobs, Ina Dean? If that's what it took to get him, I would have gladly gotten mine made bigger. I've been in love with him since sixth grade and he doesn't even know it," voice number two said with a sigh.

"I think it was just a fluke that she sat beside him in church. Andy let her sit there rather than making her walk all the way around to the other end of the pew," Ina Dean said.

"Oh, it's his girlfriend, all right. They shared a hymnbook and Melody, Janice Delford's granddaughter who runs the snow cone stand over in Bells, well, she told Janice that they were over there last night together. I tell you it's his girlfriend, without a doubt, Ina Dean. You should have told us that you had a crush on him, Cynthia. We could have arranged some dinners," the third voice said.

"Well, it's too late now," Cynthia said.

"Maybe not. If things don't work out with that woman, you could still make your move on him and wind up with all those beautiful dollars," Ina Dean said.

"Ina Dean Hawkins, how could you say that? I liked him before he was a billionaire," Cynthia declared.

"Tell me I'm right, Patsy," Ina Dean said.

"Hey, don't get me to gossipin' in the church. My niece can tell her lies any way she wants to spin them. But I'll tell you one thing—that girl ain't near as pretty as you, Cynthia. She'll never clean up good enough for him to take to all those fancy things that he has to go to. Did you see her fingernails? They aren't even polished, and those thick glasses make her look like she's an old maid Sunday school teacher. He'll never marry her, darlin'. It's just a passing fancy that they are covering up by calling her an assistant. Assistant to whom, I wonder?" Patsy said.

Laura pressed her face against the crack between the stall door and the cool metal. She got a clear vision of a tall, somewhat thin woman that had to be Cynthia because the other two were too old to have gone to school with Colton. No matter which way Laura turned her head or how hard she flattened the side of her cheek, she could not see the other women.

"Well, it's too late now, Cynthia. That rodeo is done over and you didn't make it the eight seconds," Ina Dean said.

"Whose side are you on anyway?" Cynthia sulked.

"I don't take sides," Ina Dean declared. "But if I was a bettin' woman, which I ain't, I'd bet you dollars to corn puddin' that something fishy is goin' on and I intend to get it out of his momma before the day is done."

"Maudie ain't his momma," Cynthia said.

"She raised him from just a little boy. Only momma

he's known since his folks died in that car crash, and besides, she's his granny," Patsy said.

"Well, we ain't gettin' the dinner on the table in here. Y'all ready to go play nice? He says she came from out in west Texas, but with that blond hair and blue eyes I wouldn't be surprised if he didn't buy her from Russia or one of them foreign places. I haven't heard her say a word. Just mark my words, I bet she's got a foreign accent. And if she doesn't work out, he'll just send her back and buy another one." Cynthia sighed.

"Guess we ain't got a choice. But you mark *my* words, something ain't right. There'd be a lot more fanfare if he was really involved with a woman. She's just a play toy to him and he'll be done with her soon enough. He's got too much money to be getting involved with a plain woman, even if she does have big breasts," Ina Dean said.

"But she was sittin' with him, and Maudie looked like she was pleased as punch, and Roxie was smiling too. If Colton wasn't involved with her they'd have different expressions, I just know it. If he sits by her at dinner, I swear there is something going on." Cynthia sighed.

Laura waited until she was sure they were gone before she peeked out. She checked her reflection in the mirror before she pushed out into the hallway and headed toward the noise coming from the fellowship hall. It was either that or walk home and it was still raining. Besides, she had a big bone to pick with Andy. That's what they were talking about the night before when they said they could set it in motion and it would all work out.

They'd planned for her to sit by Colton and to share a hymnbook with him. Did they finagle that snow cone trip too? She was so pissed, she had red dots in front of her eyes. Damn that Andy Joe!

She made it inside the fellowship hall just in time to see the tall brunette make her way through the circle of cowboys, bat her eyelashes, and kiss Colton on the cheek, letting her lips slide over to graze the corner of his mouth. "So tell us more about your assistant."

"She's not my assistant. She's Andy Joe's," he said.

Cynthia winked. "Sure she is. If she was Andy Joe's she would have been sharing a hymnbook with him, not you. I'm hurt that you didn't tell me you were looking for an assistant. I could have filled that job very well for you."

Colton looked over Cynthia's shoulder and there was Laura not three feet away. From the look on her face, she was not a happy woman and in a sudden flash of understanding, it dawned on him what had happened that morning.

Damn that Andy Joe! He'd fire him, but he'd never find another financial advisor like him; besides, the whole bunch of them had to be in on the deal to pull it off so smooth right under his eyes. That's why Granny and Roxie were both whispering the whole way to the church. Just when did they cook this little fiasco up anyway? And why?

The night before and because he'd gotten drugged was the reason. One question remained: Did Laura know about it and had she instigated the snow cone trip someway? No, she couldn't have because he invited her, and her expression said that she'd just figured out their shenanigans too.

They were all in big trouble when he got home. He couldn't remember the last time he was so pissed. If he hadn't spent a whole day in bed after being drugged, he'd have realized that he was being set up. There wasn't a thing to do at this point but let it play out. There was no way he was going to hurt Laura's feelings by causing a big stink in the church fellowship hall, but there was also no way Andy and the rest of them were going to get away with the stunt.

She crossed the rest of the space between them and asked, "Where's Andy Joe?"

Cynthia stuck out a hand and looked down at Laura. "I'm Cynthia Talley. Colton and I went to school together and we've been friends forever."

"Well, hello." Laura put on her best Texas drawl. "I would have sworn with your beautiful height and eyes that you were from Sweden."

Cynthia waved her hands in quick flustered motions and blushed scarlet. "Oh, no, but I thought you might be from Russia."

"No, ma'am. I'm from west Texas. Andy is my cousin," Laura said.

Ina Dean stepped in front of them and raised her arms. Colton bent down to hug the tiny, frail-looking woman. Her jet-black hair was slicked back into a tight little bun at the nape of her neck. She wore a navy blue dress buttoned all the way up to the white Peter Pan collar. The only frivolous adornment was her gold watch and it barely peeked out from the white cuffs of her long sleeves.

"I'm looking forward to the party out at the ranch in a couple of weeks. The whole community is getting fired up for the games. Me and Maudie is putting together a whole new set of rules this year. Is your assistant going to be there?"

"I'm sure Laura will be on hand. She works at the ranch, but like I told Cynthia, Laura is Andy Joe's assistant, not mine," he said.

"I help Andy in the office." Laura hoped that her explanation cooled the hot rumors.

"Sure you do, honey." She stepped back and narrowed her eyes at Laura, scrutinizing her from sandals to blond hair. "How long you been out on the ranch, anyway?"

"A little more than a week," Laura said.

"Uh-huh." Ina Dean nodded. "Well, I guess you pulled the wool over our eyes for a little while, Colton, but I'm old enough to see things in the right light and it wasn't Andy that she was hugged up to in church services."

"Ina Dean, we need you in here," a lady singsonged from the kitchen.

"Holy shit!" Laura whispered under her breath.

"Little pissed, are you?" Colton asked.

"No, honey, I'm a whole lot pissed," she said.

"Well, so am I. We'll get through this lunch and then we'll go home and pitch a fit. Deal?"

"You got it," she said. "Now where is Andy Joe?"

"Whole bunch of them left us to the wolves. Andy said he got a phone call about taxes or some other folderol, and Rusty said that Roxie had a headache so he was taking the ladies home. He said for me to bring you after the lunch."

"Uh-huh," she used Ina Dean's expression. "Who is that woman, anyway?"

"Which one?"

"The elderly one that just went to the kitchen."

"The head she-coon of Ambrose." Colton chuckled.

"Andy said that was Maudie's title. He told me that when he hired me. You are the richest cowboy in north Texas. Roxie is the new member of the household. Maudie is the head she-coon of the whole county, and Rusty is the one who really knows what is going on with the ranch," Laura said.

"Oh no, darlin'. You got to have been born in Ambrose and lived here your whole life to get the head she-coon title. Cynthia is probably next in line for it, but she can't have the crown or the right to the benediction on Sunday morning until Ina Dean is dead," Colton whispered. "But she does know how to organize a dinner. I have to give her that much."

Laura looked at the two eight-foot tables full of food and the one off to one side filling up with desserts. "I haven't been to one of these things in years. I'd forgotten how much food gets brought in."

"Haven't been to church in years or to a potluck?"

"Both. If I even eat a taste of everything on those tables I'll have to run twice as far tonight."

"You jog every night?"

"At least three times a week, but usually always on Saturday and Sunday. Do you?"

"No, I have a gym. When we get back home I'll show you where it is located. After working outside all day, I'd rather exercise in air-conditioned comfort without mosquitoes or people to stop and ask me if I want a ride. You don't have to leave the house to exercise, so eat all you want."

"We'll bow for a word of grace." The preacher

raised his voice above the noise. Instantly, conversation stopped, ice quit rattling its way into tea glasses, and even babies stopped crying. He gave thanks for the food, for the hands that prepared it, for the forgiveness in all their hearts toward their neighbors, and kept right on going for a good five minutes. Laura stopped listening after the forgiveness thing… she wasn't going to forgive Andy Joe. He did not deserve it. No sir!

But she would like an explanation as to why he'd want everyone in Ambrose to think that she was the rich cowboy's new lady love. Of all the women in the world, it was evident that he wouldn't want to throw in his lot with a nerdy woman who wore thick glasses. And God knew, it would take a whole lot more than a billion dollars to make her even think about a relationship at this time of her life. She was barely getting her own affairs in order. She sure didn't have time for a boyfriend.

"Amen! Now Colton and our visitor can start the line," Preacher Roger said.

Laura felt a hundred eyes on her as she and Colton filled their divided Styrofoam trays. Would there be talk later that she didn't eat Ina Dean's casserole and took a double helping of someone else's chicken and dressing? There was no way she could eat some of everything on the table, so she bypassed the corn casserole and the tuna salad but when she got to the end, her tray still needed sideboards. Maybe she'd made enough women happy that they wouldn't show up at the Circle 6 with a big wood cross to hang her on.

Cynthia was the hostess at the drink table and it was a very good thing she wasn't a poker player because she couldn't hide what she was thinking. She looked down at Laura's plate and her expression said, *That woman eats like a horse. No wonder she's so fat.*

Her face softened when she touched Colton on the arm and said, "I'm glad to see that you both have a good healthy appetite today. Sweet tea or lemonade?"

"Tea, thank you," Colton said.

"The same." Laura smiled.

"Laura, I do hope you are happy here in Ambrose," Cynthia purred.

Laura managed a smile, but she didn't feel it in her heart. "Thank you so much. You've got more trees and less mesquite than we do, but Texas is Texas. We all speak the same language. This actually reminds me of northeast Arkansas where I lived when I was a little girl," Laura said.

She could feel dozens of eyes on her as she carried her plate to the nearest table. Colton set his plate and tea glass down and pulled out a chair for her. Two jar candles burned brightly in the middle of the long table. A plastic fork, knife, and spoon had been wrapped up in an oversized white paper napkin that marked each place.

"Where is Maudie?" Ina Dean sat down across from them.

"Roxie had a headache so she took her home. She's got allergies and she was playing with the cats yesterday," Colton said.

"I hope that's all she's got. Her momma was a rounder and blood will have its way," Ina Dean said.

Laura filled her mouth so that she couldn't say a word back to Ina Dean. She'd been that girl when she was a teenager. The one who had a momma with a reputation, a momma who'd died in her late twenties because she'd lived too hard, drank too much, and couldn't fight off lung cancer.

"I'm sure it's just a headache. Granny keeps a real tight rein on her," Colton said.

"Well, I hope so. Her momma was a handful and couldn't nobody tame her down. Roxie is lucky to have Maudie."

Laura had been lucky to have Aunt Dotty too, but she sure didn't take the place of a mother. Janet came closer to filling that spot and that's why she owed Janet all the help she could give her when she made mistakes.

"This is really good potato salad. Did you make it?" Colton asked.

"Yes, I did. I figured you'd recognize it. Old family recipe that I don't share with nobody," Ina Dean said seriously.

Patsy sat down on one side of her and Cynthia on the other. Pretty soon they were in a heated discussion about how much mustard to put in potato salad. Laura thought they'd forgotten all about her until she caught Cynthia giving her sidelong looks across the table. She wanted to stand up between those two scented candles and announce to the whole congregation that her boobs were real, they were not bought, and Colton hadn't spent a dime on them.

Preacher Roger sat down beside Cynthia and she beamed, batted her lashes, and flirted blatantly with him. Laura watched the whole process with a smile on her face. Evidently, if the woman couldn't be rich, then by damn she'd be holy. Or maybe she was trying to make Colton jealous. After all, he hadn't made an announcement about being engaged to the ugly duckling in the glasses, and all was fair in love and war, especially when there was a billion dollars at stake.

"I hear there's a big party at the ranch in a few weeks," the preacher said.

"Oh, yes, there is, and we're playing games," Cynthia answered.

"You should make a point to come this year, Roger. We'd love to have you. Miss Roxie is in charge of the game pairing and Ina Dean and Granny take care of the rules. I hear there are some changes this year," Colton said.

"Hunger games?" Laura whispered.

Cynthia answered Laura but looked right at Colton. "Not quite that bad. But just as cutthroat. Who are you hoping to get paired with this year?"

"That's up to Roxie. I'm sure she will surprise all of us," Colton said.

Cynthia turned to Roger. "Maybe you'll get paired with me. I'm very good at the games and we could probably win."

"And what all do these games involve?" he asked.

Colton chuckled. "Lots of hard work and crazy rules."

Laura made up her mind right then and there that she wasn't going to be a part of any games. She might not even be present at the party. She'd take the day off and read a really thick good book in her apartment. With her luck, she'd get paired up with the preacher and Cynthia would have more reason to want her out of Ambrose.

"We're having dominoes and checkers after we eat today. Y'all interested?" Roger asked.

"Count me in," Cynthia said.

"Not us. We've got some prior engagements we have

to take care of this afternoon, don't we, Laura?" Colton turned his head slightly so that he was looking right into her eyes.

The depth of his dark green eyes said there was a lot more to him than dollar bills. She could have gone exploring in his soul for days, but he blinked and looked away.

"Oh, yes, we do. Business that cannot be put off," she agreed.

Chapter 3

THE RAIN HAD STOPPED WHEN THEY LEFT THE CHURCH, but dark clouds still hung low in the sky and a few drops splattered against the ground every few minutes. The dinner was over and Laura's hair didn't have to be perfect for her to show Andy just how mad he had made her. She was there to do a job and it had nothing to do with putting on a false front with Colton.

Colton was a gentleman and opened doors for her, but his angular jaw worked like he was chewing gum and every few seconds he gritted his teeth so hard that his dimples deepened. He fired up the truck and backed out of the parking space.

"Are you mad at me?" she said.

"Why would I be mad at you? Were you in on this conspiracy?"

"Hell, no! But believe me, the rumors are already breaking the speed of sound. And they think you are crazy for even looking at a nerdy woman like me. Don't worry about it. They'll figure out real quick that it's all just rumors," she said.

"What about you, Laura? Do they think I'm too nerdy for you?" he asked.

"Why in the devil would you ask a crazy question like that? They think I'm after your money which is downright stupid."

"There's been a lot of women after my money so why is it stupid for them to think you are?" he asked.

"Don't pick a fight with me. I didn't start this but I'm damn sure going to end it when we get home. I owe Andy a lot but not this and he didn't even ask me about it. Did he talk to you before he and the rest of the crew did it?" she asked.

"No, ma'am. Not a peep. I thought he was being nice by letting you sit on the end by me so you wouldn't have to go all the way around or else make all of us scoot down."

"And last night?" she asked.

"I wondered if they'd put you up to that or if you were on a scam of your own, but you didn't answer my question," he said.

"It's stupid because love can't be bought with money. Trust can't be paid for with dollars. And besides, you aren't my type," she said.

He parked the car in front of the house and she bailed out before he could say another word. She didn't knock on the front door but plowed right inside ahead of him and was on her way to the office when Maudie poked her head out the living room door into the hallway.

"I expect you'll both be looking for us. We are in here," she said.

Laura turned around and had to put her hands out to keep from running right smack into Colton. They landed on a chest full of hard muscles and his arms went to her waist to steady her.

"Whoa! You got to signal before you turn a rig around that fast," he said.

"Don't sneak up behind me like that," she said.

"Y'all going to stand out there and jaw all day or come on in here and scream at us?" Andy hollered.

She moved her hands and glanced at them. They felt as if she'd held them up to a raging fire for several minutes, but they weren't a bit red.

Colton stood to one side and made a sweeping motion with his hat. "Ladies first. Go on and begin the fight. I've got your back."

Maudie looked at Andy Joe. "You want to talk first or should I?"

"I will." Andy pointed at a chair. "Sit down, Laura."

She glared at him. "I'll stand. I'm so pissed, I can't even think straight. I had to stay at that church and listen to rumors and eat with those gossiping women and be nice and you ran off and left me."

"Ina Dean, Patsy, and Cynthia, right?" Maudie giggled.

"Has Cynthia dragged out her black mourning britches yet?" Roxie asked.

Laura jerked her head around. She couldn't believe that Roxie had spoken up or that she'd said such a thing. Maybe she wasn't as shy as she appeared and that tough interior was surfacing.

"Why would you say that?"

Roxie ducked her head and blushed. "Plain as day to me that she's got her sights set on Colton. She flirts with him every Sunday."

"Ahhh, hell! Not her too!" Colton slumped into a rocking chair. "I'm about ready to give every dime I've got to charity and go back to being a ranch hand."

"You're not pissed at us?" Rusty asked.

"Yes, I am! Why would you do that? Start rumors like that?"

"We didn't start anything and last night wasn't any of our doing," Maudie said.

Colton shot a look across the room. "Yes you did, Granny. Y'all knew exactly what you were doing."

"Well, if we did, it's for your good. Another night like you had Friday and we'll be attending your damn funeral, Colton," Andy said. "So now the people in Ambrose think you have a girlfriend. Is that so bad?"

"Yes, it is, when it's a lie," Laura said.

"And when the two adults are not consenting," Colton added.

"Play along with it for a while. The news will get out and the women will leave you alone. It'll give the whole area something to gossip about and it'll keep the women out of your hair," Andy said.

"If I wanted a fake girlfriend, I could pick out my own. I don't need y'all's help," Colton said. "And besides, Laura doesn't deserve that kind of gossip. You know what they'll say about her living at the ranch now that Ina Dean and Patsy have something to gossip about."

Laura could have kissed him right between his sexy green eyes.

"And I'm quite capable of finding my own boyfriends," she said.

"Okay, okay, slow down," Rusty said. "We had a talk last night among the four of us. We knew neither of you would agree so we created a little scenario that would start the gossip on purpose. It seemed like the perfect answer. Laura is already here at the ranch so that worked out real well. No one knows her so it's all intriguing like the good stuff that they make gossip out of. Think about it, Colton. It's an answer to a prayer. You can go to the feed store without worrying about some woman saying that you slept with her in a motel on that day and suing you for child support."

"And what can I do? Go to the feed store and not worry about some man suing me? Or maybe I better stay away from all cafés for fear that some woman who had her eye on Colton will poison me to get another chance at him?" Laura asked.

"Here's the deal we've worked out," Andy said. "Colton gets some breathing room that doesn't involve drugged beer and almost death. And you get..."

Laura butted in before he could finish. "What? What could you possibly give me for my part in this farce?"

"I'll talk to Janet tonight and invite her to the ranch party. I'll even pay for a plane ticket and a rental car so that she can come visit you," Andy said.

Laura's heart skipped a beat and then raced. That changed the whole scene in a second. Who gave a rat's ass what her reputation was in Ambrose, Texas, anyway? It would require so little and she'd get to see her sister.

"Can I talk to her on the phone?" she asked.

Andy shook his head. "No. She needs to stand on her own two feet. This won't change much at all, Laura. You still come to work every morning at eight and leave when we are done at the end of the day. You still make the same amount of money and get overtime for anything over forty hours a week. It's just pretending that you are Colton's girlfriend. It won't require much of anything. Make-believe when you are out of the house because the hired hands on the ranch carry tales home."

She looked over at Colton. "You good with this?"

He raised one shoulder. "I can live with it for a few months. Can you?"

She shifted her gaze back to Andy Joe. "I'm still pissed."

"I can deal with pissed. I'm tired of dealing with problems. You'll have to pretend to like each other. That going to be an issue?"

"I don't know her well enough to like or dislike her," Colton said.

"I don't know you either, but I can sure enough put on a good show if I can see my sister in a few weeks," she said.

It was the only way she'd get to see Janet for a long, long time. Colton could suck it up. What all did it involve anyway? Holding hands when they walked around the yard a few times. Maybe a couple of kisses. Hell, she'd hold hands with a porcupine and kiss a toad frog to get to spend a whole weekend with her sister.

"And in the meantime if I meet a woman that I really fall hard in love with, what then?" Colton asked.

"Then you break up with Laura. Until then our jobs are to make people believe that we are all really happy with you dating her and with her work here on the ranch," Maudie said.

"And if I find a man that I really love?" Laura asked.

"While you are dating Colton? I don't think so," Maudie said.

"Then the deal is off," Laura said. "I get the same consideration as he does or I won't do it."

"Not even to see Janet?" Andy begged.

"I'll see her when my debt is paid. I'm going to my apartment."

"Deal!" Maudie said. "But no shenanigans from either of you. For six months you are dating when you are outside of this house. Understood?"

Laura walked over to the rocking chair and kissed Colton on the forehead. "Isn't it nice that the cat is out of the bag, darlin'? Now the whole world can know that we are in a committed relationship."

Colton grabbed her hand and pulled her down on his lap. He cupped her face in his hands and kissed her hard right on the mouth.

"Practicing for the stage," he said hoarsely when he ended the kiss.

She pushed herself up and away from him. Every nerve in her body hummed like that damned old sewing machine that Aunt Dotty used for quilting. Blasted fickle hormones anyway—just because she hadn't had sex in over a year didn't mean they had to fire up right then.

"You want to see the gym?" Colton asked.

"I'd love to," she said. "How are we doing?" She turned toward the judge, jury, and hangmen, all speechless for the first time since she'd walked into the room.

Roxie shook her head slowly from side to side.

"What?" Laura asked.

"You better do some practicing. That looked phony," she said.

"I thought it was pretty damn good," Colton said.

"Overdone?" Laura looked at Andy.

"Little bit," Andy said. "Be natural. Make people believe it could really be happening so that Colton can have some peace of mind."

Colton chuckled. "I never was much of an actor."

"But you've always been a ladies' man," Rusty said from the corner.

"Just not with a nerdy girl, right?" Laura asked.

Colton grabbed her hand. "I did not say you were

nerdy so don't go blaming me for it. I promised to show you the gym. Are you ready?"

Colton dropped her hand until they were out in the yard and then laced his fingers in hers again. Hot to cold and then hot again. The shifting back and forth created a strange sensation deep down in her insides that pitched like a ship on angry seas.

Laura had never cared if people liked her or not. She was who she was and they could take it or leave it. She didn't have the ability or the desire to change and there wasn't a person in the world worth changing for. Her former therapist would write all kinds of code down on his little yellow notepad if she told him what she had just agreed to do just to get to see her sister. He'd told her repeatedly that she and Janet had a love/hate relationship and that neither emotion could survive without the other.

They argued constantly when they were together. Janet was always griping at Laura because she wanted things kept orderly and Janet was a complete slob when it came to housework. Laura wanted Janet to accept responsibility for her actions and grow up. But underneath all the bickering they really did love each other.

Colton led the way around the house and out across the backyard. The original owner had a good landscaping idea. Flower beds had been defined with landscaping timbers or natural rock to make a garden maze that folks could walk through. But the whole thing was overgrown with weeds and looked pitiful. She absolutely loved flowers and yard work. Working in a greenhouse had been her very first job right out of high school and she'd always kept a few plants in the apartment. They'd probably die with no one but Janet around to water them.

With a little work, she could transform this yard into something of beauty and grace. There were flowers and shrubs that flourished in Texas heat, like lantana, marigolds, and dianthus. She'd have to ask Andy if it was all right to play in the dirt in the evenings and on her days off work.

Colton slapped a palm down on the rail fence and agilely hopped right over it. She put a boot on the bottom rung and climbed over leaving thoughts of the yard behind her as she looked ahead to cows, calves, and barns.

"You aren't afraid of cows?" he asked.

"No, I'm not. And not snakes or spiders, but I hate mice. My sister and I were six and eight when our mother died. We lived up in northwest Arkansas in a little bitty town called West Fork at the time. Aunt Dotty took us in and brought us out to her place south of Amarillo. She was a cousin to Andy Joe's grandmother. She lived on a ranch and we learned as much as she could teach us whether we liked it or not," she answered.

She looked out across the rolling hills and pastures. There wasn't a gym in sight. She saw two barns close by—one with the big doors wide open showing stacks of small square hay bales, the other with a bunch of Angus cattle standing to the south side taking advantage of the cool shadows. So where was he taking her?

He bypassed the first barn and kept walking. "So how long have you been away from it?"

"Since I was eighteen. Aunt Dotty said that once we were eighteen we were on our own. I graduated from high school one day and moved in with Janet the next, went to work the day after that, and have been working ever since. Are you sure there is a gym out here?"

Gym, her ass! Probably his idea of a good workout involved restacking small bales of hay and doing chin-ups on the barn rafters. Running sounded a whole bunch better than that.

"So why is Andy using your sister as a bargaining chip? Why can't you see her anytime you want?" he asked.

"We had a three-way deal. He gave me a job and paid off her gambling debt to a loan shark. I work for him until I get him paid back. He gives me a free place to live above the old carriage house."

"That didn't answer my questions. Why can't you see her?" Colton asked.

"Because," Laura took a deep breath, "I am an enabler. Aunt Dotty told me that. My therapist told me that and Andy did too. As long as I keep bailing her out, she won't ever learn to accept responsibility for her actions. So the only way Andy would loan me the money to keep the loan sharks from hurting her was if I promised not to see or talk to her for six months. And she has to go to Gambler's Anon meetings twice a week, keep her job, and stay out of casinos for that long."

"So why did you have to call Andy Joe? If you've taken care of it in the past, why didn't you take care of it this time?"

Laura bit the inside of her lip. "I lost my job and I had just about used up all of my savings. I tried to keep a couple of thousand dollars in reserve all the time, but this time I didn't have a job and it was ten thousand she owed. Andy paid it but, well, you know the rest."

"He's a good man but I got to admit I didn't think

he'd do what he did today. I'm sorry you got dragged into my problems," Colton said.

He opened a rough, unpainted wooden door and stood to one side so she could enter before him. A blast of cool air raised goose bumps on her arms and neck. Two doors were right in front of her and she could swear she heard water running. More than likely Rusty was behind one of those doors filling up a galvanized trough for either cows or horses. Nobody put a gym inside an old weathered wood barn.

"Gym is the one on the left," he said.

She swung it open and bright lights flooded a gorgeous fully decked out gym with every kind of equipment imaginable. The walls were pure white and everything was spotlessly clean. There were treadmills, gliders, and things she'd never seen before, not even in those fancy magazines beside the checkout counter in the grocery store.

She went right to the treadmill and ran a hand over the controls. She'd always wanted to buy one, but it would take up too much space in her tiny apartment and there were plenty of streets where she could jog. She could hardly wait to try it out and see if it gave her as good a workout as natural rolling hills.

Colton pointed to a button. "The television remote is built into the treadmill. Right here." He pushed it and a forest complete with singing birds and gorgeous ferns, clematis, and wood violets appeared on the big screen right above the treadmill. "It's hooked up to normal television, but this is what I like around me when I jog. It's make-believe but it's peaceful."

"Wow!" she whispered in awe.

"Come on and I'll show you the rest of it," he said.

Holy-damn-smoke! There was more?

"My trainer comes in once a week on Thursday evening if you want him to work out a plan with you. This is the sauna." He stopped at a door with a steamed-up window. "We keep it set at a good sweating temperature, and the showers are right next door to it so you can cool off once you've sweated the soreness out of your muscles."

"What other surprises are there on the ranch?" she asked.

"A swimming pool. Do you like to swim?"

Until that moment she didn't know that speechlessness affected the ability to nod.

"No? Yes?" he asked.

She managed to tilt her head forward.

"I love to swim but did not bring a swimsuit," she said.

"No problem. We keep suits of every size and shape in the shower room. And the pool is heated to the same temperature, winter and summer, so we can swim whenever we want." He grinned.

A picture of him in one of those skimpy Speedo bathing suits popped into her mind. Who needed a sauna? She could sweat the aches out of her muscles by just letting her imagination out of the chute. It came out romping and kicking just like a wild bronc at a rodeo and it was all she could do to stay in the saddle for eight seconds. And the images that it put into her mind of Colton were downright sinful.

She reminded herself emphatically that this was all make-believe and there was not one real thing about their crazy new relationship. She told herself to kick those sexy images of him to the curb and leave them there.

"Why would you have..." She stopped. It wasn't a bit of her business how many women had been invited to swim in his pool or why there were bathing suits in the cabana room. She'd only met the man the day before and she'd probably never see him again, no matter how much he stirred her imagination by kissing her or holding her hand.

He smiled. "It's easier to keep bathing suits at the pool in case someone forgets to bring theirs. What do you say we go work off some of that potluck dinner?"

"Are you serious?"

"Yes, I am, but if we want privacy we'll have to get our laps in now because Dillon and Roxie will be out there pretty soon and they get real noisy when they play. Plus, some of the hired hands love to get in a workout and then a swim on Sunday afternoon."

"So you let others play with your toys? And who is Dillon?" she asked.

"Roxie's boyfriend. I worry about her sometimes. She clings to him like he's her rock, and he's the only real friend that she has. It hasn't been easy for her with her mother being so wild," Colton said.

"She's in a good place now and maybe that will help her get through," Laura said.

He nodded seriously. "I hope so, and to answer your question about my toys, it's part of the package when I hire someone. They get a fair wage, room and board if they want to live in the bunkhouse, and access to my toys."

"But you didn't hire me," she said.

"Andy has needed an assistant for a long time. He's interviewed dozens of applicants. If he hired you, then you get the same privileges as anyone else on the ranch."

A pretend girlfriend. A hired hand. An enabler. She'd have to remember to wear the right hat on the right day to avoid confusion.

She thought that she could not be surprised any more after the gym, but she was dead wrong! He threw open another door and there it was. Radiant glory wouldn't come close to describing the pool room. She had seen pictures of waterfalls in remote areas of the world with ferns and flowers surrounding them, but not in her wildest imagination had she ever thought to see one in a barn in north Texas.

Crystal clear water tumbled over rocks into a pool surrounded with natural-colored stones. No wonder the flowers around the house went begging; a full-time crew would have to work twelve hours a day to keep the waterfall in such perfect order.

"Oh, my!" she gasped.

"I'm pretty low maintenance myself, but the gym and pool are my two luxuries. I never had much of a hankering to travel, but I always dreamed of swimming at the base of a tropical waterfall, so I made it happen. This old barn was sittin' empty and it seemed like the perfect place. From the outside, no one would ever guess that it's not housing hay and cattle feed. Restrooms and changing rooms are this way."

The pool was surreal with its emerald-green tile sides and bottom. She half expected to see dolphins or at least flashes of minnows darting around. But there was nothing but cool, clear water reminding her of the ocean in Florida.

He walked behind the waterfall and she followed, not caring if her dress and hair got soaked, but a sheet of glass protected her from the splash as the water tumbled down to its final destination.

"Here's the ladies' room." He swung a thick wooden door open. "See you in the pool when you get changed."

"Holy shit!" She sat down on a white wrought-iron bench before her legs turned to jelly. "I could sure enough get used to this. No, no! I'm just the hired help. Barely a step up from a call girl. Now that's a sobering thought, but it's the truth. I'm getting paid to be his girlfriend. Maybe not in money for that job but in benefits, because if I don't, I can't see Janet before six months are up."

She slipped the thin straps of her dress over her shoulders and shimmied out of it and her undergarments. Just like he'd promised, bathing suits of all kinds and sizes hung on a rack. She paid attention to the sizes as she flipped through them. Size twos came in bikinis of all colors, but the half a dozen size eights were all black one-piece suits.

There were four bathing suits in her size. She picked out a hot pink bikini with fringe around the bottom of the bra top but then remembered that he'd said the hired help and Roxie could possibly be there before long. She hung it back on the rack and chose a tankini printed with brilliant blue peacock feathers. The bottoms were bikini cut and the top had an apron-like front, leaving most of her back bare except for the tie string that kept the thing on.

He was in the pool when she came out of the cave-like dressing room and waved to her. "Like the old line says, 'Come right in, the water is fine.'"

He had a beer in one hand and his chest was bare,

water streaming down his ripped abs. He reached up and combed his brown hair with his fingertips and hopped up on the side of the pool.

He reached over to a table and settled his straw hat back on his head and she came close to swooning. Forget the damn Speedo. That skimpy piece of Spandex couldn't compare to Colton Nelson, sitting on the edge of the pool in that getup.

What was it about a woman in a bathing suit that was far more appealing than a totally naked one? Could it be that just enough was covered up to let the imagination run wild? Colton didn't have the answer to either question, but his imagination kicked right up into high gear when he saw Laura.

Her hair had been set free and she wasn't wearing those thick glasses. Her waist nipped in above well-rounded hips and below a bustline that was slightly bigger than the bottom half. She was built like the sexy movie stars of the past rather than the skinny stars of the present. Her skin was so translucent that it shimmered when the sun rays filtered through the skylight and the dense greenery surrounding the waterfall.

She sat down on the edge of the pool and dangled her feet for a few seconds before she slithered down into the water like a cautious otter. She disappeared and swam down the length of the enormous pool before coming up for air. That only lasted a moment and she was back under the surface, turning when she reached the other end. Her body brushed against his bare leg and the water suddenly felt ten degrees hotter.

The next time he saw her she was sitting on the edge of the pool at the deepest end, the waterfall behind her, sunlight dancing on her wet blond hair. He sucked in a lungful of air, remembered to give his hat a toss, and did two laps before he popped up in front of her, braced his arms on the edge, and looked up.

"It's beautiful," she said.

"Yes, it is." He continued to stare without blinking.

Was she blushing? He didn't know women did that anymore.

"I'm talking about the pool," she said.

"Oh, well, that too."

Laura's lungs seized up and forgot to inhale when he used his massive biceps to haul himself out of the water to sit beside her. She coughed to cover the gasp. Unlike Janet, Laura did not talk when she was nervous. At least, she'd never had that problem before that minute when words started flowing out of her mouth so fast that she had no power over them.

"This is such a beautiful place. I feel like I'm in the middle of paradise. All it needs is birds and butterflies, not that this isn't wonderful all by itself, but I was just thinking about the thing on the television above the treadmill and..." She stopped abruptly.

"Think about why I don't have birds." He chuckled.

They were alone in the pool house, so she couldn't even pretend that kissing him was for show, but it didn't keep her from wanting to see if a real kiss could be hotter than the fake one back in the house. She forced her thoughts away from kissing his wet lips.

"Oh!" She slapped a hand over her mouth. Maybe that would keep her from babbling on and on like a thunderstruck teenager. "I guess that might get messy."

"And they'd eat the butterflies and that would make Roxie cry."

"How long have you known Roxie?"

"Her whole life. Her mother was a couple of grades above me at the Bells school and Roxie has been Granny's project since she was a little bitty girl. Granny was a cook at the Bells school until I won the lottery so she knew all the kids, but she had a soft spot for Roxie's momma. Said she never got a break in life. She was always searching for love in the wrong places."

"Project?" Laura asked.

"Roxie's mother was a sophomore in high school when she got pregnant. Smart girl when it came to books but didn't have a lick of sense when it came to boys. Granny says that she was like a butterfly that flitted around all the pretty roses and then landed on a fresh cow pile. Roxie's father was a rascal and wound up in prison. Her mother had too many responsibilities too young and liked to party. Granny took care of Roxie a lot from the time she was a baby."

"Then Maudie was her babysitter?"

"Something like that, only more. More like a surrogate grandmother, but since Roxie's momma called Granny Aunt Maudie, Roxie grew up doing the same. Two weeks ago her mother ended up in the emergency room after too much liquor and too many pills. They were going to put Roxie into the foster care system but Granny went to battle for her. She'll be living on the ranch until she graduates."

"And the mother?"

"She'll be in rehab for a long time. When she gets out she can visit Roxie, but she can't take her away from the ranch."

"Maudie is a good woman," Laura whispered. "And what's in this barn is your only luxury? No fancy cars or mansions or your own private island off in the tropics?"

Colton grinned. "I got a good truck and that big old farmhouse is mansion enough for me. That's enough luxury for any rough old cowboy. If you won a million dollars, what would you want?"

"I'd have to think long and hard about that," she said.

"What's your favorite vacation?"

"Florida, but it wasn't nearly this pretty." She fell into the water and splashed it all over him.

He dove in right behind her and beat her to the other end by one lap. When she came up for air and grabbed for the side of the pool her hands came to rest on his arms. She was still treading water with her feet when she opened her eyes to see him staring down at her. His green eyes went all dreamy and soft.

His eyes slowly closed and thick brown lashes rested on his cheek. She really wanted the kiss but noisy teenagers jerked Laura back to reality. She moved away from Colton and was swimming toward the other end when Roxie and Dillon made it to the pool's edge.

"Where are your glasses?" Roxie asked.

"Back in the dressing room. I can see well enough to swim without them," she answered.

Dillon wasn't as tall as Colton, but he still dwarfed Roxie. He wore his blond hair cut above his ears with enough left on top to comb over for Sunday or let hang on his forehead any other time. His brown eyes seldom strayed from Roxie, and his smile was genuine and honest. His arms and body testified that he was used to hard work and his hands bore the calluses to prove it. Laura recognized Sunday jeans, boots, and Western shirt and wondered if he was in the same church as they had attended that morning. She didn't remember seeing him there but there had been lots of people.

The kids had barely made their way to the backside of the waterfall when Andy and Rusty arrived with two of the hired hands. They were already dressed for swimming in cutoff jeans and wasted no time crawling up the ladder to the diving board.

"Hey!" Rusty waved from the end of the board.

Laura made her way to Colton's side and propped herself on the edge with her elbows. "Water is fine," she called out.

"We don't mean to disturb y'all," Andy hollered.

"We were just getting ready to leave anyway. I'm going to take Laura on a tour of the whole ranch," Colton said.

"In one afternoon?" Andy Joe's eyes widened. "That will be one fast tour."

Laura opened her mouth to say that she would rather stay behind and swim all afternoon but curiosity snapped it shut. Just how big was a billion-dollar cowboy's ranch, anyway? And what other surprises might be hiding in the barns that he didn't even consider luxuries? Being alone with him put her in dangerous territory, but she really did want to see the ranch.

Chapter 4

Colton poured a cup of coffee and sat down at the dining room table. Roxie was the only other person up and around and she had her nose in a book. From the hunky cowboy on the cover, it didn't have anything to do with schoolwork.

"Granny know you are reading that?" he asked.

"No, she does not," Roxie said. "You ought to read it before she does. You old people might need a little refresher course in how to kiss and all that so the acting will be more convincing."

Colton grinned. "I'm not that old. I think I can remember how to kiss a woman. And what made you so sassy today?"

"I'm not sassy. I'm just statin' facts. If you know how to kiss a woman then you need to do it and quit just lookin' at her with moony eyes."

The smile faded. "I am not lookin' at her with moony eyes."

Roxie raised her eyebrows and looked at him over the top of the book. "You just blew the bottom right out of that commandment about not lying."

"I'm glad you have to go to summer school to make up for all those times you skipped school," he muttered.

"Me too. I get to see Dillon and enjoy his moony-eyed looks."

"You use that word one more time this morning and

I'm sending Laura and Granny to shop at Tressa's without you this afternoon."

Roxie tucked the book in her backpack, slung it over her back as she stood up, and flicked bread crumbs from her shirt. "I don't reckon it would kill me." She lowered her voice as she walked past him. "She's coming in the back door and headed toward the office right now. There it is—your eyes are all dreamy just thinkin' about seeing her. Remember, this is supposed to be make-believe."

"I warned you."

"I didn't say that word I wasn't supposed to say." She giggled. "Good mornin', Laura."

"Mornin', Roxie. I hear the school bus. Have a good Monday," Laura said.

"I'll be waiting at school for y'all to pick me up." Roxie waved over her shoulder.

Laura wore snug-fitting jeans that nipped in at a small waist, a bright blue tank top, and scuffed boots. Colton wished that he'd met her at a NTAA—North Texas Angus Association—dinner or even a cattle sale instead of being thrown together with her in a fantasy world.

"You are runnin' behind this mornin'. Roxie is sassy. Something tells me it's going to be a crazy week. Roxie never ever acts like that," he said.

She shrugged. "Maybe she's finally finding her rebellious wings. You would do well to hope that she does before she leaves the ranch. You and Maudie will still have a little bit of control while she is here. Once she's gone to college, if she hasn't let the inner person out, it'll be hell to pay."

"Are you speaking from experience?" he asked.

"Let's just say that I understand that girl and let it go at that. Where's Maudie?"

"She'll be along after a while. She cooks on the weekends, but through the week we have a staff that takes care of the house and cooking so she doesn't get up so early. Have you met Sally?"

"Did I hear someone call my name?" The door to the office opened and the woman in front of Laura was at least six feet tall. She had the blackest eyes Laura had ever seen on a woman with dishwater blond hair. Her face was round and her shoulders as broad as a Dallas Cowboy linebacker's. She could be any age from late twenties to early forties.

"I'm Sally and I just cleaned that pigpen of an office. Tell Mr. Andy that I'm going to clean twice a week from now on whether he likes it or not. I hear you work in there too. Is there anything special that you like done?"

"I'm Laura and I..."

"I know who you are, missy. I hear you're keepin' company with Colton and y'all done been over at the snow cone stand and you've sat together in church two Sundays. I thought I'd run across you before now but you been holed up in that office with Mr. Andy all the time. You just remember one thing, girl. You can't keep one thing from Sally, so don't even try. I wasn't here last week because I was off down to Whitewright visitin' with my sister, but I'm back now and I'll be here every day."

"Yes, ma'am." Something in those dark eyes said that Sally could smell a lie a mile away.

Sally looked hard at her, starting at her boots and traveling all the way up to the top of her head. "You'll do but you sure ain't what I figured he'd come draggin' home. You let me know if you want something special done in that office." She whistled all the way up the stairs, but when she opened a door the whistling stopped and grumbling began.

"She's in my room. You'd think I was thirteen the way that she and Granny treat me," Colton said.

"It wasn't easy to lie to her," Laura whispered.

"It's because we've had it so easy this whole week. Hardly crossed each other's paths until yesterday and then it was just an hour in church," Colton said. "But so many people are aware of it now that Granny thinks you'd better start having supper with the family every night."

"Well, shit!" Laura mumbled.

Colton bristled. "Hey, if it's that big of an imposition, I could always bring supper out to your apartment and we could eat there."

"Hell, no! Do I have to get dressed up every night?"

"Just whatever you wear to work that day is fine. We don't stand on formality around here," he said.

He threw an arm around her shoulder and kissed her on the cheek. When he whispered in her ear his breath was warm and seductive even if the words were nothing more than information. "Sally helps Chester in the kitchen and she'll know if you aren't here for supper. They set the table before she leaves and sometimes Granny even invites her to eat with us before she goes home."

"Starting tonight?" Laura asked.

"That would be nice. Now you don't work too hard, darlin', and I'll see you at supper," he said.

"Colton Nelson," Sally leaned over the railing and yelled. "I'll be cleaning your room twice a week from now on too."

"Was she..." Laura asked.

"Oh, yes. They all are paying close attention," Colton whispered as he brushed a kiss across her lips.

Laura raised her voice slightly. "Has Sally worked here a long time?"

"She was the first person that Granny hired when we bought this ranch. She used to work at the school with Granny."

"How many more folks work in the house?" Laura asked.

"Chester, the weekday cook, and Molly, a lady who comes in four hours a day to help Sally. If you didn't stay so cooped with Andy Joe, you would have met them before now, but that's one of the things I love about you—your dedication to work."

Laura narrowed her eyes and gave him a drop-dead look. Love was a strong word that did not have room in a fairy tale world.

"Gardeners?" Laura asked.

"One comes twice a week to take care of the pool flowers," he said.

"Could I start working in the yard in the evenings?"

Their eyes met and Colton could feel the moony, so Roxie would have seen it for sure. Laura worked hard, complained very little, and she was asking for more work. She might be up to her pretty little nose in a scam, but if she was, she was damn good at it.

"Sure, I'll even pay you extra if you want to tinker around out there. Just keep up with your hours and tell Andy to add them to your paycheck each week."

"Thank you. You said that you had to get going. What's on your agenda today?"

"I'm going to round up the new calves and vaccinate them."

"Four-wheeler or horses?" she asked.

"Four-wheelers."

She gave a brief nod. "Poor little critters. They probably don't like shots any better than I do. Is that all they have to suffer through today? No working 'em or taggin' 'em?"

"You've done that?" he asked.

"If it has to do with cows, pigs, chickens, gardens, tractors, milking, or mucking out, I've probably had a hand in doin' it," she answered. "But right now I've got a whole day's work to do in three-quarters of a day because Maudie says that Roxie and I are going shopping for things to wear to some party that's going on. Want to explain what that's all about?"

Colton settled a straw hat on his head and started for the front door. "Ask Andy. He's the producer of this blockbuster film that we're starring in."

"What are you talkin' about?" Sally asked from the bottom step.

"It's a joke between me and Laura. Andy kind of introduced us when he hired Laura to help him so we have this inside joke about him creating a love story out of our lives," Colton said quickly.

Laura ducked into the office and covered her bright red face with her hands. She'd kicked the door shut with her foot and something darted across her foot, something with fur and soft feet like a mouse. She threw her hands in the air and landed in Andy's office chair. A shadow of something as big as a possum darting under the desk sent her to the top of his desk and trying to climb through air to the ceiling.

Andy heard her squeal and he rushed into the office with Colton right behind him. They took in the scene with one glance and Colton said, "Snake?"

"Mouse or maybe a possum or could be King Kong," she said in a shaky voice.

He eased over to the desk and looked under it. "Dammit! I hate snakes."

Andy stayed by the door. "If you see one, I'm out of here. I'll get Rusty to bring something to kill it."

"Two big strong men to protect me. My world is complete today," she mumbled.

"Hey!" Andy said. "At least we're not standing on top of a desk."

"Only because I haven't figured out how to get up there," Colton said.

A pitiful wail came from the corner and a big yellow cat strutted toward Andy. He chuckled as he stooped down to pet the animal. "It's just Daisy. She brushed against your leg. I bet you scared the devil out of her when you sprouted wings and flew up on that desk."

"Are you sure? That cat is yellow. I swear what I saw was gray." Laura scanned the floor and glanced up and down the draperies.

"You saw a moving shadow probably," Colton said.

Laura hopped down off the desk and did another visual sweep of the floor. "Why haven't I seen her before?"

"It's a big house and she's got free rein, both inside and out. She might have been visiting the bunkhouse. The guys all love her. But she's here now so come on over here and make her acquaintance. She'll probably show up in your apartment. When I lived there she came to see me about once a week," Andy said.

Colton bent over and scratched the cat's ears. Her purrs were loud enough that they echoed off the office walls. "You wouldn't let a nasty old mouse in our house, would you, sweet baby girl? Where is Donald? I haven't seen him in a couple of days."

"Who is Donald?" Laura asked.

"That'd be her best friend and Donald is a duck." Andy laughed.

Laura rubbed her ears and accidentally brushed her hand against Colton's arm. Sparks jumped around the room that had nothing to do with static electricity from the cat's fur. She wasn't even surprised. Colton was a fine-looking cowboy and she'd always been attracted to men with green eyes. Too damn bad they hadn't met in different circumstances, but then if they had he would have taken one look at her and thought she was after his money.

"You'll get all the scholarship funds in place before the weekend, right?" Colton said to Andy as he raised up and started for the door.

"That's what I'm working on today. You want to increase the donation this year or keep it the same?"

"Increase it to include one more senior but make it for two years instead of a four-year ride. We've had a couple of dropouts after the first year. Let's make it for two years and then optional depending on grades for that last two," Colton said.

"That seems like a sound plan to me. You going to bring that idea up at the meeting?"

"Thought I might. Right now I'm off to ranch. Daisy, you could stick around a few days and scare any mice off that might wander in from the fields." He tipped his hat at Laura. "See you at supper. Chester is making prime rib tonight and it's better than any you'll ever get in a restaurant. And I understand Sally is putting together one of her fresh peach cobblers."

"Sounds scrumptious," Laura said.

Daisy left Andy and purred until Laura picked her up and carried her to her desk. "You can sit in my lap while I work, but if you get all squirmy, you'll have to go. What's this about a scholarship meeting? I thought there was a party this next weekend."

Andy sat down behind his desk, hit a few computer keys, and waited until his screen came up. "I've been meaning to tell you about that party. Had to convince Colton first but he's on board with the idea."

"What idea?"

"It's time for you two to take this relationship out into the public if it's going to work. Y'all did real well in church again last Sunday. After two Sundays, I don't think there's any doubt that you're really dating. Even Ina Dean believes it now. That first Sunday you were caught by surprise but I got to hand it to you, last Sunday was a stellar performance. Now it's time to take it a step further. The party is in Dallas on the fourth weekend in June every year. It's a weekend affair that Colton always attends. You'll be the first girlfriend he's taken to it so it'll be a big thing."

She gasped and the cat jumped off her lap. "You have got to be joking! When were you planning to ask me? And now that you have the answer is no. Not just no, but hell no and spelled all in capital letters. Pretending here in Ambrose is one thing. In Dallas at a formal affair? I don't think so, Scooter!"

"They put him up in a penthouse suite with two bedrooms so you'll be fine. Maudie and Roxie are going shopping with you over in Sherman to buy a new dress or outfit of some kind for the formal dance and dinner. Maudie is happy as a drunk in a winery that she doesn't have to go this year. The ranch will foot the bill for whatever you buy to wear so have a good time," he said.

"Didn't you hear me? I said no!" she yelled.

Andy put a finger to his lips. "Shhh! Sally has real good hearing and she's everywhere."

Colton eased the door open and Daisy darted out. "Not going so well, is it, Andy? I told you she wouldn't go for it. I'm not her type. She said so."

She grabbed an ink pen from her desk and lobbed it across the room at him. It bounced off the door frame and rolled across the floor. He laughed aloud. "Our first fight brings out the worst in her. Hope that Sally's cobbler softens her up tonight. See you later and good luck convincing her that it's time for us to go public."

She leaned over Andy's desk and didn't stop until her nose was barely an inch from his. "I'm not Colton's type either. He didn't have to tell me. His type is cheap barmaids who doctor his beer. That has nothing to do with why I'm not going."

"If you go, I'll call Janet and give her your new cell phone number and you can talk to her all you want from now on," Andy said.

"You are a bastard," Laura said.

His smile was crooked, innocent, and wicked at the

same time. A devil wearing a halo and wings. "My momma and daddy were married so I think that is a false statement."

She returned to her chair. "I wish I'd never called you for help."

"Sweetheart, you are having a wonderful time. Admit it. It's the first time in your entire life that you've gone this long without worrying if and when the phone was going to bring news that Janet was in trouble again. It's the first time in her life that she's had to stand on her own two feet for that long. Now say you'll go and I'll leave a message on her machine. She's at a meeting right now because this is Monday and the beauty shop is closed, but you could talk to her tonight after you go shopping. I'll give her your new cell phone number and you two can talk, text, and fuss and argue all you want from now on."

Laura straightened papers on her desk and got ready to input numbers that boggled her brain. Colton was a billionaire but he was also a smart rancher and everything he touched turned to gold.

So she wasn't his type and he thought she was afraid of him, did he? There was only one way to show him that he had cow chips for brains just for entertaining such insane thoughts.

"Okay, you win. But this is the last card you have to pull out for bribery. Are you sure this party is important enough to use it?" she asked.

Andy smiled. "Oh, yeah, it's that important."

Chapter 5

Tressa had thinning gray hair that she wore pulled back into a bun at the nape of her neck. Bright red lipstick had bled into the wrinkles around her mouth, and there were crow's-feet around her deep-set green eyes. But she commanded attention when she folded her arms over her ample chest and eyed Laura.

"You are not model material, but you've got a lot to work with. I'll play up the curves like you are the next Marilyn Monroe. I'll make an appointment with Jimmy to come to the hotel room to do your hair. You got a problem with taking a few inches off so that it floats on your shoulders when he styles it?"

"I do my own hair," Laura said.

"Not if you're going to wear one of my creations. Roxie, darlin', there's a brand-new shipment of jeans over there on that rack." Tressa talked as she made her way across the room.

Laura picked up the price tag on a cute little blue halter dress. Surely there was a mistake. No dress in the world was worth that kind of money. She looked at Maudie and shook her head.

"I am not paying this much for a dress. Let's go," she said.

"Colton said for me to get you outfitted and that's what we are going to do," Maudie whispered. "Colton is paying the bill."

"Not here, we're not. I'll wait in the truck if you and Roxie want to shop here. I don't care if he does have all the money in Texas; I'm not paying these prices for something I'll only wear one time."

"He and Andy said to bring you here," Maudie said.

"Take me to that strip mall we passed by Walmart. I saw a Ross store there. I like that place."

"But Tressa's things are one of a kind."

"They should be."

"We'll be back later in the week," Maudie called out. "Come on, Roxie. Laura is getting a headache and we've got to go home."

Tressa waved as they left the store. "Call me with your hotel and room number and I'll make that appointment with Jimmy."

"I really did like that pair of jeans with all the bling-bling on the pockets," Roxie said.

"Evidently you didn't check the price tag," Laura said.

"I don't understand what's the big deal. So Tressa's stuff is expensive. You are going to a fancy place, girl," Maudie said. "She's been outfitting me ever since Colton's been on that scholarship committee. But I've got to admit I'm tickled pink that I don't have to go this year."

"I don't care if I'm having dinner with the Queen of England. I'm not paying that much for a dress. And she is not sending some guy named Jimmy to my hotel room to cut my hair either," Laura declared.

Maudie's laughter rattled off the dashboard, bounced into the backseat, and hit all four windows in the club cab truck. She pulled out onto the highway heading north toward Walmart and was still chuckling a mile down the road. "Guess you aren't going to let Ling Chi come to your room, do your nails, toes, and give you a hot oil massage, either."

It wasn't funny! Not a blessed bit. Laura looked straight ahead at the tailgate of an old dented-up truck with rusty spots.

Roxie sighed. "I'd just love to get to go to Dallas. The farthest I've ever been in my whole life is over to Sherman and to Bonham."

"You have been over the line into Durant, Oklahoma. I took you up there for college day last spring!" Maudie looked into the rearview at the teenager.

"We didn't shop," Roxie said.

"Did you look at the price on those jeans?" Laura asked.

Roxie shook her head.

"They were over two hundred dollars."

"Holy shit!" Roxie gasped.

"Roxie!" Maudie said.

Roxie slapped a hand over her mouth. "Sorry. I didn't know anything cost that much. How much was the dress?"

"Two thousand," Laura answered.

"Aunt Maudie, do you really have things that came from there?"

"I do and it was money well spent. Colton is going to be mad, let me tell you. He might play like she's his girlfriend in her jeans and cotton dresses on the ranch, but in Dallas, he's going to want a trophy girlfriend."

Laura turned as far as her seat belt would allow. "Two thousand dollars for a dress with only a yard and a half of material in it is ridiculous. I'm not that kind of woman."

"What if you had as much money as Colton? Would

you spend that much on a one-of-a-kind dress?" Roxie asked.

"I would not. But I'm not rich. And I won't ever be rich. And I'm not impressed by rich people or money. There's the Ross store, Maudie. That's where I want to go."

She pulled off onto an access road and parked in front of the store.

Roxie smiled. "I love this store. Momma let me shop in there sometimes. And Aunt Maudie took me there when I went to live at the ranch, but I can't believe Aunt Maudie is going to let you buy something for the big party here."

"Honey, I'd take her to the Goodwill store to get out of having to go to this affair," Maudie said.

Laura unfastened her seat belt. "You might have to if I can't find something in here. Why is the party such a big deal anyway?"

"He's a big contributor to a scholarship fund for kids who want to be ranchers and this is the annual meeting and formal dinner. You going to take very long in there?" Maudie said.

"No, ma'am. One hour tops and I'll have what I need," Laura answered.

Roxie groaned. "We can't even see one rack in an hour."

Laura slung an arm around the girl's shoulders. "I'll teach you how to shop in a hurry and you can have ten pairs of jeans in this store and still not pay what that one pair cost at Tressa's place."

Roxie's shy smile grew bigger. "Do I really get ten pair today, Aunt Maudie?"

"You can have one pair and one shirt on the ranch ticket because Colton promised that much to you, unless you want to take the money out of your next Friday's paycheck. I'm going to that bookstore on the corner down there while you two shop. I'll come back in one hour with the ranch credit card to pay for what y'all buy. If you get finished before that, call my cell phone."

Roxie flipped through a rack of jeans at the front of the store. "They don't have as much shiny stuff on them as the pair did at Tressa's."

"Would all that shine make you a better person?" Laura asked.

"No, but they'd make Rosalee Roche stop lookin' at me like I'm trash," she said. "Oh, look at that dress. You'd look great in it. They're showing those in all the magazines for the spring."

Rosalee Roche.

Dee Darnell.

Dee had been the thorn in Laura's side during her high school years. Maybe being a bitch had to do with double initials.

Laura snagged a cart and draped the bright blue floral dress over the side. "We are allowed eight garments at a time in the dressing room. Choose your eight while I get mine and then we'll try on. If nothing works, we'll start again."

"Aunt Maudie says I can only have two things, a shirt and a pair of jeans."

"That don't mean you can't try on lots of things. Woman has to see which one looks best before she chooses, right?"

Maudie picked out four romance books, three new mysteries, and a cookbook. She'd barely gotten through the checkout line and was looking forward to half an hour of perusing the cookbook in one of the store's comfortable chairs when her phone rang. She dug it out of her purse and looked at the ID. Roxie could beg until the sun fell out of the sky; she was not getting more than one pair of jeans and one shirt that day.

"The answer is no before you even ask," Maudie said.

"No, that you won't come get us or no that I can't even have an ice cream on the way home because it will ruin my supper?"

"You can't be finished. Am I really going to have to take Laura to the Goodwill store? Colton is going to have a fit."

"We're finished and you don't have to take us to the Goodwill, but Laura says she wants to go by the greenhouse she saw on the way here. There's a Braum's store right next to it where I can get an ice cream cone. She promises she won't take up too much time because she already knows what she wants. We are standing beside the truck."

When Maudie stepped out into the warm sunny day, sure enough there was Roxie in her bright yellow shirt, blond hair tied back with a ribbon, denim shorts, long dangling hoop earrings, looking very much like a little gypsy child leaning on the back fender of the truck. And Laura right beside her in worn boots, tight jeans, bright blue tank top, and a chambray work shirt tied around her waist.

Neither of them had a single sack in their hands, which meant that she'd be wasting another afternoon that week. Laura had to be ready for the weekend. She couldn't begin to know how important it was that she look good for Colton, and there was no way she'd found anything in that store in that length of time. In the past, Maudie had seen Roxie run around dress racks for two hours and agonize over which shirt would look best with jeans. In Maudie's opinion, anything went with jeans so it didn't matter which one the child bought.

She opened the truck door from across the parking lot with the remote. Roxie and Laura were inside when she tossed her books through the door on the driver's side. "So y'all didn't find a thing in there?"

"Oh, yes we did," Roxie said cheerfully. "See." She waved a hand over several bags resting beside her in the backseat of the truck.

"But..." Maudie looked at Laura.

"Oh, I guess you didn't see the bags. We had them stacked up on the other side," Roxie said. "When you unlocked the car we shoved them all inside."

"But..." Maudie started again.

"But I pay for my own clothing," Laura said.

Maudie looked into the rearview at Roxie. "And you?"

Laura laid a hand on Maudie's shoulder. "I bought her a pair of jeans and a shirt for the party, and a new pair of shorts and a shirt for school. And she is going to pay me."

Maudie started up the truck. "How?"

"I'm a bought woman." Roxie giggled.

The sound was music to Laura's ears. She would have bought twice that much just to see Roxie happy and acting like a sassy teenager.

Roxie went on. "I have agreed to do Laura's nails and toenails and iron her outfits for the Dallas weekend. It's my second job and I won't let it interfere with my first job, which is doing whatever you say on the ranch. I'll iron her jeans and outfits on Thursday night and we're out of school on Friday, so I can do her mani-pedi in the afternoon."

"It looks like you two have things all worked out then, so we are ready to go to the greenhouse?" Maudie asked.

Laura put her hand back in her lap and said softly, "Thank you."

Flats of green plants and brightly colored flowers along with buckets of bigger plants were lined up beside the back door when Colton came in from the fields that evening. He kicked off his dirty boots, hung his hat on a nail, and caught the tail end of something Roxie was saying.

"You should've seen Maudie's face, Sally. I don't think she believed us until we got home."

"Well, Miz Roxie, I can't say as I blame her. Laura, you sure got that shopping business down to get it all done that quick. You must do a lot of it," Sally said.

"Not me. I hate to shop so I've got a system and it works. It was a whole lot harder to leave the garden shop. It was three times the size of the one where I used to work and the plants were all so pretty."

Colton leaned against the cabinet. "So Tressa fixed y'all up, did she?"

Maudie shook her head. "Afraid not. Laura says her prices are too high."

"But we are both fixed up and she's got a pretty dress for the big party and it don't even look like it came from a cheap store," Roxie said quickly.

Colton tucked his chin and rolled his eyes up at Maudie. "You want to explain."

Laura took a step toward him. "Look at me, not at her. I'm right here. I can talk for myself. I got everything I need for a tenth of the price of what Tressa charges, and FYI, darlin', I paid for it with my money."

"And she paid for my stuff too, and I'm going to work for her to pay off the debt," Roxie said.

"I told you…" Colton looked from her to Maudie.

Laura took another step forward. "I said to look at me. Even if we are dating you don't get to tell me what to do. I'm ready for your party and Chester is putting the final touches on supper. Afterwards I'm planting all those flowers in the yard. You can help or go play in your gym. It doesn't make a bit of difference to me."

"You get bitchy every time you get hungry?" Colton asked.

"Yes, I do, and if you don't like it, keep me fed."

"The ranch paid for the flowers," Maudie said.

"Looks like she ain't after your money like folks is sayin'," Sally said seriously.

Laura whipped around. "Is that what they say?"

Sally tilted her chin down in half a bob. "Wouldn't matter who you are, that's what the people would say, so either prove 'em wrong some more or else live with it."

A smile turned the corners of Laura's mouth up in an impish grin. "How do you know what people say, Sally?"

"I got ears, don't I?"

Rusty came in from the foyer and dramatically swiped

his forehead with the back of his hand. "Is this the first fight in paradise?"

"I believe it might be, so we'll have to make up later, won't we?" Colton put his hands on Laura's waist and picked her up like a bag of chicken feed. When he'd set her down a foot to his right, he stepped around her and headed for the stairs. "I'm going to clean up a little bit for supper. I'll only be a few minutes. Don't start without me."

He'd never wanted to kiss a woman so much in his entire life. Her blue eyes sparkled in the sunlight flowing in from the kitchen windows. Her upturned chin dared him to say another word. If fighting with her created this much sexual energy, he couldn't imagine what would happen if they ever had sex.

His hands trembled when he filled them with water to wash his face. The pressure behind his zipper testified that she'd just flat turned him on with her sassiness. He straightened up and looked into the mirror above the sink. Drops of water hung to his dark eyebrows and Roxie was right. He had a moony-eyed look about him.

Laura held the shovel with both hands and stomped it into the ground. It sunk easier than she'd hoped, seeing as how the yard didn't look like it had seen a good tilling in years. She turned over the dirt, chopped it up with the shovel's sharp edge, and repeated the motions until she had loosened all the soil in the four-by-sixteen-foot flower bed. From the looks of the place, someone had once thought about making a mini-maze in the yard with landscaping timbers defining flower beds.

It was downright sinful the way it had been neglected. There were even stepping-stones down under the grass between the flower beds and cute little wrought-iron benches placed in just the right places to watch the sunrise. One evening with a Weed eater would uncover the stones and a good washing would make the benches shine.

Colton dug up the flower bed right beside hers and got finished ten minutes quicker than she did. He leaned on the shovel and eyed the other eight. "We could use the garden tiller. I think it would fit in between the timbers."

"Lazy, are you?" she teased. "Digging takes a while longer but the tiller would chew up the timbers if you got too close to them. We can take a breather and plant flowers in these two and then work on the next ones."

"Well, thank you, boss lady," Colton said.

"Don't be catty to me. When did you last work on this area, anyway?"

"I bought the ranch two years ago. This has been in a live or die situation ever since I've owned it," he said.

"How's that?"

"It can live or it can die. It's up to the rain and how tough whatever comes up in the beds is," he said.

"That's horrible. This could be a lovely garden by fall with just a little bit of maintenance. And next spring it would reseed and all you'd have to do is water it."

"Write down the instructions. It can be Roxie's job if you leave."

If!

If?

He'd best be learning how to pronounce *when*. There

was no *if* to it. She'd signed to work until she got her debt paid. After that she was going to put in her resume at every greenhouse in Texas until she found another job. Hell's tinkling little bells! She couldn't stay on the ranch, not with the physical attraction she had for Colton.

"You could be a gardener. I'd hire you to take care of the yard if Andy gets to the place where he doesn't need an assistant anymore," he said.

"Then Andy can hire one." Using a tiny spade, she dug a hole in the loose dirt, tapped a lantana from a black plastic container, and planted it.

For several minutes neither Laura nor Colton said a word. She thought about her comment about Andy hiring a gardener and remembered when he'd said that he would hire her.

It had all happened when she called him after she and Janet had gone to lunch at the diner. She remembered every single word that was said that day when she met with Janet. She'd been so stupid that she had thought for the first time in years that Janet had called her for something other than money.

She'd gotten to the little café early and ordered two bacon cheeseburgers, onion rings, and a couple of glasses of sweet tea. The waitress had just set the food on the table when Janet slid into the seat across the booth from Laura. Her face was pale gray and her blond hair hung in limp strands. Her eyes were sunken and bloodshot.

"You are in trouble again. What is it this time?" Laura had almost wept.

Janet had immediately taken a defensive stand.

"What makes you say that? Can't I call and ask you to meet me for lunch without you thinkin' I'm in trouble?"

"Not when you look like hell."

"Well, you don't look so hot yourself. Have you gained five more pounds?" Janet had said coldly.

"I will never be as skinny as you, but I'm a long way from being obese," Laura snapped back. "Now what is going on?"

Janet had put her head in her hands. "I've stepped off in a real shit storm, sister. I need help and I don't know where else to go."

"How much?" Laura didn't have five hundred dollars in her bank account and found herself hoping that Janet didn't need all of that.

"Ten grand and if I don't have it by tomorrow there will be a funeral."

"Ten thousand dollars!"

Janet had nodded emphatically.

"Holy shit! How did that happen?"

"I won a couple of times at the blackjack tables." Janet had shrugged.

"I don't have that kind of money. My truck isn't valued at half that and I don't have anything to pawn that would bring in that much. And I got laid off. I didn't tell you because I didn't want you to worry and I've had to use what I had saved to keep afloat. I've been putting in applications, but nothing so far."

"Well, your name is better than mine. You'd best come up with it by this time tomorrow or else have your black suit dry cleaned. You've got my number. I'm living out of my car. I haven't even got five dollars for a hamburger. I'll just take this one with me. I wouldn't blame you if you threw me to the wolves, but I give you my word, if you get me out of this one, I won't even play bingo again. And that's a promise."

Laura shook the memory from her head and looked across the flower bed at Colton. "Tell me about what it was like before you got rich."

"I was a ranch hand on a spread down near Ravenna. I bought one lottery ticket a week when I went into town to put my paycheck in the bank. Just one dollar a week. I'm not a gambling man, but I figured a beer cost more than that and it was fun to think about what I'd do if I ever won. And one day I hit pay dirt. Won a million-dollar lottery. The first thing I did was hire Andy Joe. The second was to buy this ranch. A year later he'd made some investments and I had ten times that much so I bought the three ranches surrounding me. Last year he worked his magic and made me a billionaire."

"And now?" she asked.

"I'm still the same old ranch hand, only now I have money. I still make a tractor work until bubble gum and bailing wire won't keep it together anymore, and I squeeze a penny until Abe groans. Guess I'll always be that poor boy who grew up over in Bells and whose granny was a cook in the lunchroom." Colton went back to the task of getting the soil prepared in the next flower bed.

Laura sunk her little shovel into the ground again and set another lantana plant in the hole.

He talked as he worked. "My folks left me with Granny one night and were killed in a car wreck on the way to dinner. Drunk driver in a semi broadsided them. They said that death was instant and that they didn't suffer. Granny finished raisin' me. I was ten that summer. She made me mow the lawn once a week for an allowance." He chuckled. "I like that you are making Roxie work for you to pay back whatever you spent on clothes today. She'll appreciate them more."

"It's nice to get paid for your efforts, and Roxie is coming out of her shell a little bit," Laura said.

"I noticed and it's great," he said.

She had never gotten paid for all the work she did at Aunt Dotty's ranch. It just came with the territory. Dotty handed her five hundred dollars the morning that she left and said it was to help her get started. Janet had gotten her the job at the greenhouse and had moved from the garage apartment into a bigger one with her boyfriend of the month. So she'd moved into Janet's old place and walked to work until she could save enough money to buy a used truck.

He finished spading up two more flower beds while she planted the first two. Then he leaned on the shovel and asked, "You goin' to water those?"

"Of course," she answered.

"I'll get a couple of hoses. If I help, we might still have time for a swim. Don't reckon we'll need a workout in the gym after this," he said.

He snaked two green hoses out across the yard from the back of the house. He handed one to her and started watering one of the long flower beds. She turned the spraying attachment to "mist" and began to soak down the flower bed closest to her.

In a month the flowers would spread out. By the end of the summer there would be an amazing garden to walk through early in the morning or late in the evening. She could imagine what it would all look like and almost feel the cool stones covered with morning dew under her bare feet.

She shut her eyes to get a clearer picture of the garden in full bloom and then *boom!* Cold water hit her square between the shoulders. She spun around and the water got her at neck level.

She instinctively turned her hose to shoot right back at Colton, but the mist setting wouldn't reach that far. However, the jet one would so she quickly readjusted and the powerful blast had no trouble reaching his chest.

"Ouch! Turn it to spray. You aren't playing fair," he yelled.

"Fair. I'll show you fair." She flipped the dial to spray and ran to the nearest pecan trees for cover. "I can beat your sorry old ass on any setting. I'm a pro at garden hose war."

He took off toward the hedges at the other end of the yard. "I'm a bigger pro."

Colton defended the south end of the yard and Laura protected the north end. Using two big pecan trees to hide behind and a couple of yew plants as cover, she made her way inch by inch to his fortress, the big box hedge up against the south corner of the house. When he peeked out she hit him at the waist and quickly soaked his jeans all the way to his boots. But the win was costly because he took up the chase as she headed back to her pecan tree fort and there wasn't a dry stitch on her when he ran out of hose.

She couldn't remember the last time she'd played or laughed so hard. Jimmy-the-fancy-hairdresser would be aghast at her blond hair hanging in wet strands. If her shirt had been white she would have looked like she was competing in a wet T-shirt contest. She looked down to make sure that the water hadn't made it transparent anyway and got a blast at knee level that almost dropped her on the spot. Her feet made sucking noises inside her boots as she turned to take shelter behind her trusty old pecan tree.

She took a deep breath and peeked out around the side of the tree. He was gone. Time for strategy, sprint like a gazelle, hit him hard in the face, and get back to the tree before he could get the water out of his eyes.

Two long strides into the run he popped up from behind a bush. She tried to apply the brakes but her boots were slick and the ground wet from the last onslaught. She and Colton met head-on in the middle of the yard like a gazelle and an Angus bull and the last thing she saw was two hoses dancing around in the grass like snakes spewing out venom as she fell forward onto the sloppy wet yard.

When she opened her eyes she was sprawled out on top of Colton. His arms held her tightly and her wet breasts were pressed against his hard chest. His green eyes had gone all dreamy and soft. One hand left her waist and his fingers twisted their way into her wet hair. She barely had time to moisten her already-wet lips when he drew her mouth to his.

She expected it to show her that the first pretend kisses were a fluke, but it didn't work the way Laura thought it would. She didn't want to pull away. She wanted the kiss to go on and on. His tongue found hers in a mating dance that left no doubt that if they were somewhere other than the backyard, this could lead to something hotter than the blue blazes of hell.

Roxie quickly turned off the water supply. "Old people are not supposed to do that in front of kids."

Laura rolled off Colton but he kept her pulled up to his side with an arm around her. Crazy thing was that it felt right for Laura to be there.

"Y'all are still playacting, aren't you?" Roxie whispered, her eyes darting around to see if someone was looking.

"She fell on top of me," Colton said.

"Looked to me like you liked it too much," Roxie said.

"Where is that shy little girl that used to live in your body?" Colton asked.

"I'm letting her out sometimes." Roxie giggled and went back inside the house.

"Teenagers! Best birth control on the planet," Colton said.

"Your kisses must be almighty potent to get a woman pregnant," Laura said.

"It's not the kisses, darlin'. It's what they lead up to."

"Who won?" Rusty yelled from the side of the house.

"I did," Colton yelled.

"He did not. I got him wetter than he got me," Laura said.

"Well, the winner gets to come on out to the barn and help me pull a calf. That damn bull you bred your prize heifer to is throwing one big calf and the momma needs some help."

Laura wiggled out of Colton's embrace. "Give me two minutes to get into dry clothes."

"Me too," Colton said.

"I won so I get to bring the baby into the world," she argued on the way to the porch.

"I won and it's my baby."

"Stop your bickering." Rusty grinned. "You are worse than two-year-old kids. You remind me of your mom and dad. Remember how they were always carryin' on like teenagers?"

Colton nodded. "Oh, yeah, I remember well. We'll meet you in the barn in ten minutes and we'll just see who gets to lay claim to that new baby."

Chapter 6

Laura rubbed the heifer's velvety ears and spoke softly to her. "Come on, sweetheart. You can do this. The first one is always the toughest. After this you can tell all the other heifers what a sweet little daughter you've got. Hell, honey, she might even win the blue ribbon at the state fair."

"It's going to be a prize bull, not a heifer calf, and I don't enter my calves in the fair," Colton said.

"Not anymore. He did when he was a kid. Maudie always let him buy a calf and show it," Rusty said.

"Trade places with me. My hands are smaller. I can get in there better than you can," Laura said.

Colton moved to one side but she could feel his eyes watching her every move.

Laura walked on her knees back to the heifer's back end. She shucked her chambray work shirt and greased up her hand and arm with petroleum jelly. Without even the faintest shudder, she shoved her hand into the cow's uterus and grabbed hold of a leg. She worked her fingers around until she found the other leg and pulled hard with the next contraction.

"It moved a couple of inches. Come on, momma; you push and I'll pull," she said.

The next contraction hit and Laura put all her weight and energy behind the pull. Several minutes and three contractions later she could see two hooves emerging.

As long as she kept talking to the heifer, the cow worked with her, but when she quit, the critter rolled her eyes and Colton had trouble keeping her on the ground.

"Keep talkin'," he said.

"You talk. I'm pullin'," Laura told him.

"She don't like me," Colton said.

"I wouldn't either if you'd bred me to a bull that was too damn big."

Rusty leaned on the stall door and chuckled.

"I see the nose. Push, girl, push. You get the head out and..."

Before she could blink a baby calf was lying in her lap and Colton was everywhere at once. Swabbing out its nose and mouth with a towel, yelling at it to breathe while Rusty took care of the afterbirth. The heifer stood up and started licking the little feller. He must've been waiting for his momma's touch because after the second lick up across his face, he sucked in air and let out a bawl.

"Congratulations, you two. You are the proud parents of a brand-new bull calf," Rusty said. "You done good, Laura."

She looked down at her messy shirt and jeans. Had it really been only two hours since she was sprawled out on top of Colton in the backyard? Well, he'd sure enough seen her at her worst. Every time he shut his eyes, he'd shudder at the memory of how she looked right then. He might even like the nerdy girl with the glasses better than the way she looked right then.

She should go to the house and get cleaned up, but she couldn't force herself away from that baby calf. He was so darn cute looking up at his momma with those big dark eyes.

"Please tell me he's not going to be a feeder calf. Tell me that you will keep him for breeding stock."

Rusty chuckled. "He chose that heifer because she comes from the best stock in this part of the state. He's been sittin' on pins and needles just hopin' this calf is a bull. Ain't no way that new baby boy is going to be hamburger."

The black calf stood on its wobbly legs and nosed its momma's udder. It was going to be a prize bull for sure. One that Colton could use to make a lot of money for breeding. And Laura was absolutely fantastic. Her hair had escaped the ponytail and strands were glued to her sweaty face and she didn't have a drop of makeup on. He wanted to scoop her up, carry her to the house, undress her slowly, and then give her a hot bath with his bare hands.

"Took both of you to get him into the world. Which one of you gets to name him?" Rusty asked.

"He's *going* to be hamburger," Colton said.

"No!" Laura hopped down and bowed up to Colton.

"Oh yes he is."

"But he's a bull calf and you wanted him to be a breeder bull. What's the matter with you? You can't send him off to the slaughterhouse. His momma worked too hard to bring him into the world and it's your fault that she had such a hard time. He can't be steak on someone's supper table, Colton. He just can't."

She fought the tears but finally one lonesome one escaped and trickled down her cheek.

Colton wiped it away with the tip of his dirty finger, leaving a smudge. "Shhhh, don't cry. I was just trying to pick a fight for fun. His name is Hamburger. I'd planned to name him that all along if he was a bull. His daddy is T-Bone."

Laura slapped him on the arm. "That was not funny."

Rusty laughed. "It was a little bit."

Laura whipped around and pointed at him. "You hush. You knew what he was saying because y'all talked about it. I would have bought him for my own before I let him go to the calf sale this fall."

Rusty nodded. "Guess I did. But what were you going to do with a bull calf in an apartment?"

"I would have figured something out. Look at those sweet little eyes."

"You're not a vegetarian, are you?" Colton asked.

"You saw me eat that steak and rib eye at supper, didn't you?" she answered.

"You might be doing that to throw me off the real you. Like Blake Shelton sings about in that song when he asks about who are you when I'm not lookin'."

"Honey, I am what you see. I wouldn't put on airs or change who I am for anyone, not even a rich cowboy," she said.

"Hey, that's a low blow," Colton shot back.

"Y'all can stay out here and argue until daylight. I'm turnin' in for the night." Rusty disappeared into the darkness. His whistling grew fainter and fainter until the noise of a couple of tomcats disagreeing about territory drowned it completely out.

"I need a bath," Laura said.

"Want me to wash your back?" Colton asked.

Laura's heart stopped, then took off like a bat out of hell, thumping so hard that it made her chest hurt. Did she want him to wash her back? Hell, yes, she did. She wanted more than that, but it wasn't going to happen because if it did, she just knew deep down in her soul that she'd leave her heart behind when she finished her work at the ranch. And it didn't take a genius to know that a body doesn't survive long without a heart.

"I can manage," she said.

In a couple of long strides Colton was beside her. He wrapped his big hand around hers. She wondered how he could even touch the hand with all the goop on it. She'd wiped it as clean as she could on an old towel after the calf was born, but it wasn't clean by any means.

"Thank you," he said softly when they reached the bottom of the stairs leading up to her apartment.

"For what?"

"For helping with the calf and for playing your part in this so well that it looks real."

"You are welcome."

For a split second, she thought that he might kiss her but then he took a step backwards and she realized no one was around so he didn't have to keep up with the ruse. When he dropped her hand, she felt as if something was missing—something vital and life-giving. Surely to God, she wasn't falling for Colton Nelson. It was all just for show and it had nothing to do with love, trust, and commitment.

She had turned on the light in her apartment and was on her way to turn on bathwater when her cell phone rang. She fished the phone from her pocket and looked at the caller ID, squealed when she saw her sister's name pop up, and almost dropped the phone in her haste to answer it. "Hello! How are you? Did you talk to Andy? Move over, Daisy. How'd you get into my apartment anyway?"

"And who is Daisy? Are you into something kinky like a threesome?" Janet's words tumbled out in a high-pitched squeak.

"Are you crazy?" Laura said. "Daisy is the ranch cat and I don't know how she got into the apartment unless she snuck in when I opened the door. And you know very well I'm not that kind of woman, Janet. For God's sake, don't start an argument on the first rattle out of the bucket. I haven't talked to you in what seems like a hundred years even though it's only been since the first of the month and I've been worried sick about you. All I can get out of Andy is that you are fine and going to meetings but I know that..."

Janet yelled into the phone, "Whoa! Catch your breath." Then she lowered her voice and said, "I'm fine. I haven't even been in a casino since I took you to the airport. I think I'm going to make it through the addiction this time. Gambler's Anon is great. And I was teasing about the kinky stuff. You never could take a joke worth a damn, sister."

Laura sighed. "Like I said, Daisy is a cat. I'm glad you are staying out of trouble. But I was afraid you were just pulling the wool over Andy Joe's eyes. Tell me the absolute truth, Janet."

"Pinky swear. No casino since you left. That last time scared the shit out of me. I realized I'm an addict," Janet said. "Now tell me about this billion-dollar rancher you've hooked up with. You'll never believe how I found out that you already have a boyfriend."

"How?" Laura whispered.

"One of my clients, Lacy Ann Walker, has a grandmother who lives in Bonham. The grandmother has a sister who lives in Ambrose and attends church with your boyfriend and his family. Lacy said that she tried to make a move on your cowboy a year ago when she was over there visiting but didn't get anywhere. How in the hell did a..."

"A what?" Laura asked.

"A goody-two-shoes like you get his attention?"

"And I thought we weren't going to fight." Laura sighed again.

"Ain't possible with us, but that don't mean I don't love my goody-two-shoes sister." Janet laughed.

"You should. She'll be working double hard for months to pay off your stupid debt."

"But I promise, I even pinky finger promise, it's the last time so that should count for something," Janet said.

"I'll believe it when I see it," Laura said. "Promise me that you are really going to the meetings and you are not going to gamble."

The line went quiet for several seconds before Janet spoke. "I promise. And I'm sorry, Laura. I mean it." Several seconds elapsed before Janet spoke again. "I saw his picture on the ranch website. He's not ugly. What's the matter with him?"

"He got tired of women chasing him for his money. I don't give a rat's ass whether he's got money or not."

Janet's laugh was brittle. "Well, that is definitely the gospel truth. You never did have any sense when it came to men. Always falling for the underdog. Is this relationship going to get serious?"

Laura had to think quickly. She'd promised that she wouldn't tell anyone that the whole thing with Colton was just a ruse and that included Janet.

"Well?" Janet said impatiently.

"Hell, I don't know where it's going. I'm taking it real slow," Laura said.

"Don't get bitchy now. It doesn't suit you. You are the sister who usually quotes self-help Scripture. I'm the bad sister," Janet said.

"Janet, you are not a bad sister but you've got to get past this addiction. I really mean it, so I hope you are telling me the truth."

"I am. I've lied to you in the past but this time is different. I'll call often now that I've earned the right. That Andy has a God complex and you can tell him I said so. Good night, little sister."

"Good night, Janet."

Laura laid the phone on the nightstand and headed straight for the shower. Daisy followed her, weaving around her legs and purring as if she was telling a story. The phone rang again. Laura stumbled over the cat and answered without checking the ID that time.

"Andy said that there's a ranch party coming up and he's making arrangements for me to fly from Amarillo to Dallas. He'll have a rental car waiting at the airport. What should I bring? I told him that I have Monday off. Could I stay that long? Can I come on Friday night after I get off work? I promise I'll make the GA meeting during my noon hour that day," Janet asked.

"I'm sure he won't mind. Just talk to him and tell him what you want to do. He's making the arrangements. I'm not."

"Formal?" Janet asked.

"Barn dance. Jeans, fancy shirt, and boots. You've got all that."

"I don't have good memories of a ranch," Janet said.

"I loved it," Laura told her.

"You loved the animals and growing things. You didn't love the life there," Janet said.

"It wasn't so bad."

"It was military camp with no pay and Aunt Dotty was the major general," Janet said.

"Throw out the bad memories and hang on to the good ones. We were together and we had our own cat. If she'd have let them put us in the system it could have been a lot worse." Laura laughed.

"But the cat stayed on the ranch when we left."

"Couldn't take him to the apartment anyway, and besides, he would have died if we would have cooped him up inside. He liked roaming free in the barns and catching rats and mice," Laura said.

"How in the hell you can stay so positive has always amazed me. I've got to go clean the shop and get it ready for tomorrow. See you soon."

Laura tossed the phone on the bed and headed for the bathroom one more time, but Daisy opted to stay curled up on her bed.

"Lord, please let her be telling me the truth about not gambling," Laura prayed. It wasn't the first time she'd uttered that prayer and probably wouldn't be the last.

Laura knew he wasn't there when she walked into the dining room. There were no flutters doing backflips in her stomach; her hands weren't clammy and her heart didn't thump one time.

Roxie looked up from the end of the table and said, "Good mornin'. Rusty and Colton just left. They're all wound up about buying a new tractor over in Sherman."

She was disappointed. She'd taken extra pains with her makeup and hair that morning and had dressed in a flowing gauze skirt and tank top.

"Oh, and Andy said that he had to go into town and talk to some tax people this morning so you were free to do whatever you want on the ranch. So what's it going to be?" Roxie asked.

"I'm going to change clothes and work in the flower gardens," she answered.

"You really like that stuff, don't you?"

Laura nodded. "I really do."

"Do what?" Maudie joined them.

"She likes to play in the dirt," Roxie said.

"I've got to make a trip to Sherman today. You want to go with me and buy some more flowers? You didn't get a fourth of what it's going to take to make that backyard presentable." Maudie went to the buffet.

Laura followed her. "No, but if I give you a list, would you bring back what I want? You'd just have to give it to the lady at the greenhouse and she'll load it in the truck for you."

"Sure thing. I'll drop off the list on the way to the hairdresser and pick it up when I get done," Maudie said.

Laura put her plate on the table and sat down. That first night at the supper table had broken the ice and pretty soon she'd found herself eating more and more meals at the big house.

Roxie pushed her plate back and said, "Aunt Maudie gets her hair done on Tuesday every week. Ten o'clock in the morning. She needs to change up her schedule. Someone is going to kidnap her and hold her for ransom. She's so predictable that it won't even be a hard job."

"You've been watching too much crime television. We live in Ambrose, not Chicago." Maudie cut up two fried eggs and talked between bites. "I'm wondering if one trip will get enough flowers for the yard. That greenhouse owner is going to get rich off of us this year."

"Are you telling me that I'm spending too much?" Laura asked.

"If I thought you were overspending, I'd say it outright. I don't beat around the bush when I've got something to say, young lady, but who is going to do the maintenance once you are gone?"

"I will," Roxie said. "I'd rather pull weeds and water pretty flowers as sniff hay dust and plow pastures."

Maudie glanced down the table at Roxie. "I'll hold you to it, girl."

"Yes, ma'am. Got to go. School bus gets here in five."

Maudie shifted her gaze to Laura. "I'll be leavin' at nine. Get your list ready. I'm glad we've got a minute by ourselves. I want an honest answer to an honest question. You willing to give me one?"

"Yes, ma'am, if I'm able, I will."

"You aren't taking advantage of this situation to pull a scam on my grandson, are you? It seems like this is all going too well for it to be right. I just want to know that you didn't plan something like this before you ever got here. Andy would have talked about Colton and it would have been easy to do," Maudie said.

"No, ma'am. There is no scam," Laura answered.

"Okay, I believe you and I hope you aren't lying to me."

Laura remembered her last conversation with Janet when she'd wished for the same thing. She would never, ever take advantage of Andy's job and respect that the family had for him by swindling Colton. But if the situation were reversed she could have thought the same thing.

"Believe me, I'm not lying. Money doesn't impress me. I like the security that it buys but I'm not that kind of woman. I'm just here for the job but I'm glad y'all are letting me play in the dirt, as Roxie calls it. I love gardening."

"Thank you," Maudie said.

The morning went by swiftly. She turned the soil on the rest of the flower beds. Maudie returned just before dinnertime with a pickup bed full of perennials, annuals, three buckets containing four-foot crepe myrtles, and several bags of mulch.

She stopped long enough for a bowl of Chester's wonderful potato chowder and two of his big, fluffy yeast rolls and went back to the yard. At four o'clock she heard the bus roll up in the front yard and five minutes later, Roxie stood in front of her. Tears flowed down her pretty cheeks like tiny rivers and dripped from her delicate chin onto her new shirt that Laura had bought the day before.

"What's wrong? What happened?" Laura whispered.

Her whole body went stone cold and her first thought was that Colton was dead. He'd gotten killed on the way home with that damn new tractor and she'd never know what might have been between them. Fate was truly a bitch for giving her a tiny taste of ranch life and putting Colton into her life, only to snatch it from her again.

Roxie sat down and laid her head on Laura's shoulder. Her sobs broke Laura's heart and she cried with the child. Roxie had known Colton her whole life, so the hurt had to be deeper for her, but Laura had kissed him, had felt whatever that was between them when he simply held her hand.

"That Rosalee has gone and taken Dillon away from me," Roxie said and burst into more tears.

"What happened and why do you think that?" Laura asked.

"She's used her witchcraft to steal Dillon away from me and I hope she dies," Roxie dragged the last word out into a long sobbing moan.

"This isn't about Colton?" Laura asked cautiously.

"No, is something wrong with Colton?" she asked.

"Not that I know of. It's just that I thought it might be the way you were crying."

"I'm mad at Rosalee. She's mean and hateful and she made me and Dillon fight and now she's going to steal him tonight. She's wanted him ever since she moved up here from Louisiana and he's more than just my boyfriend. He's my best friend in the world. He's probably my only real friend."

Laura patted Roxie on the back. "Suck it up and quit crying. She's not worth your tears. Now tell me what happened, and I'm your real friend, Roxie, and don't you ever forget it. And so is your Aunt Maudie."

"It was in Family Living class. We were taking this personality quiz the teacher handed out. And when we got finished she told us what the test said that we would be best suited doing for our whole lives. It was just a stupid test." Roxie swiped the back of her hand across her cheek.

"And?" Laura asked.

"Dillon and Rosalee would be best at something in the agriculture field. And I'd be good at fashion or interior design. She cheated. I know she did. She looked over his shoulder and filled in the same dots he did so he'd notice her."

Laura patted her on the knee. "You are right. It was just a test. Stop worrying. Dillon isn't going to break up with you."

Another burst of tears flooded Roxie's face. "But Rosalee played it up and said that I'd be a horrible rancher's wife. She lives in an apartment complex in town. I live on a ranch. So maybe I like clothes and maybe I like to pretty up my room. It don't mean I don't know anything about ranchin'. I bet if she'd been honest that it would've said she was a Cajun witch. I told Dillon that and he took up for her and said I was being mean."

It took lots of pats and reassurances before Laura calmed Roxie down.

"She is a witch because she put..." Roxie stopped mid-sentence, unzipped her backpack, and pulled out a rag doll with yellow yarn hair and blue eyes colored in with a Magic Marker.

It was dressed in jean shorts and a tank top and right where the heart would be in a real person, there was a straight pin jabbed in all the way to the round red pin head. It looked like a single drop of blood. There was a noose made of red yard around its neck, and its legs and arms were bound together with more of the same yarn.

"I found it in my locker at the end of the day," Roxie whispered. "I think it is supposed to be me and she's put a curse on me."

"It's too crude for a real witch, but it is a voodoo doll and she's just trying to scare you. Throw it away; it means nothing unless you let it get to you," Laura said through clenched teeth.

"And this." Roxie brought out a tiny cloth bag tied together at the top with another length of red yarn. She dumped it on the ground.

"That's a lock of my hair and one of my bracelets that I thought I'd lost."

Laura recognized the curse immediately.

"We'll put a counter curse on it," she said.

"You know about these things?"

"I worked with a woman who was Cajun. I've seen that kind of thing before and I know how to take the curse away."

Roxie stopped weeping altogether. "Can I watch?"

Laura hugged Roxie close to her side. "Give me the doll and the bag. I'll take care of it while you do your homework. To be effective, I'll have to take care of it in darkness and secrecy. But believe me, I know how to fix this voodoo doll."

Roxie handed over the doll and the bag. "Promise."

"Oh, yeah! Trust me, honey. Rosalee Roche's power is nothing compared to mine."

Chapter 7

"What in the devil are you doing?" Colton whispered.

She looked up at him and wondered if that deep drawl came through when he mumbled in his sleep. It damn sure did when he talked and when he whispered.

"Are you planting flowers in the dark?" He stepped out of the shadows and peered down into the hole she had dug.

"Shhh! Where is Roxie?"

"Sitting at the dining room table working on her algebra."

"I'm taking care of a voodoo doll."

"You are kidding, right?" He sat down on the edge of the raised flower bed and took a closer look.

"A girl at school is after Dillon and she's messing with Roxie. She put a silly fake voodoo doll in her locker and tried to make her believe she'd put a curse on her. I'm undoing the curse."

"For real? How do you know how to undo a curse?"

"Well, it's not by burying a silly dime-store doll in a flower bed. But Roxie trusted me to take care of it, so I am," Laura answered.

"But how do you know the difference between a fake and a real voodoo doll?"

Laura pushed dirt in on top of the doll that she'd torn apart, limb by limb. She drew a ring around the area with her finger, and said, "Dust to dust. Doll is dead and so is curse."

She rocked back on her heels and sat down on the ground beside the flower bed. "I knew a lady who was a real Cajun and who put real curses on people. Believe me, I do know the difference."

"Then why did you say that and draw a circle?"

She giggled. "It takes the curse away. It can't get out of the circle so it's doomed to stay in the ground forever. It's a lot of hocus-pocus, but hey, if it makes Roxie feel better, that's what's important."

"Is it done?" Roxie asked from the back door of the house.

"It is done. Curse over," Laura said.

"I've got my homework done. Aunt Maudie says I can go swimming. Y'all want to go with me?"

"You betcha," Laura yelled back. "You ready now?"

The door slammed. "Last one in the pool is a rotten egg."

Colton jumped up to give her some competition, but Laura grabbed his knee. "Let her win. She needs it today."

He took off in an easy lope. "You cheated, girl. You got ahead of me."

Roxie's voice rang through the night air. "You are old and slow."

"Hey," Laura yelled a few steps behind him. "Who are you calling old?"

"Both of you," Roxie hollered.

She was pulling on the bottoms to a bright blue bikini when Laura opened the door to the dressing room. "See, you are old," she teased.

"Yes, but age knew how to take that curse off so be careful," Laura said.

Roxie clamped a hand over her mouth to keep the giggles back, but it was useless. "It's gone. I feel all better, but you and Colton are still old."

Laura peeled out of her dirty jeans, donned a cute little tankini, and followed Roxie out of the ladies' cabana room in time to see Colton do a cannonball dive off the side of the pool into the deepest water. He surfaced and ran a hand over his face. "Looks like you are both rotten eggs because I beat you into the water. Now who is old, Miz Roxie?"

Roxie pushed her hair back behind her ears. "Did Laura tell you what Rosalee did? Thank goodness Laura knew exactly what to do."

"I suppose you could feel it in your bones when she said her chant?" Colton said.

"Yes, I did. All the bad feelings in my chest went away. It was just before I opened the back door, wasn't it?"

Listening to Roxie weep that afternoon had come close to breaking Laura's heart. Memories flooded back to the day that she'd felt just like that. The social worker had come to the trailer right after their mother's funeral. She said that they were wards of the state and she couldn't guarantee that they'd wind up in the same home. Laura had felt like crying but she had to be strong for Janet, who was sobbing so hard she couldn't breathe.

Laura had marched right up to the social worker, popped her hands on her hips, and said, "If you take me away from my sister, I will starve."

"What do you mean?"

"I will not eat. I won't even drink water. I will die and it will be your fault."

That had made the lady uncomfortable and she'd tried to reason with both little girls. But Laura simply shook her head and told her the same thing over and over. They had to stay together or she would die.

That's when Great Aunt Dotty had come from the kitchen and told the social worker that no one was taking her blood kin anywhere. She would be responsible for the girls until they were of age. If there was paperwork to be signed then bring it to the trailer that afternoon because she'd be taking the girls home with her the next day. Looking back, that had been the beginning of the time when Laura became the oldest sister. That had been the day she'd taken care of Janet for the first time, but it sure hadn't been the last time.

"You sure are quiet. Does removing the curse mean that you aren't supposed to talk until the sun comes up?" Roxie asked.

"Just wool gathering," Laura said.

"What's that?"

"Thinking," Colton answered.

"Wow! You mean you old folks can think?" Roxie teased.

Laura splashed water toward her. "Honey, blink twice and you'll be the age we are right now."

Roxie made a big show of opening and closing her eyes two times. "Look, I'm still just sixteen. It didn't work." She sunk into the water and did two laps before coming up for air. "Y'all are still old. Must be the age that keeps drawing you to each other. When I went under you were across the pool from each other and now you are together."

"Be careful who you're calling old, young lady,"

Maudie said on her way from the door to the falls. "Thought I might take a dip tonight, but if you think they're old then maybe you won't want to play pool basketball with a creakin' old fossil like me."

Roxie pulled herself up over the edge and sprawled out in a lounging chair. "Aunt Maudie, you won't ever be old. I bet I can beat you by three points."

"We'll see about that." Maudie disappeared into the cabana.

Teenagers had always amazed Laura. Their emotions were as unstable as water and changeable as the weather. Teenage girls were either whining or giggling and the boys were ready to fight at the drop of a hat. She'd watched them for hours as they strutted around in the mall or outside the school parking lot across the street from where she'd worked.

Colton swam over next to her, sat on the side, and dangled his feet in the water. "You really are quiet tonight."

"I wouldn't want to be a teenager again for all the dirt in Texas."

"That's a lot of dirt," he said.

"That's a lot of emotions. I'm going to get dressed and go check on Hamburger," she said. "Maudie can keep Roxie's mind off that little witch at school. I did my duty by taking the curse off her."

"I'll go with you but we don't have to get dressed. We can go in our swimsuits. The night is warm. Sally will get your clothes tomorrow morning when she cleans down here."

"I'll get my own clothes, and besides, I'll need my work boots first thing tomorrow."

She passed Maudie coming out as she went inside.

With her height and slim build, Maudie still looked good in a bathing suit.

"I wish I had six inches of your height," she said.

Maudie smiled brightly. "I always hated being tall and gangly. When I was a girl I would have robbed banks if they'd had boobs like yours instead of just plain old dollar bills."

Laura giggled. "I'll trade. You give me some height and I'll share my boobs."

"I'd do it in a heartbeat if it was possible. Time to go show Roxie that age and experience often wins over youth and beauty," Maude said.

"Colton and I are on our way to see about that new bull calf," Laura said.

"I heard you did a pretty good job bringing that baby into the world. See you tomorrow," Maudie said.

"He's a gorgeous calf. He's going to grow up to be a prize bull."

The tankini Laura had chosen that evening was a multicolored swirl of bright colors against a blue background. She put a chambray work shirt over the top, leaving it unbuttoned, jammed her feet down into her boots with no socks, folded the rest of her clothing neatly, and tucked it under her arm.

Colton was waiting beside the door when she came out. He wore cutoff denim shorts, boots, and the shirt he'd worked in that day, unbuttoned and showing ripped muscles underneath. A foot of space separated them when they reached the pool where Maudie and Roxie were already in a heated argument over the rules.

He slipped her clothing out from her arm, laid them

on a chaise lounge, and said, "Hey, Roxie, lay this on the steps up to Laura's apartment, okay?"

"Sure thing, but I'll be glad to just take them inside for her."

"Thank you, that would be great. The door is open," Laura said.

Colton threw an arm around Laura's shoulders. His legs were longer than hers but he shortened his step and they kept perfect time. It was about two hundred yards from one barn to the other. She could have sprinted that far without even losing her wind, but when he slid the big barn door open and there was no sign of her new calf or its mother, she gasped.

"Did he die?"

"No, he was fine this morning so I turned them both back out to pasture. He's been romping around all day. He's a happy little bull calf and there are other calves his size to play with him."

"Then why did you bring me in here?"

He sat down on a bale of hay and patted the one beside him. "I want to talk. I want straight answers and nothing else. And I didn't want Roxie or Aunt Maudie to hear."

"Then talk," she said.

"Are you for real?"

"That's a weird question, Colton. Real what? Real hair color, yes, it's all natural. My eyes are this shade of blue even when I use my contacts. My glasses are really this thick because I'm half blind without them. My boobs are real and my lips have no collagen. They're all what God blessed me with. I do have pierced ears, if that counts as fake."

"Okay, I'll put it plainer. Did you agree to this pretend thing because of my money?" he said.

She opened her mouth to give him an angry answer but snapped it shut and thought about what she'd say for a long time.

"Well?" he asked.

"I'm thinking."

"About how to beat around the bush?"

"Words are just words, Colton. If I was trying to con you, then I'd lie so well you wouldn't even catch me, wouldn't I? I'd say what you wanted to hear, maybe bat my eyelashes, and reassure you with kisses or sex. But it would all be part of the trick to swindle you."

"Then you admit that you did see an opportunity?" he asked.

"No, I don't admit that. I'm an honest person. I'm not playing any kind of game. Whether you believe that or not is up to you. What you see is what I am. No bells. No whistles. Just plain old hardworking Laura Baker. No intrigue and no fraud."

The silence when she finished was almost suffocating. She felt like she did when she was a little girl and the social worker said that she and Janet were going to different homes. Her chest hurt and her stomach felt queasy. But she couldn't make him believe her or trust her, either. He'd been running from women and people with an agenda ever since he won the lottery.

His hand covered hers. His fingers inched their way between hers with the tips resting on her palm. He scooted over until his thigh was pressed against hers and whispered, "I believe you but..."

"But you are a billionaire and most folks see money when they look at you, right?"

He was nodding when she looked up.

"Well, Colton Nelson, I don't see money. I see a hardworking cowboy with a sense of humor who is a lot of fun to be around. I don't believe that money is evil, but it is worthless when it comes to the important things in life," she whispered back.

He untangled his fingers from hers and slipped his hand around her back. It felt hot on her cool skin but not as hot as his lips when they claimed her mouth for a long, lingering kiss that felt very, very real and not the least bit make-believe.

His tongue flicked through her slightly parted lips, slowly and methodically making love to her. Kisses were so personal, almost more so than sex. Words couldn't describe the feelings they stirred within her. Emotions were exposed that she had never, ever felt before.

Liquid heat boiled inside her, creating a desire for more and more. She shifted her body until she was sitting in his lap. One hand pressed against his rock-hard chest, the fingers on the other hand combed their way into his thick dark hair. The kisses went from hot to scorching as she pressed her whole body hard against his.

His hand moved around her rib cage and under the top of the bathing suit to cup a breast, at first cautiously and then more daring as he toyed with it. She gasped. God Almighty, didn't he realize that his hands were hotter than blue blazes? She wiggled even closer and moaned, not caring if she woke up tomorrow with burns all over her body from his touch.

He pulled away from her enough to move his hand downward toward her bikini bottom. If Roxie came running in the door right then, she intended to dig that damned doll back up and create a real voodoo doll from it.

But it wasn't Roxie who stopped the progress.

She was unzipping his wet jean shorts when Daisy jumped onto her lap and laid a half-dead mouse on her bare thighs. It made a chirping noise like a baby bird and flipped around on her leg, tail swishing back and forth until Daisy batted it with her paw, sending it flying through the air to land on her other leg.

Colton's hand stayed in the bikini bottoms when she jumped off his lap and together they went sprawling in the hay. Daisy grabbed her mouse and darted away with it straight up the stacked hay to a higher place.

"What was that all about?" Colton asked.

She wiggled free of his hand and rolled away from him. The quiver started at her neck and traveled to her toes, then shot back up through her body and to her cheeks before it stopped.

"Mouse."

"Where?"

"Daisy put it in my lap. It touched both my legs." She swiped at her skin, trying to wipe away the feel of the critter's legs trying to get traction against her bare skin.

"Damn cat," he muttered.

"I hate mice. Absolutely hate them."

He sat up and combed his hair back with his fingers. "Good."

"Good? What's good about them or hating them?"

"I thought the reaction was against me. It's good that it wasn't."

She opened her mouth but nothing came out. She'd never, ever—not one time in her life—gone that far that fast with anyone. She didn't even do kisses on first dates, and her two relationships had taken six months of serious dating to make it to the bedroom.

She swiped at her bare leg for the hundredth time. It took all of her willpower just to keep from running the whole distance to the carriage house. It would take a bar of soap and an hour of scrubbing before she felt clean again.

He ran a hand up her arm. "Don't suppose we could start where we left off."

"Not a chance. I need a bath to get the feel of mouse off me. You?"

"I think I'll go back to the pool and see if the cold water will take care of my problem." He chuckled.

She rocked up onto her knees and then stood. "Sorry about that."

"Wasn't your fault, darlin'. But that damned cat best stay out of my sight for the next week."

She didn't use a whole bar of soap but she did scrub until her thighs were red. When she finished she tucked the ends of a big fluffy towel under her arm and padded into the bedroom. There was Daisy, sitting on the extra pillow and licking her paws.

"I'd lick my paws too if they'd touched a nasty old mouse." Laura said.

The cat ignored her.

"Please tell me you didn't bring that thing to the bed."

She looked up and meowed.

Laura carefully checked every inch of the bed but found nothing. She dropped the towel, stepped into clean underpants, and a pulled a nightshirt over her head.

"How do you get in here through closed and locked doors?"

Daisy turned around twice on the pillow and curled up in a ball, putting her paw over her nose.

"Well, good night to you too. I'm going to figure out how you are getting in and out of my room and when I do, I intend to fix it. Until then, you'd do well to remember that cats who bring mice to me are not my friend. Do you understand?"

Chapter 8

Daisy was gone the next morning when Laura awoke. She checked under the bed, in the bathroom, and even the window ledge. She did find a paw print on the rim of the potty and a faint one on the tile floor leading back to the bedroom. They ended there and no matter which angle she looked, the carpet yielded no clues. But while she was on her hands and knees trying to figure out if the cat was magic, she noticed a tuft of yellow hair stuck in the air vent at the bottom of the door. She crawled over to it and there was a shadow on the other side right along with some serious purring.

Laura fussed at the cat. "Don't beg me to open that door. You know how to get in and out of every room in this house. Your purring don't charm me. You are spoiled. Cats don't belong in the house. They belong in the barn, catching rats and mice. And that sounded just like Aunt Dotty!"

The vent popped to the inside. Daisy pushed her head inside and her body followed. She meowed at Laura and began to weave around her legs, begging for attention. Laura ran her hand around the vent and found that it was hinged on the top but the bottom was completely free.

"So this is your magic. Well, darlin', if you ever bring a mouse near me again, I'll duct tape it shut. You can butt your little brains out and this vent won't open."

Daisy meowed again and pushed her way right back

out onto the landing at the top of the staircase. Laura dressed in jeans and a knit shirt, heated up a cup of coffee in the microwave, and drank it on the way to the house. Daisy followed so close to her heels that she had to be careful to avoid stepping on the cat.

When she opened the door Daisy rushed in ahead of her. Laura peeked into the dining room to find it empty, snagged a piece of toast, and was in the hallway when she heard a crash followed by Roxie fussing at the cat. It was a good thing that Aunt Maudie had her own suite of rooms off the dining room. And that Daisy could not tattle because what Roxie called that cat would have gotten her in big trouble.

Laura had grown up with a mother that had a large repertoire of cuss words, sometimes strung together so well that they would blister the paint off of a car, so she understood just exactly where Roxie's vocabulary came from. She smiled and waited to hear her apologize to the cat but it didn't happen. Daisy trotted down the stairs, her tail straight up, as if she were pissed at the whole world.

Colton was sipping coffee when Laura made it into the dining room. "Good mornin'. Have any mouse problems last night?"

"No, but I figured out how that pesky cat gets into my room."

"Through the vent in the door. I would have told you if you'd asked. Folks that built this place had a little Chihuahua. If Daisy gets much fatter, she'll have trouble using the vents. I'm just glad that Donald doesn't think he belongs in the house too."

"Donald?"

"Remember, Andy told you about him the first day you met Daisy. And for the record, Daisy is named after Daisy Duke, not Daisy Duck. She gets her feelings hurt when anyone thinks that she's a duck. Donald is named after Donald Duck so that's why most people think that when they meet Daisy. Donald stays down at the pond most of the summer but when food gets scarce he comes waddling up here to beg for scraps or for a cup of the special grain that Rusty gets for him." Colton smiled.

She heard the words but she felt the smile. It generated enough electricity in the room to crackle. "I betcha Sally would have something to say about a duck in the house."

"I imagine she would. At least Daisy is trained to a litter pan. Sally would have our hides if she had to clean up after Donald." He chuckled. "I've got a question."

She poured a cup of coffee and carried it to the table. "If you get to ask one, then I do. That's the rule of twenty questions, and I believe we still have fifteen left for each of us."

"Fair enough. Do you have a real boyfriend waiting in the wings for when you leave here?" he asked.

"Do you have a woman you are already wishing you'd asked out before you agreed to this situation?"

"No, I do not," he answered quickly.

She sipped her coffee. "I'm not in a relationship with anyone. I have been in the past. Twice. Neither worked out. If I was in love with someone else, I would not have agreed to the arrangement and I would not have kissed you or made out with you in the barn."

"Then you give your whole heart when you give it?" he asked.

"I'm not sure I'd know how to give my whole heart to anyone. That would involve a lot of trust. The only person I've ever trusted that much is my sister."

He rubbed a hand across his chin. "Your sister? You have to bail her out of trouble every time you turn around and you trust her that much?"

"She's always in trouble, but through it all I know she loves me and she would never, ever forsake me."

His dark eyebrows knit together. "Kind of like Granny has been to me, I guess."

"I suppose so. Why did you even want to know?"

"Because I would never trespass on another man's territory."

She believed him. "Never have?"

"No, ma'am. Could have lots of times even before the money, but if it's got someone else's brand, it's not mine. Seems dishonest as well as immoral."

She had to swallow the mouthful of coffee fast to keep from spewing it across the table. "Women are not cattle!"

"No, ma'am, they are not. A man should respect them far more than he does his livestock and a decent man wouldn't steal another man's heifer. I could use some help in the hay field this morning. I asked Andy if I could borrow you since he's going into town for the day to meet with the tax people. You up for doing some baling today?"

She wasn't sure if he'd just called her a heifer or if he'd paid her a compliment or what he'd said. Sitting inside a tractor cab would give her plenty of time to think it through and figure out exactly what Colton Nelson was beating around the bush about. Mercy, but the man's deep drawl was intoxicating. He could describe the method of making manure and it would mesmerize her.

"I'll be ready soon as I eat. Meet you on the porch. Well, good morning, Roxie. You are running late," she said.

"I'm sick. I can't go to school," Roxie said.

"That's bullshit," Laura told her. "Go back upstairs, put on that pretty new shirt I bought you for the party next week and those fancy jeans. And get out that fancy headband with the sparkly stuff on it for your hair. You are going to school!"

"I can't go, Laura. I really can't."

"You want Rosalee to win? The curse won't be undone unless you face her within twenty-four hours."

Roxie mumbled all the way back up the stairs. When she reached the top she yelled back down, "If I wear my new things to school, what am I going to wear to the party?"

"I'll bring you something special from Dallas or we'll go back to the store. Get dressed. You've got fifteen minutes. I'll make a sausage biscuit and pour up some juice for you to take with you to eat on the bus," Laura hollered back.

Roxie's voice floated to the dining room. "I'd rather have a container of milk from the fridge. You may get paired up with the preacher for the games since you are making me go to school when I'm sick."

Colton chuckled. "I'm not sure that I like this new rebellious Roxie."

"Of course you like her and she'll grow up to be a strong woman if you give her a few gentle pushes," Laura told him. "Now, tell me more about these games."

"The barn party will start in the morning and last all day. The games are a big part of it. She gets to play matchmaker for the first time this year. You and I will be a couple, naturally, and she and Dillon will be one. She'll pair your sister up with one of the guys from the bunkhouse," Colton explained.

"But she and Dillon are broke up," Laura argued.

"They'll make up and break up a couple of times before then. Don't you remember what it was like when you were sixteen?" He laughed.

"Not if I can help it," she muttered under her breath. "Want to tell me what to expect on the games?"

"It's all about teamwork and we have to trust each other if we want to win. And I really, really want to win, so expect to work hard." He settled his straw hat on his head and headed toward the porch.

At the end of the day she was hot and sweaty. She'd listened to a Creedence Clearwater Revival CD she'd found in the cab of the tractor at least a dozen times. The twang of the guitar and the words to "Green River" stuck in her head.

Her boots made little dust devils in the loose dirt when she hopped down from the tractor. Rusty and Colton drove up, leaving clouds of dust mixing together behind the trucks in their wake. Rusty didn't waste a bit of time getting out of his big black truck and hurrying over to the tractor.

"I'm just here to get my favorite Creedence CD. I drove that tractor yesterday and left it in there by mistake. Missed it today," he said.

"So you are a Creedence fan?"

"Oh, yeah! I cut my teeth on their music. My momma and daddy played it all the time."

"I might've worn a couple of hours' worth of listenin' off it today."

"That's all right. Anyone who appreciates good old CCR can borrow my music." He stood on the running board and grabbed the CD. "You even made sure it was back in the case."

"Oh, yeah! It would be a sin to get a scratch on a Creedence CD."

Colton held the truck door open for her. "You really like that kind of music?"

"Listened to it all day, though." She hopped up into the seat. "I like country music better than anything, but CCR has a life and pulse of its own. My sister loves it so I know the lyrics to just about everything they ever did. And before you ask, yes, she knows the lyrics to every Marty Stuart, Travis Tritt, and Miranda Lambert song too."

Colton turned the truck around and headed toward the house. "Blake Shelton?"

She nodded. "And the G Kings."

"Who or what are the G Kings?"

"You don't know?" she asked.

He shook his head.

She smiled. "That would be George Strait and George Jones. Have you seen Roxie yet?"

He shook his head. "I hope she gets off that bus with a smile on her face. I want to strangle someone when she's unhappy. That kid's been through enough upheaval in her life."

"So she's been in and out of Maudie's life ever since she was a little girl?"

"Not a little girl. Ever since she was a three-month-old baby. I was just fourteen the first time Granny brought her home from church. Her momma asked Granny to keep her for the afternoon and didn't show up to pick her up until Tuesday. It was summertime so it didn't interfere with Granny's job."

"Maudie's a good woman to give her support and stability. I hope that she showed Rosalee who is really the boss today."

Colton flashed one of his brilliant smiles. "Oh, I'm sure that little girl won't mess with her anymore, and poor old Dillon better hit the ground with apologies spewin' out of his mouth."

"Bless her heart. It's not easy growing up. She reminds me so much of Janet that it's eerie. Who do you think she'll pair my sister up with for the party?"

"Who knows, but it's Cynthia that is going to make her rich. I swear she's got pure gypsy blood in her. She can figure a way to con a dollar out of anything. Rusty and Andy both will pay her big bucks to keep from having to spend the whole day with Cynthia. I'm going to give her all the names of the folks who'll be participating in the games tonight. That'll keep her busy all weekend while we are gone."

Roxie bailed off the porch, slung both her arms around Laura, and hugged her tightly. She'd taken the cute little headband out of her hair and had pinned it up off her neck in a messy bun. She'd changed out of her fancy jeans and new shirt and wore an oversized faded Western shirt over a pair of cutoff jean shorts.

"It worked! You did it! You are a better witch than Rosalee. She called Dillon and admitted that she'd cheated on the test so that he'd notice her. She must've thought that would impress him, but he told her that he didn't like cheaters and he apologized to me. You are a genius," Roxie said.

"You are a genius," Colton whispered.

"What's he talking about?" Roxie asked.

"Nothing. See, I was right. You needed to go to school today."

Roxie looped her arm through Laura's. "It wasn't easy but you should've seen her face when I got off the bus with Dillon this morning. I don't think she'll be messing with me anymore."

"Sometimes it's tough wanting what's not yours," Laura said.

"Don't I know it. Come up to my room with me and we'll pick out fingernail polish for your trip."

"I'm a mess. Why don't you get the polish and bring it out to my apartment. I'll get a quick shower while you are gathering it up."

Roxie nodded and Laura made her way through the flower beds to her apartment. She'd barely gotten out of the shower and slipped into lounging pants and a tank top when Roxie rapped on the door.

"Come on in," Laura yelled.

Roxie carried a shoebox into the apartment, set it on the bed, and slouched down in a rocker beside the window.

Daisy pushed through the vent into the room and jumped up on the bed. She curled up on the pillow and eyed Roxie with an evil look.

"Look at that animal. She hates me and I didn't do a

thing," Roxie said. "They say that cats don't like gypsies. Do you think it's true?"

"I wouldn't know. Are you really a gypsy?" Laura asked.

"Momma says that my daddy's momma was one and that I look and act just like her. She said that Grandma was horrible and I'd probably grow up to be just like her," Roxie said.

"You'll grow up to be whoever you want to be. Set your goals and keep your eyes right on them. If you fall, get up and go again and don't let anyone push you around," Laura said.

"You believe all that?" Roxie asked.

"I do because I lived through being sixteen in the same situation you've got," Laura said. "Now I bet Daisy is just playing hard to get. Ignore her. Let's look at the fingernail polish."

Roxie opened the box and picked up a bottle. "Crimson red. You should definitely wear deep red with that dress and your toenails should match. Let's put diamonds on your big toes. I've got some left from the Christmas party."

Tears hung on Laura's lashes and she wiped them away with the back of her hand. It would be wonderful if by magic a person could pour a little bleach or some kind of miracle drug into their gene pool. Roxie would always be plagued by genetics just like Laura was. Neither of them had much to offer when it came to reaching into the DNA pool for parenting role models. But maybe, just maybe, with Maudie's firm hand and gentle love, environment could override the murky gene puddle enough that Roxie would be a well-rounded woman when she grew up.

"Are you crying?" Roxie asked.

"I rubbed my eyes with lotion on my hands and they're watering. Let me see that crimson red you were talking about." Laura nodded toward the lineup of polish on the dresser.

"Okay, but you got to look at a bunch so you know you made the right decision. Starting here, they're rated from one through ten. I tried to match your dress from memory but red is such a fickle color. This is my favorite." Roxie held up the first one.

Laura pulled her dress out of the closet and laid it out on the bed. "Put the bottles right on the dress and see which one is the true match," she suggested.

Roxie clapped her hands. "Look at that. I got it right."

"Perfect match. You've got an eye for fashion."

Roxie beamed. "No one says a ranchin' woman has to look all trashy!"

Laura giggled. "No, they don't. And you might turn out to be the first woman in Texas who can work on a ranch and design clothing, too. Tomorrow right after school, I'll be ready for a manicure and pedicure. Colton says we're leaving the ranch at five. Does that give you enough time?"

Roxie frowned. "Remember, we don't have school tomorrow. We are going to start the beautification at one o'clock. I've got it all lined out, step by step."

"I'm in your capable hands, but right now let's look through those magazines over there and see what I should do with my hair," Laura said.

The frown turned into a grin and for the next hour they turned page after page, earmarking some to look at later and giggling over some that looked downright ridiculous. It was a few minutes until six when Laura stretched and said that she'd better change into jeans and put on some shoes so that they could go to the big house for supper.

"I am hungry. I didn't eat much lunch and we got to talking and I forgot all about an after-school snack," Roxie said.

She continued to chatter on and on about what she had planned for the next day as they left Laura's apartment and went arm in arm across the yard. But Laura heard little of it. Something had triggered a faint memory of Janet standing on a stool, making sandwiches for them. It had to have been before Aunt Dotty took them to Texas because their mother was lying asleep on the sofa.

Laura tried to hang on to the vision but it faded. The lady on the sofa had long, curly blond hair, and light brown lashes fanned out on a delicate face.

Colton winked at her from the buffet. Standing there in snug-fitting jeans, a plaid Western shirt, and freshly shaven, he looked like a magazine advertisement for Stetson or maybe Jack Daniel's. She inhaled deeply and caught a whiff of shaving lotion. All that, plus the sexy wink, was enough to put her firmly in Rosalee's boots: she wanted what she could not have.

Chapter 9

Laura was nervous but she didn't panic until the elevator doors slid open. Straight ahead a glass wall gave them a gorgeous view of the sunset behind the Dallas skyline. The bellboy rolled the luggage carrier into the sitting room and set the suitcases beside a brass and glass table with two chairs pushed up under it.

Colton handed him a bill and he pushed the carrier back into the elevator. Both of them looked at Laura, who was still in the elevator. She managed to take a step forward but it wasn't without great effort. She wasn't one to let anything intimidate her but the sight of that room did a fine job of doing so. She did not belong there and worry wrapped its cold arms around her like a blanket of ice.

The bellboy smiled brightly and pushed the carrier back into the elevator. The doors shut behind her and she whipped around. Yes, there were buttons to open it again if she wanted to run away.

"It is a two-bedroom suite. Both are exactly the same." Colton threw open the door to the right of the glass wall. "You got a preference?"

Laura shook her head. She did but it had nothing to do with which bedroom was hers for the weekend.

"Then you can have this one." He picked up her suitcase and carried it inside with her following behind him.

It was a lovely room with a king-sized bed and a

huge bathroom with a Jacuzzi, separate shower, and enormous mirror above a two-sink vanity. It wasn't the room, the view, or the bathroom that struck her mute. It was a sudden case of acute anxiety about what was in her suitcases.

She shouldn't have been so quick to leave Tressa's Boutique in a snit about the prices. She would look like Cinderella had come to the ball in her scrub rags. She glanced at her hair in the mirror above the dresser and bit back a moan. Jimmy was probably already booked solid so she'd have to manage on her own. Thank God Roxie had helped her pack a curling iron and hair dryer.

"Is something wrong?" Colton asked.

"Not a thing. I wasn't expecting all this." She took the whole suite in with a wide sweep of her hands.

"It is a little overpowering, isn't it? But since I'm the biggest contributor in their scholarship fund, they give me the penthouse suite each year. Granny says it's sinful to stay in a room that costs more a night than she made in two months when she was cooking at the school, and you got to admit, it's not nearly as big as the ranch house." He laughed.

"I agree with her," she said.

"I've already ordered room service to be brought up at six." He looked at the clock beside her bed. "Ten minutes from right now. Then I have a meeting at seven which will last until at least ten. You are invited to go with the wives and girlfriends for drinks at the hotel bar. I'll introduce you to Karen. She's the one who plans the itinerary for the ladies. You will like her."

"How many ladies are there?" Laura asked.

"Seven usually, but I understand two didn't come this

year. One is getting over a heart attack and another one just had a baby last week. So that makes five. There are seven on the board of directors. Number has to be an odd one so we can't hang up a vote. They are all over fifty except me. Most of the women are middle-aged. The one that had a heart attack is about seventy. You will be the youngest one among them."

Her eyebrows shot up to her hairline. "A new baby at fifty?"

"She's the third or maybe fourth wife. He's sixty. She's about thirty."

"Are they all billionaires?"

"I'm the poor kid on the block amongst them." He laughed.

"Are you joking?"

"Not a bit."

"What do their suites look like?" she whispered.

He laughed so hard that they didn't hear room service arriving.

"Excuse me..." a lady said loudly from the elevator doors.

Laura peeked out around into the sitting room. "Yes?"

"Your supper, ma'am."

Colton brushed past her and pulled a money clip from the pocket of his jeans. He handed the woman a tip and she removed the silver domes from the plates after she set the plates on the small table. "Just let me know if you need anything else, Mr. Nelson, and I'll get it up here within minutes."

"Thank you." He was already pulling out Laura's chair when the woman disappeared into the elevator.

The butterflies in her stomach had to have been

feeding on pure sugar, the way they flitted around. There was a steak the size of a plate, baked potato dressed up with sour cream, butter, bacon, and cheese, and steamed broccoli—and she didn't think she could swallow a single bite.

"I hope steak is all right? I remembered that you like yours medium well."

"It looks delicious."

"Butter?" He held up a dinner roll.

"Yes, please."

He split the roll and slathered the inside with softened butter from a crystal dish in the middle of the table.

She cut off a small bite of the steak and surprisingly enough it chased the butterflies away when she swallowed. "Tomorrow? Tell me what's going on tomorrow. I feel like I just walked into another world."

"I'll be in meetings all day. Karen plans the day for you ladies so I can't help you out there. Ask her tonight. Meetings end at five and we'll have a snack in the room, then at eight we have the formal dinner. After that, there is a dance. Sunday we sleep late and go home in the afternoon. Checkout is at noon."

She fidgeted with her hair, curling the ends and putting on makeup. Roxie said that she'd picked Maudie's brain and on the first night jeans and boots were acceptable. So Laura dressed in starched jeans, a Western-cut shirt in brown silk with lace inserts on the yoke, and brown boots that had been shined.

Colton whistled when she walked out into the sitting room which helped so much that she wanted to kiss him.

"Well, don't you look stunning," he said.

"Thank you. I wasn't sure what your girlfriend would

wear to one of these things," she said. "So I asked Roxie to talk to Maudie."

"Honey, you are going to turn heads, believe me." He smiled.

She stole glances at him in the mirrored sides of the elevator on the way down to the lobby. She wouldn't turn nearly as many heads as he would in his creased black dress jeans, eel boots, and white shirt topped with a Western-cut sports jacket. He was today's modern cowboy all decked out to rub elbows with the Texas elite.

The doors opened and he threw an arm around her shoulder. It amazed her how well she fit there beside him as they crossed the floor to a table where four women waited.

"Well, would you look at this, girls," the oldest of the women said. "Our Colton has done grown up and brought a guest with him. This should be interesting."

He said their names but not a one of them stuck in Laura's head, and she was usually really good at putting names and faces together. Then he said, "Karen, sweetheart, I'm going to leave Laura in your hands. Don't y'all scare her off now. I kind of like her."

He brushed a sweet kiss across Laura's lips. "See you later, darlin'."

She was so nervous that her hands were shaking and his kiss, however sweet, didn't help a bit when it turned her knees into jelly. A real relationship couldn't be one damn bit hotter than the false one had been since day one. She watched him disappear behind double doors into a conference room and then turned to face the other women.

Karen looped an arm through hers and led her to the

bar. "I'm Karen and you've been left in my care. We'll take two longneck Coors," she told the bartender who had stopped at their table. "I hope I'm right in assuming you drink beer."

Laura nodded.

"Good. Then me and you are going to get along just fine, honey."

Karen wasn't any taller than Laura. Her red hair was ratted up into a French twist and her eyebrows were painted on, expertly arched halfway to her hairline. "These other broads like their Kool-Aid drinks but give me a beer or a double shot of Jim Beam any day of the week."

"Don't pay no attention to her. She's full of shit. And as fast as Colton said our names I bet you don't remember a damn one of them. He probably introduced me as Barbara but I'm Bunny to my friends. Bartender, make me a White Russian. Kool-Aid drinks my ass."

With her three chins and beady little eyes she looked more like a bulldog than a bunny. Besides, bunnies never prop a boot heel on the bar rail and order up a White Russian.

"And then whip up two margaritas," a third woman said before turning to Laura. "I'm Tootsie. That's not my real name but the only people who know that information is the courthouse personnel where my birth certificate is registered and my parents, and they are both dead. And this is Melanie. Pull up a chair, honey, and tell us how you landed that sexy cowboy. Or maybe tell us how he landed you—that might be a better story."

Tootsie was tall, thin, and had blond hair. The wrinkles in her face said that the hair color was right out of a bottle. Next to Laura, Melanie was probably the youngest one of the four and she had to be close to fifty. Her brown hair was cut in chin-length layers, and her hazel eyes were enormous behind thick lenses in her glasses.

Laura stole a chair from a nearby table.

Tootsie scooted over to make room for her. "How did all this come about? We figured no one was fast enough to catch Colton Nelson. Lord, that boy has been outrunning women so long, we'd begun to wonder if he was straight."

"It's kind of a long story," Laura stammered.

"We ain't goin' nowhere," Bunny said.

"My cousin is his financial advisor. His name is Andy and he hired me to be his assistant. I met Colton when I went to work at the ranch and this just kind of happened."

"Oh, we thought he might have bought you." Tootsie giggled at her own joke.

"Honey, there ain't enough money in the world for any man to buy me," Laura said.

Bunny giggled. "I like a good sense of humor. If a man did try to buy you, how much would it take?"

"A hundred grand." Laura smiled.

"You work cheap." Melanie laughed. "That wouldn't support my shoe habit for a year."

"I'm low maintenance."

"Yeah, right. Anyone built like you can't sell that brand of bullshit, darlin'. If he offers to buy you, hold out for a cool million, and that's just to date you," Karen said.

"Well, thank you. I understand you are the one who

has planned the day tomorrow. What are we doing?" Laura changed the subject.

Karen picked up her bottle of beer and took a long draw. "We're meeting right here at ten o'clock and getting drunk."

Tootsie air slapped Karen's arm. "As good as that sounds, it's not you. Now what are we doing?"

Karen smiled. "We're having a day of beauty. We'll start at ten with a brunch here in the hotel. Then I've got a limo ordered to take us to a spa where we will be pampered and spoiled all day. Massages, hot oil baths, hair, and nails. We'll get back here at five, only slightly tipsy but enough to get through that boring-as-the-devil dinner."

"And the dance?" Laura asked.

"That's the best part," Tootsie said.

"But there's only what? Ten of us?"

"Oh, no, there will be a couple of hundred at the dinner. We'll have to sit at the head table with the husbands since they are the committee heads, but as soon as dinner is over and the band strikes up, we get to mingle and dance," Tootsie answered. "At least this year we won't have to steer clear of the stampede toward Colton."

Bunny almost snorted in her White Russian. "Karen, you best order a truckload of hankies brought in and set beside all the single women's plates. There is going to be weeping and gnashing of teeth."

Laura raised her shoulders in a semi-shrug and asked, "Do you think I should order some Kevlar?"

"Wouldn't hurt, darlin'. Wouldn't hurt one bit. I can already tell you that Mindy Colbert is going to be the number one bitch you'll have to contend with. She's had her sights on Colton for a whole year."

"How much would he have had to pay for her?" Laura asked.

Melanie laid a hand on Laura's arm. "Honey, he couldn't have bought her underpants for a hundred grand."

Laura leaned forward and whispered, "How much to get into her underpants?"

Tootsie howled. "I like this girl. She's one of us."

Bunny nodded in agreement. "Darlin', Mindy's underpants go to crawlin' down around her ankles when she sees more than six zeros after a number. Poor old Colton did good to stay up there in the boondocks or she would have pushed him backwards and mounted him before he knew what happened. But she hates cows and hay and tractors, so as long as he stayed out of the city, he was in pretty good shape."

Colton listened to figures, facts, and the budget for the next year. With the donations and the dinner the next night, funds would let them give at least twenty more scholarships than they had the previous year. That was wonderful, but his mind kept sneaking out the door to the bar where he'd left Laura.

It seemed like they'd been together forever and that it was real, not a sham. He wondered if she was doing all right out there with the rich hens. He felt bad about throwing her in the mix without sticking around to see that she got settled, but it couldn't be helped.

Willis closed his laptop. "That's the end of the business. Everyone want a shot of whiskey to celebrate?"

The other six committee members all nodded. A waiter who'd been keeping their water glasses filled loaded a tray with glasses, an ice bucket, and a crystal decanter of whiskey. He set a glass in front of Willis and poured until the man held up a hand. Then he proceeded around the table doing the same thing at each chair.

Willis held up his glass. "To another good year."

They touched glasses and sipped the whiskey.

"What's on the agenda for tomorrow?" Colton asked.

"Meeting right here at ten with the essay committee for this year's entries. We'll break for an hour at noon to eat and then listen to more essays. Y'all ever get tired of hearing why kids think they deserve our scholarships?"

Colton shook his head.

"Well, by the time you've heard fifty years' worth of them, you will. Hey, I heard that you brought a girlfriend along this year. Congratulations. I got a text message from Bunny a few minutes ago that said that they all liked her. She must be special. Bunny don't give out high praise to just anyone."

Colton smiled. "Thank you."

"Where'd you find her? Or did you finally slow down and get caught?"

"Out in the panhandle. She's an assistant to my financial advisor at the ranch. You've heard me speak about Andy."

"According to Bunny, she is pretty as a picture. And she works and she likes livin' on a ranch? Boy, you'd better hang on to that one!"

Colton chuckled. "Bunny tell you all that in a text message?"

"She gets a little wordy when she's had a couple of drinks."

"I got one big word of advice. Prenup!" Richard said.

Colton raised his glass as if in agreement. It was crazy how easy it was to convince people that he and Laura really were together without saying hardly anything at all.

"Smart man. First wife damn near wiped me out. I made Tootsie sign a prenup," Richard said.

"Yeah, but she made you sign one too, didn't she?" Willis asked.

Richard nodded.

Willis stood up. "Well, I'm going to go to my room and get out of these boots. It's going to be a long day tomorrow. See y'all at ten right here."

Laura stretched out in the Jacuzzi and let the warm water and jets work on her tense muscles. She'd made it through the first item on the agenda. If she had a gold sticky star she'd paste it on her forehead.

The ladies damn sure didn't act like rich women, but then Laura had never dealt with a billionaire before so she didn't have a ruler to go by. These old gals were funny, sweet, and Karen even drank beer. They were all a far cry from Viola Cranston, the fussy rich woman who came into the greenhouse in her high heels, floppy hats, and dripping diamonds from every finger.

The water finally grew lukewarm, so she reluctantly crawled out and wrapped a luxurious towel around her body. Roxie had worked hard on her fingernails, but two of them were already chipped. Her blond hair hung in damp strands.

"Thank you, Karen, for planning a day of beauty.

I'm going to need it." She talked to her reflection in the mirror.

She padded barefoot from bathroom to bedroom and dug her nightshirt and underpants from her suitcase. When she was dressed she headed for the living room. Using the arm of the sofa for a pillow, she snuggled down with a fluffy throw over her body and turned on the television. Reruns of *Friends* popped up.

She was laughing at Joey, who'd just found out that Monica and Chandler were sleeping together. Would Janet's eyes bug out like that if she found out that Laura and Colton were sleeping together?

Damn, where did that bizarre thought come from? This was as made up as playing paper dolls in the yard with her sister when they lived in Arkansas. In their make-believe world the paper dolls kissed each other and hopped across the grass to live happily ever after. They did not take off their paper clothes and sleep together.

"You got home before I did. Bad night?" Colton said.

She blushed and looked up to see him leaning over the sofa. "No, it was a great night. We just got all our plans made and beers drank early and I came back to the room and had a long bath. I didn't hear the elevator."

"You were laughing too hard to hear anything." He kicked off his boots and moved around to the front of the sofa. "I like that episode too. Joey's eyes tell the tale, don't they? I'm glad you had a good time. I worried about leaving you."

She caught a whiff of his shaving lotion and her breath caught in her chest. She pulled the throw up tighter, but it didn't ease the quivering mass of raw nerves. "I had fun. So you watched this too?"

"Oh, yes. It was the first grown-up sitcom that Granny let me watch. I couldn't wait for the nights it came on. I was just a teenager when it started and up into my twenties when it ended. I never missed an episode. I own all ten seasons, so if you ever want to have a whole weekend of watching it, just holler at me."

He removed his jacket, tossed it over a nearby chair, and scooted to the middle of the sofa. She started to jerk her feet up to give him room to sit, but he picked them up and laid them in his lap. "So you did fine with the ladies?"

They weren't in public and there wasn't even a bellboy in the room. He didn't have to play the dating role, so why in the devil was he so close to her?

"They are great. Not what I was expecting, but great," she mumbled.

He unwrapped one of her feet and started massaging it. "What were you expecting?"

How had he gotten to be thirty years old and still be single, with or without money, when he could rub a foot like that? Her skin tingled all the way to her scalp.

"I expected them to be all hoity-toity," she said.

He grinned. "Amazin', ain't it? I figured I'd be treated like a redheaded stepchild when I first met them. But folks nowadays don't care where you got the money. They just want to know what you're going to do with it. People are people. Sometimes moneyed folks have toys that are a higher quality but they all take their britches off the same way at the end of the day."

He could have massaged her feet all night without mentioning taking off britches. The sensation of his thumbs working on her arch and a picture of him slowly removing his jeans fanned a roaring hot fire of desire.

"That feels wonderful. Can I take your hands with me when I go back to Amarillo?"

"Sorry, darlin'. I go where they go and my ranch is in Ambrose. Why don't you just leave your feet with me?"

"But how would I walk?"

"You wouldn't. You'd have to stay with them."

She propped up on her elbows. "So you are offering me a job as a permanent assistant on the ranch?"

He raised one shoulder in a half shrug. "You are doing right well at the ranch. Andy isn't nearly as stressed. Yesterday, he was even whistling like he used to do all the time."

"And how long do you plan on keeping up the dating ruse?" she asked.

He shrugged. "It's working out pretty good for me. I'm usually knee-deep in women by now at this thing, but after I walked in with you and you were seen with the ladies, no one has come on to me. Andy and Granny are geniuses, but don't tell them I said that."

He tucked her feet back under the throw and stood up. "Hungry?"

He could have sat right there until daybreak, but since he stood, so did she. "No, Karen ordered a couple trays of appetizers for us while we were drinking. You?"

"We had snacks on the table."

She had the gut feeling that they were not talking about food, but she had no idea what to do next. No, she did not want food. Yes, she did want something else, but the desire terrified her. Definitely she had no idea how to tell him in words what she felt.

"Sleepy?" he asked.

She flipped the throw back and stood up. "I'm way too wound up to be sleepy."

He stretched and looked up. His green eyes felt as if they were shooting flashes of heat on her skin. When he blinked she cooled slightly for a nanosecond, but then his eyes opened and there was the fire again. The depth of his gaze drew her like a magnet.

He reminded her of a sleek male panther when he stood up and stretched, undressing her every minute with no more than his eyes. Lord, if he could make her squirm with just a long, lingering look, what would happen if his hands were on her body?

He took a step forward and she could feel the warmth of his breath on her forehead when he exhaled. Instinctively, the tip of her tongue moistened her lips. It all happened in slow motion. His mouth covered hers, first in a sweet kiss and then in a hungry, lingering one, and things kicked fast-forward so fast that her head swam.

She thought she heard Janet screaming from inside the elevator, telling her to slow down and make sure she wasn't doing something she'd regret. She mentally pushed the button and sent her sister down to the lobby. After that all she could hear was the humming inside her heart.

He cupped her butt in both hands and she gave a little hop, wrapping her legs around his waist and both arms around his neck. She needed to feel his body against hers, so she pressed closer and closer. He backed up two steps and sat down on the sofa with her in his lap.

"Tell me to stop now if you are going to," he whispered.

"I can't," she said honestly.

"This is not part of the deal and it's not make-believe," he said.

She leaned back and unsnapped his shirt all in one motion. "No, it is not." She splayed her fingers out on his hard muscular chest. "I never knew that erotic zones had anything to do with my fingertips."

"Guess it all depends on what you are touching." He grinned.

His lips found hers before she could answer and his hands slipped up under the nightshirt to massage her back. God Almighty, every single inch of her skin had become erotic zones. His hands were ice and fire at the same time. Sizzling heat one second and then icy cold when his hand left that spot and moved on. She arched her back and purred like a kitten.

"Feel good?" he whispered.

"Mmmmm!"

He pulled the shirt over her head and tossed it on the floor.

Pressing her naked breasts against his chest, she bookcased his cheeks with her cool hands and brought his lips to hers again. She unbuttoned his shirt and pushed it back over his shoulders so she could touch his skin freely. His hands moved from back to breasts and she moaned out loud. His lips followed and she thought she'd melt in a puddle right there on the sofa.

As if he could read her mind, he readjusted her position, scooped her up into his arms like a bride, and carried her to his bedroom. "Sofa is too narrow. We got a king-sized bed."

He laid her on the bed and true to the picture she'd had, he slowly kicked off his boots, unbuckled his belt, slid down the zipper of his jeans, and pushed them down to the floor. Her eyes bulged when she realized he wasn't wearing underwear.

"Never learned to like them," he answered her unasked question.

"Wow!"

"Thank you." He gathered her up in his arms and started another round of steamy, hot kisses. His thumb and forefinger hooked in her panties and she raised her hips enough that he could remove them. And then his hands were everywhere on her body, touching as his mouth tasted. She ran her hands down across his chest, through the thin line of soft dark hair that extended from taut nipples to belly button. The combination of his hands on her and her newfound sensual fingertips on him created a fire that grew hotter and hotter until she thought she'd explode before they ever got around to having sex.

"My God, that feels good," he whispered.

She inched her fingers down.

"And this?" She teased the already hard erection.

"That is going to get you in big trouble."

"What kind?" she whispered.

He kissed her hard and rolled on top of her.

Her hands automatically went around his neck. She got ready for the first thrust, but he buried his face in her neck and nuzzled there until she groaned.

"Tell me what you want, Laura." It felt as if his breath was making love to her.

Nothing mattered anymore. Not whether she stayed or went at the end of the month or whether she wore a cheap dress to a formal dinner. She just wanted Colton to put out the fire.

She wrapped her legs around him. "I want you."

She arched against him and with a firm thrust he started a rocking rhythm that shot her straight upwards toward the full moon hanging over the Dallas skyline outside the bedroom window. She was frantic in her desire to find release, and yet she didn't want it to end. His hands were magic and made her float somewhere between heaven and earth where gravity had no power.

"Oh. My. God," she mumbled.

"I know," he said.

Then his mouth covered hers. They could have been in a barn full of hay or on the banks of the river. It had nothing to do with the fancy hotel room and everything to do with a red-hot fire between them. They moved in unison and groaned at the same time. She wailed his name at the same time he mumbled hers and then it was over.

Her body had no bones and her breath came in quick, short gasps. Had she died in that last moment? Was her soul floating toward heaven and her body didn't even realize that it had left?

Colton rolled to one side and six inches of space separated them. She felt lost until he laced his fingers in hers and squeezed. That kept her alive and her soul settled back into her body. She inhaled deeply several times and opened her eyes. He was inches away from her face and staring right at her. He brushed a soft kiss on her lips.

"Now I'm hungry," he said.

"For what?"

"I'd say seconds but, darlin', after that..." He let the sentence dangle.

"I thought I'd died. I don't think I could do that again tonight," she said.

"Intense," he drawled.

"Doesn't begin to cover it."

He threw his left arm around her and drew her close. "You are…"

"What?" she asked.

"I can't find the words."

It was the most beautiful line she'd ever heard.

Chapter 10

LAURA HAD NEVER SLEPT WITH A MAN IN HER ENTIRE life. In the two relationships she'd had, they'd gotten together in motels and in their apartments but never in hers. And she'd always, always gone home long before daylight. When she awoke that morning, it took more than a minute to get her bearings. When she realized what she'd done and where she was, she threw a pillow over her head and hoped it didn't catch on fire from the scarlet blush burning her face.

"Good morning," Colton said cheerfully.

She mumbled something but didn't move the pillow. She couldn't look at him and she'd have trouble looking at herself in the mirror. She still had months and months of work to do at the ranch to pay Andy and she had to sit at the supper table with Colton and... the list went on and on.

"Wake up, sleepyhead. We've got a full day ahead of us."

She wanted to crawl inside the pillowcase and flat-out die, but she sat up and managed a weak smile. She kept the pillow close in case she needed to use it again and looked everywhere in the room but at Colton.

"Hungry?" he asked.

"Mmmm," she mumbled.

Food was the last thing on her mind.

"Are you awake or are you still sleeping even though your eyes are open?" he asked.

She glanced in his direction. He wore lounging pants printed with the Dallas Cowboys' logo and a gauze undershirt with the tail hanging out. He was barefoot and he definitely had bedroom hair.

"Breakfast in bed. We'll share," he said.

"Coffee?" she muttered.

He nodded and headed back toward the door. "The beast does not wake without coffee?"

"The beast has been known to bite before coffee." She pulled the covers up over her naked body and looked around for her underpants and shirt but couldn't locate them anywhere.

Colton rolled a small cart into the room with a coffee service on the top and two dome-covered plates on the second shelf.

"Pancakes, bacon, and eggs, but first coffee. I would have pegged you for beauty, not beast." He poured two cups of coffee and handed one to her before adding lots of cream and sugar to his.

She tucked the sheet tightly under her arms and held the cup in her hands for a few seconds, savoring the steamy aroma as it spiraled up. "Thank you."

"No cream or sugar?" he asked.

She shook her head and sipped.

"So you like your coffee like your men?" A wicked, sexy grin put a twinkle in his green eyes.

She cocked her head to one side.

"Strong and hot," he answered the question in her expression.

High color filled her cheeks.

"Is that a blush I see?" he asked.

"I don't… I haven't… I mean," she stammered.

"Spit it out, Laura." He chuckled.

"That was not make-believe and I'm not that kind of woman." The words tumbled out.

He patted her bare shoulder. "It was what it was and it was fantastic. Want me to find a robe for you?"

Their eyes met in the middle of the bed and held.

"Please," she whispered.

He kissed her on the forehead. A whisper of warm sweet coffee, his very breath told her that Colton didn't think she was cheap and easy.

He handed her a thick white robe monogrammed with the hotel logo and turned his back while she slung her legs off the bed, dropped the sheet, and tied the belt firmly around her waist.

"Decent?" he asked.

"Yes, and thank you," she said.

"Good. Come on around here and sit beside me while we have breakfast. We've got about an hour before we have to be down in the lobby."

She tucked the robe in between her knees when she sat down. He set the two plates on the top of the cart and removed the domes. Her stomach growled at the smell of bacon and warm maple syrup.

"We worked up an appetite, didn't we?" he said.

She blushed again. Couldn't they pretend it never happened? In the other two relationships, the fellow called the next day but they didn't talk about what they'd done the night before. But then, in those relationships there wasn't much to talk about, not when compared to what had happened with Colton. She'd never been so hot, so wanton, or so satisfied when it was over.

"What's on your calendar for the day?" he asked.

"We're doing a day of beauty," she said.

"Then you can call Karen and tell her that you will see her at the dinner tonight because you don't need to do a day of beauty. You are gorgeous just like you are right now."

The giggle was barely there but it relieved a whole lot of tension. "That is a line of shit. I just woke up and my hair is a fright. My eyes have bags under them and are droopy. I have to wear my glasses today if I get to wear contacts tonight, and remember, I'm the nerdy girl, not the sexy one."

"I just see one lovely sexy woman in my bed eating breakfast with me, and if you don't do the day of beauty, I can skip lunch and we can spend a whole hour in bed at noon."

That time she was able to fend off the blush, but his words created a stirring of desire that she couldn't brush away.

"I don't think so. I've never had a day of beauty and I'm going to see what I've been missing."

Her mouth said one thing; her brain thought another; her body screamed for a third that sounded much better than anything else.

He slid close enough that he could cup her cheeks in his palms. The kiss was one of those hungry ones that made her forget about food, beauty, and even breathing. It ended as abruptly as it started and he went back to eating.

"What was that all about?" she asked.

"While you are getting your day of beauty, I want you to think about what you are missing," he said.

She picked up her last piece of bacon and crammed

it into her mouth. She would have thought about him all morning anyway without the kiss, but now she wouldn't be able to put him out of her mind for sure. No wonder so many women had been chasing him. If they knew what she did, they'd run even harder. Too damn bad theirs was a fake relationship. She could fall so easily for Colton and just as easily get her heart shattered into a billion pieces. No billion-dollar cowboy would ever settle for a woman who had worked in a greenhouse, who lived in boots and jeans, and could care less if her fingernails were painted pink, red, or even blue!

"It's really not fair for Laura to be in the same room with us," Bunny fussed.

"That's right, Karen. You damn sure dropped the ball on this one. We're all going to have self-esteem issues after today," Tootsie said.

"God, I'd give half of my billions to have firm upper arms like you've got, Laura," Melanie said.

Karen piped up from the end of the row of massage tables. "If they're up for sale, I'll give you more than she can rake up out of her bank accounts."

Laura smiled. "Y'all are too funny."

She swallowed a moan when the masseuse dug into the tight places in her neck and shoulders. It felt almost as good as the sex did the night before. Not *as good* by any means. Nothing was that wonderful.

"I bet you brought that slouchy old black pantsuit for tonight, didn't you, Karen?" Melanie asked.

"Jesus, I live in jeans and boots on the ranch. I hate

to shop and it's worked fine for five years, so it will be fine for one more boring dinner and dance."

Laura listened to their conversation with one ear and to the trickling waterfall over against the far wall with the other. She imagined skinny-dipping in the small pool with Colton. She had to turn off the pictures or she'd be making sex noises right there on the massage table.

"Jesus ain't goin' to help you, Karen. You are not wearing that thing again. It's out of style. We are going shopping right after the hair salon stuff. I made arrangements for an hour at a little boutique right beside the beauty shop. If we're ready except for slipping into our new outfits, it won't hurt to get back to the hotel thirty minutes later than we'd planned," Melanie said.

"Gloria's?" the lady massaging Bunny asked.

"That's right," Melanie said. "We may all buy something new, but Karen is definitely not wearing that ugly outfit she's worn for twenty years."

"Five, not twenty," Karen said.

"Well, it's damn sure ugly enough for twenty years. What'd you bring, Bunny?" Melanie asked.

"I'm not saying jack shit. I'm just going to buy something new. I don't want you bitchin' at me. What about you, Tootsie?"

"I'll buy whatever Melanie and Gloria pick out, long as it doesn't show my bat-wing arms or my flabby stomach. I swear gravity just sucks fat cells down faster and faster."

"Laura?" Melanie asked.

"You mean I can't wear bibbed overalls and go barefoot?" she asked.

"Honey, you probably could and even in that put

everyone else to shame, but you ain't goin' to. What did you bring?"

"A cute little red dress, but I'm not afraid to change my mind."

"Good girl," Melanie said.

After the deep massage, Laura felt like a wet noodle. She was amazed that her legs carried her to the next room, where curtains separated five deep Whirlpool tubs. Her personal lady-of-the-day, Sarah, waved a hand in front of dozens of containers filled with bath salts.

"What's your favorite fragrance?"

She glanced down the row and finally pointed at the warm vanilla sugar. The woman opened the top and put three heaping scoops into the bubbling warm water. She motioned for Laura to get inside, hung her robe on a hook when she dropped it, and tucked a rolled towel under her neck when she was comfortable in the tub. Then she massaged Laura's face and temples for ten minutes before applying a mud mask.

"We'll let that set for twenty minutes before we remove it. I'll leave you to relax while it does its job," Sarah said softly.

Laura couldn't wait to share what it meant to have a day of beauty with her sister. Janet would squeal when she heard about a thirty-minute soak in a Whirlpool that smelled like vanilla.

"What flavor did you go for?" Karen hollered from the other side of the curtain.

"Peach," Tootsie said. "If I wasn't already through menopause, I'd swear I was pregnant. I've been craving peaches like when I was expecting both my girls."

"Honey, you passed menopause twenty years ago.

And you have to be exposed to get pregnant." Bunny giggled.

"Hey, now! I've been exposed. Maybe not as often or as wild as I used to get exposed but I haven't dried completely up yet."

Karen's voice was louder than theirs. "You two are going to embarrass Laura. I swear, I see a red glow from behind her curtains."

"I'm not blushing," Laura protested. "Good for you, Tootsie. I'm not going to dry up when I get to be forty either."

"Forty, my ass!" Bunny exclaimed. "Forty has done bypassed her like a wild Texas tornado."

Tootsie giggled. "We were all wild as Texas tornadoes in our day, weren't we, girls?"

Melanie piped up. "I wouldn't know what y'all are talking about. Changing the subject before we do embarrass Laura… what time did you say that afternoon snack was coming around? I'm hungry."

"Soon as they wash the mud off our faces, we get to eat," Karen answered.

Lunch was served at a glass table at the edge of a bubbling waterfall. They wore their white robes as they nibbled on finger sandwiches, pepper poppers, strawberries, and grapes, and sipped chilled glasses of wine. After that they dressed in their jeans and boots to go to the hair salon. Five women waited with snap-front robes for them to slip over their clothing and then the next step began.

"Oh, darlin', I love your hair and the way it's cut; we could do it up like Marilyn Monroe in the picture where she's standing over the vent. The old styles like that are making a comeback and you've got just the figure and face to wear it."

"I agree," Karen said.

Laura nodded. "I'm at your mercy."

"Oh, let's find her a dress like that for the dance tonight," Bunny said.

"There's one in the window over at Gloria's," the hairdresser said. "I looked at it but it was too small for me to fit into. I bet it would work great on you. It's shorter than Marilyn's and there are sparkly stones on the halter, but it would have the same effect. It would be perfect with the hairstyle I've got in mind."

"You're going to knock Colton's eyes out," Bunny said.

"I don't know..." Laura started.

"Honey, in twenty years your arms are going to look like shit and your boobs won't be all perky. Enjoy your time because it won't last forever," Bunny said seriously.

Chapter 11

COLTON CHANGED INTO A WESTERN-CUT SUIT, HIS BEST black eel cowboy boots all polished to a shine, and shaved for the second time that day. He was halfway across the floor, heading over to knock on Laura's door when it swung open. And his boots were instantly glued to the floor. His mouth felt as if someone had swabbed it out with a big ball of cotton, and his brain had gone to pure mush. The reaction against his zipper said that he'd best get it all under control or he was going to be in for a mighty rough night.

He blinked and she did not disappear. It wasn't the late great Marilyn or Miranda Lambert but reminded him of a fine mixture of both. When she popped a hand on her hip, it was all Laura, turned from the nerd into the princess. He couldn't take his eyes from her or wipe the silly grin from his face.

He swallowed several times and finally said, "You look amazing."

"You clean up pretty good yourself." She smiled.

"I'd best stop by the hotel gift shop and buy all the drooling bibs they've got in stock. The other men at the dinner are going to need them," he said.

He wasn't just shooting her a line. Her white dress tucked in at her small waist and flowed out over her hips. The back was bare and there were stones that sparkled on the part that fastened around her neck. Her hair had been styled to look like Marilyn's did in that famous picture where she was standing over the air vent. He looked down expecting to see high heels but she wore brand-new white cowboy boots sporting an inset heart of bright red decorated with sparkling stones.

"Does that mean that you like it?" she asked. "I was a little skeptical about the boots with the dress but Tootsie said they were the finishing touch. Do any of the other women wear boots with a dress like this?"

"It don't matter what they wear. I won't be able to keep my eyes off you all evening. Shall we?" He crooked his arm and she slipped hers inside it.

They stepped inside and he stared at her in the mirrored sides. First at her from a side view, then a glance over his shoulder at her from the back view, and finally a full frontal shot just before the doors slid open. There wasn't a single angle that she didn't look like a million bucks.

Hell, no! She looked like a billion bucks that night.

Laura had been full of self-confidence until she stepped inside the double doors of the banquet room and everything went from a low buzz to total silence. Then she had to rely on pure bullshit bluff because her self-confidence did a backflip right out the enormous window at the end of the room.

She had overdressed. The ladies had steered her wrong and everyone would think that Colton had brought a slutty hooker to the dinner. She tried to think of a reason to cut and run but she couldn't. Her stomach wouldn't even cooperate and make her nauseous in her time of dire need.

"I told you," Colton leaned down slightly and whispered.

"Told me what?"

"That you look awesome. Everyone in the place is thunderstruck. They think I've reincarnated Marilyn and brought her to the dinner."

"They think you brought a prostitute to the dinner," Laura whispered.

"Honey, there is not a hooker in Texas who'd be as stunning as you are or as classy."

His comment gave back a tiny bit of her confidence.

Melanie appeared right beside her. "I told you that you would knock 'em dead. I bet Karen is glad now that she didn't wear that ugly old black pantsuit."

People began to talk again but Laura could still feel their eyes on her. She glanced down to make sure neither of her breasts had popped out of the halter top. Thank goodness, they were still covered.

"She is gorgeous, isn't she?" Colton said. "Did you know that she's a whiz on a computer? She can pull a calf and work magic in flower beds and then look like this for a dinner."

"Yep," Bunny said as she crossed the floor in her brand-new electric blue dress, "you done good when you landed this one, Colton. There ain't enough money in the world to buy quality goods like this woman brings to the table. You'd best hang on to her because there's a dozen billionaires in this room tonight and they are snortin' at the gate for a chance at her. Now let's go on over to the bar and get a drink. I want a White Russian and Laura here wants a good cold beer, right, darlin'?"

Laura felt like a queen again. “Coors, please. Longneck if possible.”

Colton squeezed her hand. “Make that two and we’ll be right behind you. There are a few folks I want to introduce Laura to on the way.”

She wound up sitting between Colton and Tootsie at the dinner table. Steaks, dinner rolls, baked potatoes, and steamed baby vegetables were served. A dessert cart offered a variety of cheesecakes, cobbler, and pies. Tootsie told her the gossip during dinner and she enjoyed that even more than the food. Besides, the steaks were better at the ranch, Chester made much better hot rolls, and the cheesecake was bought, not homemade.

“See that woman in the red dress with the cheesy arms?”

Laura tilted her head enough to call it a nod.

“Now look at the hunky bodybuilder next to her.”

“Her son?” Laura asked.

Tootsie whispered, “Son, my ass! That’s her fifth husband. They get younger every time and she puts on more and more makeup. I swear the next one will come straight out of high school and she’ll put on her makeup with a putty knife.”

Laura checked the couple out again and sure enough the man had his arm thrown around the lady in a possessive husbandly fashion.

“What about the one in the gold dress with all that sparkly jewelry?” she asked.

“Oh, that’s fake, honey. He probably hired her from one of the local hooker unions, but he’s finally woke up and got some smarts about him. Last two wives almost cost him his ranch and his oil wells.”

By the time dinner was finished and the band started

playing, Laura had forgotten all about how uncomfortable she'd been when she first arrived. When Colton stood up and asked her to dance, she put her hand in his and looked back at Tootsie.

The old girl shook her finger at Laura. "Don't you dare sell a single piece of your body without calling me first. I'm richer than any of those other three."

The lead singer in the country-western band strummed a guitar and started a Blake Shelton tune, "Who Are You When I'm Not Looking?" Laura stepped into Colton's open arms and when the second verse started the crowd parted. When she realized she and Colton were the only ones on the floor, she felt like she did at the church potluck when the preacher told her and Colton to head up the buffet line.

It was all even more surreal when Colton looked right into her eyes and sang along with the singer. The words said that he had not tasted all her cooking and he wondered who she was when he wasn't looking. She could answer that easily enough by simply saying that what he saw was what he got. Yes, she did break things when she got mad and she would eat a whole box of chocolates when she was sad, just like the lyrics of the song. He must have known women a whole lot better than most men because he asked if she left a path when she undressed and if she sunk to her nose in a bubble bath.

The song ended and the crowd all clapped. The singer went right into a George Strait song and Colton kept his arms around Laura.

"Who are you, Laura, when I'm not around?"

"I am who I am and I do leave a path of clothes when I undress just like he says in the song," she whispered.

"I haven't seen you break anything when you are mad," he said.

"You haven't seen me mad. And I really do all the things that he sang about except callin' my momma when all things fail. That's when I call my sister, Janet, or my best friend, Brenda."

"Why?" Colton asked.

"Because as unstable as she is, Janet is all I've got. I've been getting her out of trouble since we were kids and she's been my responsibility that long. And Brenda is the only friend I had in high school. She lives in California now and has three kids, but we try to call on birthdays and holidays and play catch-up."

Colton had a million questions and he scarcely knew where to start or how fast to go. He drew her close enough to his chest that he could hear her heart pounding. No wonder she and Roxie hit it off so well. They were cut from the same bolt of denim.

Someone tapped him on the shoulder and he turned to find a grinning cowboy who asked if he could cut in.

"I've always been a big admirer of Marilyn's and my friend is going to take a picture of me dancing with her for my website," he said.

"What kind of donation did you make?" Colton asked.

The cowboy's grin got bigger. "For two dances, I bet my donation will have another zero on it."

"Colton Nelson! I'm not for sale!" Laura said.

"Of course not, darlin'." Colton stepped back. "I wouldn't dream of selling you. I'm too selfish."

He joined Tootsie and Bunny at the table and watched

the cowboy dance with Laura from a distance. He was smooth on his feet and she kept up with every step.

"You are an idiot," Tootsie told him.

"A damned fool," Bunny said.

"Why are you two ganging up on me?"

"We didn't get her all dolled up for nobody but you. Everybody has seen her. She's danced with you. Now take her up to y'all's room. Do we have to spell it out for you?" Bunny asked.

"And put a ring on that girl's finger before the next meeting," Tootsie whispered.

"Whoa! I'm just now getting used to a girlfriend," he countered.

"Women like her don't come along every day, boy. She's one of those that heads the list of, 'What money can't buy.' She's the type that don't care if all you got is two dimes to rub together in your pocket or if you got enough money to buy the whole state of Texas," Tootsie said.

"Tootsie, you are so right," Colton said. "I think I will go find something more interesting to do than dancing."

All of Bunny's chins wiggled when she nodded. "She's a keeper, son. We'll expect you to bring her back to play with us next year and it really would be good if she came with diamonds on the right finger. We really did like her and we can't wait for Blanche and Dottie to meet her."

He waved at the ladies and reclaimed Laura just as the second song ended.

They two-stepped to an old Conway Twitty tune and he moved closer to the door with every drumbeat. "You ready to get out of here or do you want to stay and dance some more?"

"You mean we don't have to stay until the last dog is dead?" she asked.

"I've done my duty, written my check, and I can go anytime," he answered.

Laura looked around at the ballroom one more time, memorizing all the details to tell Janet and Roxie about later. She might never get to be Cinderella again. It wasn't midnight and she could stay, but she'd already captured the prince—at least for that night. Her cowboy boots weren't made of glass and she didn't intend to lose one of them on her way out of the ballroom. The cowboy that all the women kept staring at was leaving with her. It just flat-out didn't get any better than that. For the first time in her life, she was walking on clouds.

"Well?" he asked.

"I'm ready anytime you are," she said.

The twin chandeliers were sparkling crystal. The tables were covered in white and the centerpieces were red roses. The floor was hardwood, and Western artwork covered the walls. Yes, she could tell Janet the details, but she could never explain the feeling in her heart or what that whole day had meant to her.

Colton's hand was warm on the small of her back, downright hot by the time they reached the elevator. He guided her inside and used the key card in his jacket pocket to take them to the penthouse. Then he looped an arm around Laura's waist and bent her backwards for a Hollywood kiss that came close to frying her boots right there in front of the mirrored elevator walls.

"I've wanted to do that all night," he said.

He raised her up and she snaked both arms up around his neck and kissed him passionately. "And I've wanted to do that all night."

The doors opened and he walked her backwards into his bedroom, leaving a trail of clothing behind them—fancy dress, jacket, shirt, boots, pants, underpants all in a line from elevator door to the edge of the bed where the last item was her boots.

"You are as exquisite without clothes as with them," he said just before he tumbled her back on the bed.

"I bet you say that to all the girls."

"Never said it before in my life. Is it a good line?"

She kissed him and nipped his lower lip. "It's a good line."

Something in her mind reminded her that tomorrow morning she was going to wake up and throw a pillow over her head again, that two times in his bed would be asking for even more trouble and heartache. But right then, she was the rebellious child who didn't listen to common sense when it spoke. She wanted what she wanted, and that was Colton.

He returned the favor and they quickly went from teasing kisses to searching ones and then to the hot, steamy kind that left them breathless. Her hands caressed his muscles and moved lower. His teased her body into an arch that begged for more without her having to say a word.

"Just looking at you all evening made me hot," he whispered.

"Oh, yeah?"

"I thought my zipper was going to bust when you reached over and laid a hand on my thigh during dinner," he said.

"It was payback."

"What did I do?"

"You put your arm around my naked shoulders and made circles on my upper arm with your thumb."

He even had a deep, sexy drawl when he chuckled. "That made *you* hot, did it?"

"Let's just say I missed a juicy bit of gossip that Tootsie was telling me because my whole body was humming."

He grinned and her heart did a couple of flips.

His hands moved slowly from neck to knees. "Is it humming now?"

She grabbed a handful of hair and brought his lips to hers. When the kiss ended she said, "It's singing at the top of its lungs."

She'd never flirted like that before. Talking during sex had never happened before. Looking back, she wasn't sure she'd even known what a real climax was until the night before.

With a wiggle she freed herself from him, pushed him back on the bed, and straddled his body. "My turn, cowboy."

It only took a shift and another wiggle and he was planted firmly inside her and she started the slow ride. When he could stand no more, he groaned and circled her waist with his big hands.

"Laura, darlin', this isn't going to be a two-hour movie." He flipped her over on her back and took control, bringing them both to the top of the game in just a few strokes.

She buried her face in his shoulder. "It was better than a movie. It got right to the point and now I can't breathe."

He propped up on his elbows. "Is this afterglow?"

"I'm not sure. I've never had afterglow, but it's sure wonderful."

They snuggled together under the covers, taking up only a small portion of the king-sized bed. Laura intended to rest her eyes for a minute and then go over to her own room. It wasn't healthy to spend two nights in his bed. One was excusable since they were both tired and had had a few drinks. Two and she'd be thinking that was where she belonged. Just a few seconds to enjoy the pretty warm feeling surrounding them like a furry blanket in a snowstorm and then she'd sneak out of his bed and go to hers. His soft breathing said he was already asleep.

She cuddled up next to him and fell fast asleep. They both slept that deep sleep reserved for those lucky folks who have just had mind-blowing sex.

Chapter 12

She awoke the next morning angling for a fight. If they had a rousing good argument it would put a screeching stop to her feelings. Happiness didn't last forever and it was smart to clip it in the bud before it faded like yesterday's lilies.

Breakfast was awkward. Packing to leave was hurried. The ride down the elevator was quiet as she tried to make sense out of all the mixed emotions rattling around inside her body and mind.

The trip from penthouse to lobby was over in a flash, but when the doors opened, Melanie, Bunny, Tootsie, and Karen were there, arguing as usual. Colton let go of her hand and brushed a kiss across her lips. The magical weekend was over. When she had awakened that morning, her robe waited on the end of the bed and Colton was singing in the shower.

"Good morning. Glad y'all got here before we left so we could say good-bye," Karen said.

"I'll get the valet to bring the truck around. You've got a few minutes to talk to the ladies," he said.

She smiled at the ladies. "I figured y'all would be gone. We were running so late."

Tootsie smiled. "I remember back when we used to be late on the day after the dance. Enjoy it, darlin'. You'll get old soon enough and all you'll want to do after a meal and a couple of dances is put on a comfortable gown and go to sleep."

Karen hugged her and tucked a business card into her shirt pocket. "Our dear husbands have to get our vehicles brought around and the luggage loaded. If you are back in Dallas before the next board meeting, call one of us and we'll do lunch, or better yet, a day of beauty."

"You were the talk of the party last night," Bunny said.

"Really?" Laura said.

"Good talk. Everyone says Colton did well when he found you."

"I hope they are right. We have a big barn party going on next Saturday. It's going to last all day. If y'all are free, please come up to Ambrose and join us," Laura said.

"I just might do that," Tootsie said.

Laura hugged her. "Call me if you want to come the night before and you can stay at the ranch. Got to go; there's our truck."

Sunday morning traffic was sparse. At eleven o'clock folks were either sleeping off the effects of Saturday night parties or else sitting in church. Either way, they weren't on the road that morning.

Lightning streaked through the sky and thunder rumbled. Rain, so hard that it obliterated the skyline, was the last view that Laura had of the hotel.

"Weekend used to last forever. This time it was too short," Colton said.

"We had a good time, didn't we?"

He reached across the seat and laid a hand on her knee. "We had a wonderful time, Laura. Thank you for going with me and for everything."

Was she supposed to tell him that he was welcome? Was that what pretend girlfriends that got too involved in the make-believe world did? She looked out the side window at the hard rain and didn't say anything.

The lyrics from Brad Paisley's song a few years back came to her mind. It said that hard rain don't last. The man was a prophet for sure because by the time they'd made it up the highway to McKinney, the rain had slowed to a drizzle and she could actually see the white lines on the highway. A few miles farther and there was barely a drop to the acre, but water still stood in puddles and the ditches along the road were flowing.

"I hope we got some of this," Colton said.

"All the hay baled?"

It was time to forget the hot sex and go back to ranching, evidently.

"Rusty was finishing up with it yesterday morning. A good rain will be real good on the next crop that just went into the ground. And your flower gardens," he reminded her.

The weekend had been a figment of her imagination. It hadn't really happened or they wouldn't be talking about hay, rain, and flower beds. Did Cinderella feel like this after the ball when she went back to scrubbing floors and living in the attic?

Laura blinked several times to keep tears from rolling down her cheeks. She'd felt beautiful but now it was time to go home to the ranch and go back to work. She'd go to her apartment at the end of the day and he'd go upstairs to his bedroom. They'd hold hands and even brush light kisses across cheeks and foreheads, but the fire was gone now, leaving nothing but cold, gray ashes in its place.

She noticed the Ross store where she'd bought her

inexpensive little red dress. She should have worn it instead of letting Melanie talk her into charging the white dress to the hotel room. She would definitely make Andy take the price of it from her final paycheck. She didn't intend to owe anyone for anything when she left. She loved that dress, loved how it made her feel when she wore it, and in the future she'd take it out of the zippered bag and remember the most beautiful weekend of her life.

One tear escaped but she quickly brushed it away.

Colton's phone rang and he hit the speaker button. "We're about ten minutes from the ranch," he answered.

"You didn't stop and eat, did you?" Maudie asked.

"No, we didn't."

"Then I'll set the table for y'all too. Chester made chocolate cake before he left yesterday. I can't wait for you to get here and tell me all about the weekend."

"We're on the way. Bye, now." Colton touched the phone and the truck cab was quiet again.

All about the weekend?

She could tell them about the hotel, the dinner, the spa, and even the ladies, but never about what was tucked away inside her heart. It was impossible.

Colton had spent two days in another world. It had gone by like a flash of lightning zipping through the sky, but now that he was back on the Circle 6 it seemed like he'd been gone a month.

He hiked a leg on the rail fence and looked out over a pasture full of Angus cattle. The air was fresh from the recent rain, but the warm sun had brought on humidity.

Even with the sticky weather, Colton was glad to be home and even happier that those events were only a couple of times a year.

Rusty propped his elbows on the fence beside Colton. "So did she do all right in the big city?"

"She did fine." Colton removed his cell phone from his shirt pocket, touched the screen, and brought up a picture. "See?"

"Who is that? Did y'all have movie star look-alikes this year?" Rusty asked.

"Look closer."

"That's a Marilyn look-alike but I don't recognize the cowboy. Is he supposed to be Josh Turner?" Rusty asked.

"We didn't have a movie star thing. The guy is some multibillionaire who paid out the ass for a couple of dances with the lady."

"How do you know?"

Colton grinned. "Because I made him pay and I asked the president of the committee the next morning how much he'd donated."

Rusty studied the picture on the phone then touched the screen and zeroed in on the woman's face. "Shit! That ain't... is it? It's Laura. What did you do when you saw her lookin' like that?"

"Stuttered."

Rusty threw back his head and roared.

"It wasn't funny."

He wiped his eyes with his shirt sleeve and was still chuckling when he said, "Oh, yes it was. This whole false relationship idea has whipped around to bite you on the ass. Laura is everything you wanted all these years and you are probably going to lose her because she thinks this whole thing is just a front. You are falling for that woman, my friend."

Colton slapped the top fence rail hard enough to shake it. "What do I do about it?"

"I reckon you've got a while to think about it. It's going to take her a long time to pay off that debt, but you've got your work cut out for you convincing her that this has gone from false to real. Did you kiss her? Of course you did. You'd be a fool not to kiss her," Rusty mused.

Colton nodded.

"Knock your socks off?"

He nodded again.

"Then talk her into staying."

"That love shit is some scary stuff," Colton said.

"Yes, it is, and it's some serious stuff too. Don't lead her on. If you get tired of this thing that we all forced you into tell her and then tell us."

"I'm not sure I'll get tired of it," he said.

Rusty shrugged. "That's up to you, partner. We got two more calves while you were gone. Heifers were those two yearlings that you bred to Dandy Six. Cows didn't have a bit of trouble."

"Bulls?"

"No, heifers. Good stock that folks will pay high for if you want to sell."

Colton shook his head. "Anything out of Dandy stays on the ranch unless it's a bull. I'll keep one or two to replace him when he's too old to use anymore, but the heifers I plan to keep. And I'm not selling anything that T-Bone produces either."

Rusty looked at the picture one more time and handed

him the cell phone. "I hear that you're letting Roxie partner up the games for the party."

Colton smiled. "It's good for her. You worried about who she might fix you up with for the day?"

"Hell, no!"

Colton laughed. "How much did it cost you?"

Rusty blushed. "Fifty bucks not to put me with Cynthia Talley. I'd rather dig worms with Ina Dean. At least she wouldn't be squeamish about putting them in a can and squeal if she broke a fingernail."

"You got a good deal. I would've paid Roxie a hundred. Andy talked to her yet?"

"You the lucky one. To keep the gossip vines well watered, you get to play games with Laura and it ain't costin' you a thin dime. Andy had to give her sixty dollars because she already had his name beside Cynthia's and she said it cost ten extra to erase it. He said it was money well spent."

Colton threw up both palms. "Y'all just need to find a girlfriend and you won't ever have to buy your way out of partners again."

"I'll pay my fifty rather than feel like you do today. Guess who Cynthia is with now?"

"The preacher. That's who Roxie planned to put her with the whole time," Colton answered.

Rusty slapped his thigh. "That gypsy demon!"

"We don't know that her grandma was a real gypsy."

"Oh, I bet she was and I bet Roxie is just like her." Rusty pushed away from the fence and headed toward the barn with the pool and gym, mumbling the whole way. He'd barely gotten out of sight when Andy joined Colton at the fence.

"The bill for the hotel came through on your credit card. Were you aware that your new bride bought a very expensive dress and spent a wad at a spa? I hope that I didn't unleash a monster when we helped to get those rumors started." He pulled a red bandana from the bib pocket of his striped overalls and mopped sweat from his round face.

"I'd be willing to bet that she insists on you taking the money out of her final payment for both." Colton removed the cell phone from his pocket again and brought up the picture he'd shown Rusty.

Andy took it when Colton offered it to him. "Wow! Who is… holy smokin' shit!"

Colton couldn't keep the grin off his face. "If she never gives me back a penny of what she spent, I won't complain. You should've been there, Andy Joe. It was amazing to walk into that dinner with her on my arm. You done good, partner, when you brought her to the ranch."

Andy continued to stare at the picture. "You fallin' for her?"

Colton looked out across the pasture for a long time before he answered. "A man can fall for a woman without letting her have his heart, can't he?"

"If you manage to do that, you write a book about it and we'll make another billion," Andy said.

Roxie squealed when she saw the dress. "Can I borrow it for the prom next year? Please, please, please! Dillon will think I'm beautiful in that dress."

"Of course you can, but we'll have to get it altered.

And honey, Dillon thinks you are beautiful no matter what you are wearing."

Roxie looked down at her chest and whispered, "You think Colton will buy me some boobs?"

"Roxie!"

"Well, it's worth askin'. All he can say is no."

"And you've got enough nerve to ask him for new boobs?"

Roxie blushed as crimson as Laura had the morning she woke up in Colton's bed. "Probably not, but I sure would like to have bigger ones. Tell me about the dance. Was it fabulous?"

"Yes, it was. I snuck in a few pictures with my phone. Want to see them?"

Roxie crawled up in the middle of Laura's bed and reached with both hands. "Oh, oh, look at that chandelier and that room. It's like a Cinderella ball. And who is this?"

"Her name is Tootsie and she was a riot. She and some other ladies went with me for a day of beauty. It was unreal, Roxie. I really did feel like Cinderella."

Roxie looked up. "Will you take me for one of them on the day of my prom next year?"

"If you don't make a single C all year, I promise that you can have a day at the spa."

Roxie's smile was prepayment for whatever a day like that would cost. If Laura wasn't still on the ranch, then she'd come back just for that occasion.

"Did he kiss you?" Roxie asked.

It was Laura's turn for high color in her cheeks.

"He did!" Roxie grabbed her heart and fell backwards onto the pillows. "Tell me what it was like. Did it make you go all jelly inside and did you see stars and feel all tingly?"

"All of the above," Laura said.

"I knew it. I just knew it was out there somewhere just like in the romance books."

"You don't feel like that when Dillon kisses you?" Laura asked.

"No, I don't, but I might someday."

Laura's laughter echoed off the walls. "Then why don't you let Rosalee have him?"

"I'm the only girl he's ever kissed and he's got to learn, don't he?"

"Is he the only boy you've ever kissed?"

Roxie smiled shyly. "Yes, he is. I'm not going to have a baby at sixteen and repeat my momma's mistakes. I'm going to go to college and be somebody, like you."

Laura moved from the rocker to the edge of the bed. "Roxie, I was eighteen two days after I graduated high school. That's as much education as I got. I did not go to college. I went right to work in a greenhouse and when I got laid off I came here."

Roxie sat up and handed the phone back to Laura. "But you are somebody. You went to the ball and you got all dolled up and you were friends with those women. You are smart. Andy says you are and that you are the best help he could ever have."

She fished her phone out of her hip pocket when it rang. "It's Dillon. He calls when he starts down the lane."

She answered, "Hello. Yes, I'm ready. Meet you on the front porch."

She popped up off the bed in one swift movement, talking the whole time. "We're going horseback riding this afternoon and then swimming and he's staying for supper and then we're going to work on algebra. God, I hate math but I promise I'll keep a B in it if I can wear that dress and look like you did. Did you ever notice that we look enough alike we could be cousins? Who knows, maybe I'll even get some boobs by next year. Gotta run, but you got to tell me more about that spa thing later."

She'd barely made it out the door when the ringtone on Laura's phone let her know that her sister was calling.

"Hello," she said.

"Good God! I couldn't believe that was you in the picture you took in the bathroom mirror. You looked fabulous! Are you wearing that to the dance next weekend? If you are, I'll look like a poor stepsister."

Laura held the phone out from her ear. Janet got loud when she was excited. She couldn't imagine what happened in the casino when her sister hit a jackpot.

"I'm not wearing that to the dance. I bought a decent pair of jeans and shirt at Ross's. That's what I'm wearing that night," she said.

"Okay, now tell me about the spa and the dance."

Laura spent the next hour talking to her sister about the weekend. When the conversation wound down, Janet asked bluntly, "Did you sleep with him?"

"I don't kiss and tell," Laura told her.

"Which means that you did. Be careful. It would be easy to fall for that kind of security," Janet said. "See you Friday night. My flight gets in at seven so I should be there about dark."

Laura changed into a pair of shorts, flip-flops, and a faded baggy T-shirt and headed to her flower beds. With her hands in the dirt, she could solve any problem—personal, global, or even spiritual. She pulled weeds while the soil was damp from the rain, but when she went inside she'd added more problems to the list without solving a single one.

Supper was leftovers from dinner and set up on the buffet. Roxie and Dillon were making ham sandwiches when Laura came in through the kitchen door and washed her hands at the sink. Roxie kept stealing so many glances at Dillon that it was no wonder she couldn't get the algebra formulas set in her head.

"Colton said to tell you that he and Andy are going over some finances and he'll catch up to you later. He made sandwiches and took them to the office," Roxie said. "You want to take your plate to the porch with us?"

Laura shook her head. "I think I'll take mine to my apartment and have a nice long bath after I eat. I've got a big thick romance book I'm reading."

"Can I borrow it when you are finished with it? I don't care if it's contemporary or historical. I just love happy endings," Roxie said.

"Sure, you can. I brought a whole suitcase of books with me. Come on up and get any that you want, but only after your homework is done," Laura answered.

"Thanks a lot, Laura." Roxie's grin lit up the room.

It was after ten when someone knocked softly on Laura's door. Thinking it was Roxie coming after a book, she slung it open without stopping to put a robe over her tank top and underpants. Colton leaned on the doorjamb. He looked like he'd combed his hair with his fingers right after a shower and he smelled like soap and Stetson cologne.

"I came to tell you good night, Laura. I know this

weekend was kind of surreal and we were both out of our element. In a very different world, I went to bed with a princess and you kind of went to bed with a prince. But if you ever want to sleep with a plain old cowboy, my bedroom door is open. I'll never pressure you, but I'm the door at the end of the landing."

He slipped an arm around her waist, drew her to his chest, tipped up her chin with his knuckles, and kissed her hard. "Good night, Miz Cinderella."

He turned and walked down the steps leaving her standing there with her fingers on her lips. Prince, her ass! He was the king when it came to setting a woman on fire with his kisses.

Chapter 13

On Monday Laura spent the whole day at the dining room table with Maudie. Between them, they called several caterers in Sherman, a couple in Denison, and one in Bonham before they found one who was free to work all day on such short notice. They'd barely gotten their notebooks off the table when Andy Joe, Rusty, and Colton came in for dinner.

Chester had made lasagna that beat anything Laura had ever had before. Not even the Italian restaurants in Amarillo could produce anything that would touch it. He'd put together slabs of Italian bread smeared with red sauce, topped with grated mozzarella cheese and diced tomatoes, along with herbs that he grew in pots on the windowsill. And there was tiramisu for dessert.

The guys talked about the new crop of alfalfa they'd put in and how that if the summer wasn't too hot they might get at least two more cuttings of hay. Thank God! Because the previous summer had been so miserable hot that they'd had a poor crop and had to buy hay before the winter was out.

"Y'all gettin' the party ready?" Colton asked as they all three pushed back their chairs.

"We've got the caterer. Now we'll call the folks who bring the tables and dishes," Maudie answered.

"You get the wheelbarrows ordered?"

"It's on my list."

"Wheelbarrows?" Laura asked.

He kissed her on top of the head as he left. "For the games. See y'all at supper. Save me some time this evening. We'll go get a snow cone."

She meant to ask about the games, but she got so busy helping Maudie that she forgot until midafternoon when Janet called.

Laura filled her in on the day and said, "And there's games that will be played from noon until suppertime. You got someone in particular you want to get paired up with?"

"Got any more billionaires floatin' around?" Janet asked.

"Not that I know of, but Roxie is in charge of fixing up the partners and she wants to borrow my dress for next year's prom so I reckon I could fix you up with a good-lookin' cowboy."

"I've had it with good-lookin'. I want someone who'll walk a mile barefoot in crushed glass just to get to kiss my ass," Janet said.

"I might be able to arrange that." Laura laughed.

She had barely hung up the phone when she got a text from Colton saying that he and the guys would be working until midnight in the hay fields. Would she take a rain check on the snow cone date?

Date!

The word sent her into such a tailspin that her thumbs shook as she sent back a text saying that was fine. She was still trying to wrap her mind around him saying they were going on a date when Roxie knocked on the office door.

"Come in," she yelled.

The girl looked like she was going to burst into tears any minute.

"What's going on? Please don't tell me Rosalee has made another voodoo doll," Laura said.

Roxie threw a spiral notebook on Laura's desk. "I'm having trouble with this blasted game thing. I thought it would be so much fun but it is giving me a headache. I don't like playing matchmaker and I'm never doing it again, even if I did make over a hundred dollars off Rusty and Andy."

It took them thirty minutes to arrange the partners and when she left she was giggling. Rusty now was hooked up with Laura's sister. Cynthia had the preacher, and the married men who worked on the ranch would work with their wives. Of course, Roxie was with Dillon and Laura was with Colton.

The rest of the day went by in a blur. She and Andy had a whole new program to install and get set up before the fiscal year started. After supper, she excused herself and dragged her tired body up the stairs. She should have spent two hours in the flower beds, but she was brain-dead, which was every bit as exhausting as being weary of body. She took a long, hot bath, picked up a book, and was well into a juicy sex scene when someone knocked on her apartment door.

Roxie must be having trouble with the game pairing again. She swung open the door to find Colton leaning against the doorjamb, for the second night in a row.

"I missed you today. I know we go our separate ways until supper, but I missed that little bit of time with you."

"Colton, are you romancing me?" she asked bluntly.

His arms drew her close to his chest. "I'm just statin'

facts and gettin' my good-night kiss. You take it anyway you want to."

She rolled up on her toes and met him halfway for the kiss that sent basketball-sized sparks bouncing all the way to the full moon.

"See you tomorrow, Laura." He whistled all the way across the backyard, leaving her standing on her tiptoes and wishing she could follow him.

On Tuesday, Maudie had the notebooks on the table at breakfast when Laura arrived. Andy shoved back his plate and informed her that she'd be helping with party arrangements that day so she wouldn't be in the office at all.

"What color scheme do you think? We did green last year but I'm thinking something brighter this time," Maudie asked.

"Red, white, and blue. The party is just two days after July Fourth. We could hit the fireworks stands the day after the real holiday and buy up their leftovers at a good price and have a fireworks show at midnight," Laura said.

Maudie tilted her head to one side and looked at her notes. "Now why didn't I think of that? It's a wonderful idea. And you can wear the red dress you bought for the Dallas party and didn't use."

"I thought I'd just wear jeans like everyone else." That prickly feeling on the back of her neck returned. What did these people have up their sleeves now?

"You are the girlfriend. You should stand out, and besides, there will be photographers here to take pictures for the area newspapers. It will be great. We'll drape the walls in navy blue. That will be a better background for your blond hair. We'll use white tablecloths and get the florist in Sherman to put together red, white, and blue carnation bouquets."

"In mason jars," Laura added.

"Oh, I like that better than vases. And maybe instead of drippy candles we'll use oil lamps. I bet the catering service can come up with those." Maudie made notes in her book. "I'll tell the caterers to wear red bow ties and the bartenders to wear red vests. This is going to be the best party ever."

At noon they finished the last of the arrangements and Laura was free to go back to the office, but Andy said that he had things under control.

"You might ask Colton if he's got a tractor that needs a driver this afternoon," Andy said.

She felt like a bird set free from a cage when she hopped up into the tractor's seat. She turned the switch and the hum of the motor turning over was music to her ears. She pulled the lever to drop the disc that would turn over the rich black soil and slipped a Blake Shelton CD into the player before she shifted into gear.

Life was good again. She liked driving and being outside. That's why she'd stayed in the greenhouse business so long. After her vo-tech classes in high school, she could have easily gotten a job as a data entry processer in the computer department of a large firm. But she loved the smell of dirt and new plants. She liked watching something grow from a seed and selling lovely plants to the customers.

She had thought that maybe Aunt Dotty would leave the little ranch she owned to her and Janet when she passed. But she'd left a will saying that it was to be sold and all the proceeds given to her church. Apparently, raising the two girls was enough inheritance.

Blake sang the same song that she and Colton had danced to on Saturday night and she thought about turning the tables. Who was he when she wasn't looking? She'd had sex with him, danced with him, and even slept with him, but something said that she hadn't tasted all his cookin' yet, either.

"Do you listen to your music loud or soft and do you think of me when you hear this song?" she asked when Blake asked similar questions in the lyrics.

Nothing had prepared her for the upheaval that had shaken her world apart the past month. She thought back on that day when her last resort was to call Andy. She and Janet were across from each other in the booth. She'd figured Janet needed rent money or maybe fifty dollars to tide her over until payday, but she'd never thought of her needing ten thousand dollars.

The news had been delivered and Janet had fled the scene. The only person she could think of was Andy. They'd been to the family reunion back in April and he'd told her over a couple of cold beers that he was still working for a rich cowboy who had been his best friend forever. He'd laid down the conditions for the loan and offered her a job to pay it back all in one breath. It was fate and even though it could be a bitch at times, it had saved her sister's hide that day.

It had brought Laura to the Circle 6 two days later.

Was it going to be a fickle bitch and break her heart?

Daisy curled up in Laura's lap on the front porch after supper and a big white duck waddled up the steps to rest beside her chair. It had to be the duck she'd heard about. He seemed docile enough and acted like he owned the place—a whole lot like Daisy did.

It was therapy to watch the sun go down, rub the cat's yellow fur, and listen to purring while the duck put in his opinion with an occasional quack. She wished that was all it took to solve her trust and commitment issues, but like Aunt Dotty used to say, "If wishes and buts were candy and nuts, you'd all have a Merry Christmas."

"Whatever that means," she told the animals.

Daisy purred a little louder.

Donald gave his biggest quack of the night.

The front door swung open and Colton sat down in the rocker beside her. "I guess Daisy told Donald about you and he's come to see if she's right. I think he might like you."

"Why wouldn't he like me? I don't kick animals," she said.

"No, you just throw them out into the hay when they put a half-dead mouse on your bare leg."

She smiled. "Well, there is that. But I forgave her because I'm a sucker for cats."

"Think you'd hurt her feelings if you shoved her off your lap and came out to the gym with me? I need a spotter. Andy is knee-deep in figures and Rusty has gone into town for the wheelbarrows and stuff for the games. I need to work the tension out of my muscles tonight."

She set the cat to one side. "I could use a good run on the treadmill. Let me get my shoes."

"I'll wait right here."

Twenty minutes later she was standing over him while he raised the weights up and down in ten unit reps before putting them back in the rack. On the tenth time she thought she'd have to help him but he managed without her. He sat up on the bench, wiped his face with a towel, and nodded toward the machinery.

He picked up a bottle of water from the cooler in the corner and drank the whole thing. "I'm going to ride the bike a few miles while you run."

She stepped onto the treadmill, set it to a nice comfortable trot to warm up, and after five minutes hit it to speed up to five miles an hour. Five more minutes and she poked the buttons to do six miles an hour. That wasn't as fast as she could run, but it got a good heavy heartbeat going.

When she'd run thirty minutes at that rate she slowed the speed twice back to a jog and then turned it off. While he finished his bike run, she used the Gazelle, a ski-type machine that exercised the arms and upper body as well as her legs.

They were both panting at the end of the session and with a wave of the hand he said, "Might as well do ten minutes in the sauna to burn the soreness out. Grab a bottle of water and I'll meet you there."

"Want me to bring one for you?"

"No, I just drank a whole one. My stomach won't hold anymore now."

She set her water on a small table right inside the door and stripped out of her clothing, leaving it all lying on the floor. She grabbed a towel and wrapped it around her body and stepped into the steamy room. Wide benches against the walls circled the room. The floor was tile and cool on her feet.

"That doesn't make a bit of sense," she said.

His voice came through a fog of steam as he entered the room. "What? The cold floor?"

"Yes," she answered.

"I'm not sure how they did it but I didn't want the tile to be hot on my bare feet so I told them to make it cool. It's got something to do with a system up under the floor. They had to build it up in order to put it under there."

She sat down on a bench and he joined her. Moisture rolled off his body worse than when he was lifting weights. She tried to listen to what he was saying but he was so damned sexy sitting there all wet and silky looking. There was nothing but a towel between what she wanted to touch and her fingers. Temptation in a sauna with a sweaty cowboy—lord, she did not have a halo or wings. It wasn't a bit fair.

"I want to kiss you so bad I can taste it," Colton said abruptly.

"And?" she whispered.

"I'm dripping sweat."

She padded over to the door and pushed the button to lock it. She threw one leg over his and eased down on his lap, being very careful that she didn't slip off to either side.

Cupping his face in her hands, she brought his mouth to hers. His hands reached out to touch her cheeks and his tongue teased her wet lips open.

"I want you," he said.

"In here?" she asked.

"On the cool floor with the steam all around us. I've wanted you ever since we got home from Dallas."

Her pulse raced. "Sounds kinky."

"I don't do kinky, darlin'. Plain old mind-boggling sex like we had in Dallas is fine with me."

He slid onto the floor carefully, keeping her on his lap and leaned back against the bench. "Feels pretty good on a naked butt as well as on the feet."

She slipped off his lap and sat down on the cool floor. The sensation was unreal. Cold tile, hot steam.

He tugged at her towel, rolled it up into a pillow, and gently laid her on the floor, placing the towel under her head. "You are addictive, Laura Baker."

He snuggled up next to her and traced her lips with his fingertip.

"You look like a Greek god with dark hair and green eyes." She brushed his hair back away from his sweaty forehead.

He kissed the tip of her nose. "Your hands anywhere on my body make me so damned hot it's unbearable." He moved down and kissed each breast.

She ran the tip of her forefinger from his neck, down his shoulder, and to his palm. She picked up his hand and placed it firmly on her ribs. "Hold on right here while you make love to me, Colton, or you'll slip off."

He rolled over on top of her, kissed her long, hard, and passionately, and sunk himself into her body. She hadn't figured on just how big he was or how hard the tile was and in just a few thrusts she was panting. The release came in a burst and a moan.

"Now for seconds," he whispered seductively in her ear.

"Oh. My!" She gasped.

She feared he would slip off her body so she wrapped her legs tightly around him and when he said her name in a hoarse drawl, she tightened her hold.

"Wow!" he mumbled after a while.

"I know," she whispered hoarsely.

"Time for phase two," he said.

"I don't know if I'm up for phase two," she told him.

One second she was on the cool floor with him on top of her, the next she was in his arms and he was carrying her out of the sauna. "Oh, I think you are."

"Colton, I'm naked." She fussed when he unlocked and opened the sauna door.

"Yes, ma'am, you surely are at that."

"But?"

"I locked the doors when we came into the gym. No one else can get in until I unlock them."

When they reached the edge of the pool, he tossed her into the deep water. When she surfaced he was right there in front of her, his eyes locked with hers and his lips coming closer and closer. She barely had time to shut her eyes before another searing string of kisses set her on fire again.

"You ever had sex underwater?" he asked.

She shook her head. "Or in a sauna until tonight. I've never even been skinny-dippin' until right now."

"You poor deprived baby. We'll have to remedy that, won't we?"

Chapter 14

EVERYTHING WAS PERFECT.

Nothing was right.

Colton wasn't sure how both those statements could apply to his life but they did. He and a crew had worked all day on the fencing job on the far side of the ranch. Laura had spent the entire day in the backyard making it nice for the upcoming weekend. She had barely come inside for supper before going right back out.

After the absolutely awesome sex the night before, he was sure she'd invite him up to her apartment for the night, but she hadn't. And then at breakfast, lunch, and even supper she'd barely talked to him.

Dusk settled, bringing a nice breeze which was a rarity for Texas in the summer. Donald waddled around in the yard quacking at Daisy, who teased him by swatting at his beak when he got close. Was Laura teasing him? No, not Laura. She was as straightforward and honest as any woman he'd ever known.

"Hey, you want to go lift some weights?" Andy plopped down in a rocking chair on the porch beside Colton. "I haven't exercised anything but my brain in four days and that kind of exercise does not burn off the calories of peach cobbler and ice cream."

"I lifted last night so I'm going to pass and let my muscles rest until tomorrow," Colton said.

"Every other day, huh?"

Colton nodded.

Daisy shimmied up the mimosa tree and back down it on the porch side, bounced over to the porch railing, and walked it like a tightrope until she could jump into Colton's lap. She walked up his chest with her front paws until she could rest her head on his shoulder.

Andy pushed up out of the rocking chair. "That crazy cat is spoiled almost as bad as the duck. I'll go find Rusty to spot for me. You realize ever since Laura came to the ranch that nothing is the same. That cat don't even hiss at me anymore."

Colton stroked the cat from head to tip of the tail. "Guess Laura is taming her for everyone. Who'd Roxie put you with for the games?"

"Darcy Massey. I don't even know the woman except to tip my hat to her at church. She's Ina Dean's cousin's daughter. It takes teamwork to win and I don't know if she can even dig up a fishin' worm. You and Laura will probably win or else Cynthia and the preacher," Andy said.

Andy kicked at a piece of dirt like a little boy in his frustration.

Donald spread his wings and floated up the steps to nest beside Colton's rocking chair. "I could give her fifty dollars to put her with the preacher and give you Cynthia. She's not printing out the final copy until tomorrow night. After that rules say it can't be changed."

Andy shivered. "I'll keep Ina's niece, but thanks for the offer."

He headed out for the gym and Colton kept petting the cat. It didn't solve his problems but Daisy purred in appreciation. The last glowing rays of the day were slipping away when Laura marched up on the porch and propped a hip on the rail. She pulled off her gloves and leaned forward to pet Daisy. Colton got a whiff of the remnants of vanilla-scented shampoo and fought the urge to twist the strands of her hair around his fingers.

"You ready to see your sister?" he asked.

"Yes, I am, but maybe you ought to know that we don't agree on things very often. My therapist called it a love/hate relationship. I love her because she's always been my leaning post but I can get pretty mad at her. She loves me but she uses me a lot to get her out of trouble. Don't be thinkin' we'll get along the whole weekend."

Colton laid a hand on hers. "Would you be more comfortable if she stayed in the big house? Hell, you can stay here too for the weekend so y'all would be in the same place. That way you wouldn't be cramped up together in that little apartment. There's plenty of room. Just choose a room and put her in one of the other ones. I would have never built a house this big but it came with the ranch when I bought it."

"I thought Andy and Rusty had rooms up there," she said.

"Andy has a small apartment on the ground floor back behind the office. The original owner built in a mother-in-law apartment on the other side of the dining room and that's Granny's space. Rusty sleeps in the bunkhouse. We're building another bunkhouse, which should be up and ready by fall. Andy is moving to it when we get it done," he explained.

She moved into the rocking chair and set it in motion before she pulled her knees up and wrapped her arms around them. "Thank you. I think I'd like that a lot. I'll just move a few things over the day that she arrives. Tell me more about these games everyone talks about. The idea of not knowing what is expected of me makes me pretty nervous."

Daisy had evidently had enough petting because she was barely a flash of yellow as she dashed across the porch, the yard, and disappeared with the duck quacking and chasing her around the house.

"There they go. Do you ever wonder what they talk about?" Colton asked.

"You were going to tell me about the games?" Laura reminded him.

"Just fun stuff. You'll find out. It's mostly about teamwork. To be totally honest, I don't know what all will happen, because Granny changes them up from one year to the next. She's always got a twist of some kind up her sleeve, though. Roxie got to do the pairing up, but Granny, Ina Dean, and Patsy are the ones who figure out how the games will go. You like to fish? I do know we'll be fishing because she's ordered fishing rods and reels."

She shrugged. "I haven't been fishing since I was a little girl and lived in Arkansas. I thought it was exciting, but it didn't take much to amuse me."

"Why won't you sleep with me in my bedroom? We've had sex and you slept with me in the hotel and in the sauna," he blurted out.

The question took Laura by surprise. Not so much that he'd asked it but that he was so open about it. She opened her mouth to give him a curt answer then shut it tightly. He deserved honesty and that's what he'd get.

"You know part of my background, right?"

"I know you would have been in foster homes if your Aunt Dotty hadn't taken you and your sister to raise."

She shook her head emphatically. "She was good to us. We had plenty of food, a lot of discipline, and clothes on our back. She made sure we finished high school and took us to church every single Sunday morning. But sometimes I've wondered if she didn't just want a couple of kids to help run the ranch. It didn't hurt us to work and I loved the ranch, but there was no bonding like with Roxie and Maudie. When I left, the day after my eighteenth birthday, there were no tears. I've got a feeling that when Roxie goes to college there will be a lot of tears around here."

Colton reached across the distance, removed one of her hands from around her knees, and held it tightly.

That gesture melted years of hardness from her heart.

"Go on," he said softly.

"I've seen a therapist but it didn't do a bit of good. I admit and realize that I have trust and commitment issues but it'll take more than talking an hour a week to get past them," she said.

She paused and the silence hung between them like heavy fog.

"I had a couple of semiserious relationships. Both ended because I wouldn't stay overnight in their places and I wouldn't let them into my bedroom to sleep. I'm not saying I was a virgin before the hotel, Colton. I'm saying that to let someone into my personal space scares the devil out of me."

He squeezed her hand gently. "You slept in my room at the hotel."

"That was a big step for me and it was the prince and princess, not the rancher and the computer geek."

He tugged at her hand. "Come here."

She planted both feet on the wooden porch floor and stood up. In one swift movement he pulled her onto his lap, wrapped his arms around her, and drew her mouth to his for a kiss so filled with emotion that it brought tears to her eyes.

"It's me, not you," she muttered when he broke away.

"Darlin', I've got trust issues too. It comes with the territory. We'll just have to work through them."

"I saw a therapist for more than a year. He didn't help me work through them. What makes you think that we can work through anything? We don't even have a real relationship here. We've had some good sex and enjoyed spending time with each other but..." She let the sentence dangle.

Everything felt right with him rocking her. The setting sun dimmed the daylight and the gentle movement of the chair relaxed her. His arms felt good around her as their hearts beat in unison. But nothing was right. All the right could not erase the fact that in reality what they had was just a shell with nothing inside.

He tucked a thumb under her chin and tipped it up. She could see past the present and into eternity in his green eyes and she wanted so bad to shed her baggage and join him there. When his lips found hers she felt as if she was floating right up to the tops of the pecan trees.

She didn't even come crashing down when the kiss ended and he said, "It's up to you to decide whether this is real or fake. As for me, I'm ready to declare it real and tell the family that we are dating. You just tell me when you want me to make the announcement."

Thursday morning Laura awoke, touched her lips to see if they were still kiss-swollen and hot, and bounded out of bed. Maudie said they had a busy two days ahead of them and if Maudie said it, it was gospel. Besides, staying busy meant the time would go by fast and then Janet would arrive. When her sister got to the ranch everything would fall into the right place, she was just sure of it. She'd understand what she needed to do next with Janet by her side.

Maudie was at the buffet when Laura reached the dining room. Roxie was pouting at the end of the table. Colton looked up and winked. Andy concentrated on his breakfast and Rusty sipped a mug of coffee.

Laura filled a coffee cup and sat down beside Roxie. "What has that boyfriend done now?"

"It's not him. Aunt Maudie is mean to me. Make her let me stay home from school today and help decorate, Laura."

Maudie carried a plate to the table and sat down. "The answer is no and when I say no, it never becomes yes, so stop whining. You don't have to go to school tomorrow because it's a professional day for the teachers so you can get in the middle of things then. Today you are going to school and that's the end of the conversation. You'll be home by four o'clock and believe me, we won't be finished by then. You've got to make every class so that in the fall you can be counted in with the junior class. You think I'm mean?"

Roxie raised her head and nodded.

Maudie smiled. "Thank you. Mean mommas make good kids. I hope someday in the far distant future you are even meaner than I am."

Roxie looked over at Laura. "Are you going to be a mean momma?"

The room went so silent that a feather floating from the rafters would have sounded like a jet airplane taking off. Laura glanced at Colton, who was not smiling. Andy Joe's fork stopped midair between plate and mouth. Rusty's coffee cup did the same thing.

Laura shook a finger toward Roxie. "Honey, I'm going to make Maudie look like a wimp. If she says you are going to school, then I'm on her side—you are going to school. All mommas should be mean. It means they love their kids. I promise to save lots of fun stuff for you to do when you get home."

She'd said it but the idea of being a mother with her DNA background terrified her even worse than facing the commitment and trust issues. Her mother hadn't been mean; she'd been indifferent. She didn't hate her two daughters. They were just a weight tied around her neck, holding her back from having a good time. And her father hadn't even been in the picture. Not a very good genetic pool to be wading in and expecting to be a decent mother, now was it?

"You better or I'll put you with the preacher and Colton with Cynthia," Roxie threatened. "I'm not printing the final copy until after supper tonight."

"Whew!" Laura wiped her brow with the back of her hand. "That's a lot of power you've got there, kiddo."

Roxie picked up her backpack and marched out of the room.

"Well, I'm staying on her good side until tonight. I don't know a thing about your sister, Laura, but I'll take my chances with her rather than make Roxie mad. I'll be off in the west forty on the bulldozer clearing off scrub oak and mesquite if anyone needs me. I'm taking ten men with me," Rusty said.

Andy finished his last bite and pushed back his chair. "I'm hiding out in the office. There's enough work in there to keep me busy all day. I'd love to know what Darcy is like but I guess I won't know until the party."

"Even if I knew Darcy, I wouldn't say a word because Roxie might team up with the preacher," Laura said seriously.

Andy rolled his eyes toward the ceiling. "Lord, have mercy."

"I forgot the books and left them in my apartment. I'll be right back." Maudie hopped up. "Laura, would you please refill my coffee cup?"

"Yes, ma'am," Laura said.

Colton stretched when he stood up, raising his arms above his head and reaching for the ceiling. "It's time for another workout in the gym but I don't see it happening tonight with all that's going on."

A picture flashed through Laura's mind that involved cool floors, hot steam, skinny-dipping, and lots of scorching sex. Her body was already tingling when he picked her up from a sitting position to hug her to his chest. Her feet were six inches off the floor when his lips met hers and the whole world disappeared.

"Good morning. I would've done that earlier but I didn't want to embarrass you in front of everyone. But I sure couldn't think of anything else," he said.

"I was thinking about cold floors and hot steam," she said honestly.

"Well, there is that too." He chuckled. "Y'all have a good day. Never know what tonight will bring."

He was gone when Maudie came back with the books. Laura put extra food on her plate at the buffet just to give herself a few more minutes before she had to tackle another day of caterers, food, and the whole game thing.

"Why does this have to be such a big thing? I mean, all those yards and yards of filmy stuff hanging from the balcony on the sale barn seems a bit much," she said.

Maudie opened the timetable book. "One hour and the first crew will be here. And stop whining. You sound worse than Roxie and it's unbecoming."

"Yes, ma'am," she said shortly.

Maudie looked up. "Ina Dean can smell a lie all the way from heaven or hell or wherever lies go once they are put out there. She'll be expecting the party to be spectacular this year because Colton has a girlfriend, and if it's done up cheap, the word will get out what's going on over here. He will be plagued with women driving him crazy again. These past weeks have been very nice and I intend that it keeps on being nice."

Maudie's tone capitalized the word "He" like Colton was God.

"Have you liked any of his past relationships?" Laura asked.

"No, I have not. The first couple of girlfriends he had as a teenager liked him because he was on the football team and they wanted the prestige of hanging on his arm. The first serious girlfriend he had was the one right before he won the lottery. She wanted him to quit ranchin'. Mercy, he would die without dirt and cows and fences and hay in his life. So no, I have not liked his women," Maudie answered.

"Okay, what's first on the list?"

"Colton is sending six men to sweep out the barn. I expect they are already out there getting it done. At eight thirty, the first people arrive to put up all that chiffon that you are worried about. We ain't buyin' it. We're just rentin' it. That will take most of the morning and then right after lunch the folks with the tables will back their truck in and get those set up with the chairs around them."

Laura watched Maudie run her finger down the page.

"And what do I do?" she asked.

"You oversee. You tell them where to put the tables, how much chiffon you want hung. Do you want it really full or just barely there? I can help but I won't make the final decisions for you. You need to be seen, and all day people are going to be asking you questions, and believe me, the word will get out by nightfall about what you chose and how you looked. So put on your best jeans and boots and get ready to come across as his girlfriend that we all love so much that we've put her in charge of important things," Maudie said.

Laura couldn't think of a single thing to say to that so she finished her breakfast and went upstairs to put on her best jeans and boots. When she came out of her room, Maudie was waiting at the bottom of the stairs. She nodded and led the way through the foyer, the dining room, and kitchen and right out the back door.

She threw the keys across the hood of a shiny red truck and Laura caught them without even thinking.

"You are driving," Maudie said. "The van is already there so they need to see you get out of the truck on the driver's side. You can bet your sweet ass there will be pictures taken on the camera phones."

"I'm not a celebrity and this sure ain't Hollywood!"

"You got that right and there's more than one billionaire in north Texas, but people do love to put everything they know and see on them damn computers for the whole world to gaze at. You mark my words, them things is going to be the undoing of the world before it's all said and done."

Chapter 15

LAURA CAME CLOSE TO FAINTING DEAD AWAY WHEN the people who transformed the barn into a sheik's tent handed her the bill for what they'd done that day.

"This is my first time around with your company. How do you want this paid?" she asked.

"We usually just give the bill to Miz Maudie or Andy and we get a check in the mail the next week," the woman said.

Laura tucked it away in her notebook. "Thank you. We appreciate all of your hard work. I'll give this to the right person."

"One of my assistants has taken several before and after pictures for our website and scrapbook while we were working. Do you mind if we use them? I'm only asking because you are in several of the shots."

"Whatever you want to post is fine, I'm sure," she said. At least they'd asked before her face showed up on the social media sites.

Tables were set up by suppertime and ready for the coverings. Chairs were unfolded and placed exactly right. The stage for the band and the dance floor had been gotten out of storage and put together, thanks to the cowboys who knew as much about carpentry and electricity as they did pushing a broom.

By the end of the day Laura's brain was mush and her butt was dragging. She wanted a long soaking bath instead of supper, but she also wanted to see Colton and Roxie. So she washed up and went to the supper table.

"I'm worn plumb out," she announced.

"Well, it's your own fault. If you'd took my side and made Aunt Maudie let me stay home, I could have helped," Roxie said.

"You are right. Why don't you just quit school altogether and forget about all your dreams? I bet Dillon wouldn't forget all about you in a week or two if you weren't there every day. In the sight of a month he wouldn't even remember your name. And you can bet your sweet ass Rosalee would not be slinging snot all over her sexy little T-shirt because you weren't there to interfere with her takin' your boyfriend right out from under your nose. She might even send you one of them pretty little greeting cards with thank you written in purple ink on the front," Laura snapped.

Maudie threw back her head and cackled.

Andy looked like he'd been pole-axed.

Rusty kept his eyes on his food.

"That was mean," Roxie said. "If I hadn't just handed that list to Colton, I'd make you spend the whole day with the preacher."

"In that case, she's right." Andy grinned. "You've been spending too much time with Dillon. You see him all day at school and he's over here most every night and on weekends. You need to branch out and make more friends."

Roxie threw up her hands. "Is this gang up on Roxie night?"

Rusty looked at Colton. "You sure you got that list under wraps?"

He smiled and tapped his shirt pocket.

"Then it might be gang up on Roxie night. You've been blackmailing us all week, so you deserve it," Rusty said.

Roxie giggled. "Maybe so, but it was worth every minute, so give it your best shot. And Laura, I ain't about to quit school and let Rosalee win. Besides, I'm wearing that dress to the prom and I'm going to look just like Miranda Lambert in it and Rosalee can just eat *her* little heart out."

"You want to decorate, well you can decorate. Tomorrow get up real early because you are going to be my gofer all day long," Laura said.

"I betcha I'm finished with breakfast before you even get to the dining room," Roxie challenged.

"We'll see about that." Laura nudged her with a shoulder like she used to do to Janet when they were kids.

Friday arrived in a flurry. Laura's alarm went off and she bailed out of bed. Today Janet was coming to the ranch. Her sister would be there before bedtime and she couldn't contain the excitement. It had been weeks since she'd seen Janet, but it seemed like years.

Roxie wandered into the dining room when Laura was on her second cup of coffee and grunted as she filled a mug for herself. "Guess you beat me after all. When does the first round of decorators get here anyway?"

"Eight o'clock. That'll be the folks who bring the linens and tableware. The portable bar is coming at ten and those people stock it," Laura answered.

Colton crossed the room and planted a kiss on

Laura's forehead. "Good mornin'. Guess y'all are plannin' another big day, right?"

Roxie did a head wiggle. "Y'all don't have to play like you are in love in front of me. I know what's going on."

"I liked you better when you were shy."

Roxie's head wobbled like one of those dolls. "Blame Laura. She's my new role model."

Colton looked over at Laura.

She raised a palm. "Woman has to stand up for herself."

"See!" Roxie grinned.

"You two are ganging up on me so I'm going to change the subject. It looks like we've got ten teams for the games, right?"

"That's right, but me and Dillon are going to win so the rest of you might as well sit back in your easy chairs and watch us," Roxie said.

"My sister, Janet, is pretty competitive. She'll give you and Dillon a run for your money, and believe me, she does not like to lose. She was an old bear when we were kids and played cards or Monopoly," she said.

Roxie's eyes got brighter with each sip of coffee. "That will just make our win sweeter. You and Colton will be busy pretending to like each other. Darcy and Andy will be trying to learn each other's ways. The rest of them are married and they'll be fighting."

"You got it all figured out, don't you?" Colton asked.

"Easy to figure things out if you just watch and listen," she answered and then lowered her voice. "Speakin' of which, they're going to blindside y'all, so get ready to be pissed. And that means that Dillon and I will sure have a chance at winning."

"Blindside?" Laura's blood ran cold. "Who?"

"Rusty, Andy, and Aunt Maudie. That's all the warning you're going to get because I hear them coming right now. You can thank me later," she said.

"Good morning," Andy said in a cheery voice.

"Fine morning." Rusty smiled.

Maudie laid a newspaper on the table. "Take a look at this."

There was a picture of Laura in the white dress dancing with Colton. From the quality, it definitely was not shot with a camera phone. The caption said something about the billion-dollar cowboy bringing a Marilyn look-alike to a very prestigious party to honor scholarship recipients and there were rumors that they were secretly engaged. If they were she'd left her ring at home. It ended with a question about how big and flashy the diamond was."

"What newspaper is this?" Laura gasped.

"Gossip rag out of Dallas," Rusty said. "But it don't matter. Probably more people read it than the ones that read the real-world stuff in *The Wall Street Journal*."

Colton chuckled.

"What's so funny?"

"I still can't believe people refer to me as that," he said.

"What women didn't know from the local gossip that you have a girlfriend will sure know it now," Maudie said. "And they'll be burning up the roads trying to get at you, even harder than before, since there's competition involved now."

"So we've come up with a plan," Andy said.

Blindsided! Blindsided! Whatcha gonna do?

played in a loop through Laura's head to the tune of an old song that she'd heard when she was a kid. Only it said something about a bad boy and what was he going to do.

"Oh, no!" Laura's head shook emphatically. "You don't have any more bargaining chips."

"I've got one." Andy stuck his hand in his pocket and pulled out a velvet box.

"What is that? And if it's what I think it is, the answer is no," Laura said.

"Don't get all excited. I'm kin to you so I'm not proposing." He snapped the box open and the biggest diamond she'd ever seen glittered in the dining room lights. "Don't faint. It's fake."

Colton shook his head. "Just how far are y'all going to ask us to take this crazy relationship? If the women are still a problem after we are engaged, then do we have a pretend wedding?"

Maudie shook her head. "No, that would be going way too far. I just want you to propose to Laura at the party. You can dance with her the first time..."

"But we danced in Dallas," Laura said.

The soup got thicker and thicker and she was sinking faster and faster.

"That don't count. It's the first dance in Ambrose that is the lucky one," Roxie said. "It's the one that shows everyone that you two are really together. They will take pictures and put it in the paper and Andy will put it on the ranch website for the whole world to see."

Laura looked at Colton. Surely to God that man would protest the hoops they were asking him to jump through to keep the women from chasing him. But he didn't. He was actually grinning rather than cussing a blue streak like she wanted to do.

She couldn't do it! The lie was too big.

"If you agree, you don't owe me one thin dime as of right now," Andy said. "You have to stay on the ranch one more month so everyone will think you two are really involved, but after that you are free to leave."

Her head pounded. Her pulse raced. Her breath caught in her chest.

"Why not? It's no big deal." Colton reached for the ring and shoved it into his pocket. "Hollywood people do things like that all the time just for the publicity."

"We're not Hollywood," Laura gasped.

Almost ten thousand dollars forgiven for just nodding her head when he dropped down on one knee and proposed. She didn't have to say a single word. Everyone would believe that she had agreed when he put the ring on her finger and they danced. She could leave in one month.

"Well?" Andy asked.

"One month," she whispered.

"You got it and you don't owe me anything," Andy said.

"Why would you do that?"

"Because Colton is my best friend and he's made me a rich man while I've made him even richer," Andy answered.

"Want me to propose now and you can just show up at the party wearing the ring?" Colton asked.

She shook her head. The fantasy world sure did get tangled up in knots. Just when she thought she was ready to think about dating Colton in real life, now she was going to be engaged to him in the fantasy world.

"Okay, I'll say yes," she said.

"Good," Maudie told her. "Now let's get on about making this the best summer party ever on the Circle 6."

Colton dropped another kiss on her forehead and left with Rusty. Andy escaped to his office. Maudie brought out the books again and Roxie winked at Laura.

"Are you wearing that white dress to the dance?" Roxie asked.

"No, she's wearing the red dress she bought at Ross's. And she'll be wearing my pearls and her hair like it was in that picture right there," Maudie said.

For ten thousand dollars, Laura would wear a burlap bag with a rope belt and go barefoot.

"Can Roxie do hair like that?"

"I've got that covered," Maudie said with a grin. "And it's a big surprise for all you girls, so don't ask for details."

Tears streamed down Roxie's face. "I don't want you to leave in a month but I want you to be out of debt and I want you to stay because you want to, not because you have to."

Laura hugged the girl. "Always remember this, even if I'm all the way across the state: we are friends and we'll stay that way."

The barn was ready right before supper. What had been a rustic-looking old sale barn with a balcony around the top so the buyers could see the cattle being auctioned was now a gorgeous party room. All it needed was the band, the people, and the food and that was coming the next day.

At dusk, Janet pulled up in the front yard and Laura

bailed off the porch like a little girl. She and Janet met halfway in an embrace that made Colton more than a little bit jealous. First, that he'd never had a sibling, and second, that he had to share Laura for the next three days.

He hadn't meant to fall for her but she had flat-out stolen his heart and it bugged him that he'd have to take second place while Janet was there.

"Colton, come and meet my sister and my friend. This is Janet." She hugged her sister again, "Meet my…" He caught the slight hesitation even if her sister didn't.

"I'm Colton Nelson and it's a real pleasure to welcome you to the Circle 6 Ranch. Please make yourself at home, and if you need anything let one of us know." He slipped an arm around Laura's waist and drew her to his side.

There, that felt better. She belonged glued to him, not to her sister. He still had a month to prove to her that she shouldn't leave the ranch, and Janet had best not be putting crazy notions in her head, either.

"Nice place, even if it is way back in the sticks," Janet said.

Janet was a smaller replica of Laura. Blonde, blue-eyed, minus the big boobs and round fanny, but she had a hard look about her. Like maybe she'd visited one too many bars and lived a whole lot of her life on the too-rough side of the tracks.

"That's the way we like it." Colton squeezed Laura's waist.

She didn't know what was going on, but the vibes weren't right. Usually his hands anywhere on her body set her ablaze, but tonight they irritated her. She stepped out of his reach and said, "I love it out here. Tomorrow when it's light you'll have to see what I'm doing with the flower beds, Janet. Bring your suitcases on upstairs and I'll show you where your rooms are."

"I'll get the suitcases, darlin'. You girls go on and play catch-up. I know you've got a lot to talk about." He kissed her on the cheek and looked at Janet. "Backseat or trunk?"

She hit a button on the keychain and the trunk popped open. "Thank you. I'm afraid I brought too much but I didn't know what all I'd need. And all of it isn't mine. I brought the rest of Laura's things too."

"Why would you do that?" Laura asked.

"Because they were in my way and because you live here now."

"No problem. There's plenty of room for her to store her things here." Colton smiled.

"Wow!" Janet said when they were inside the house. "That is one damn sexy cowboy you are dating. You should have told me that he was movie star gorgeous. Those pictures on the ranch website don't do him a bit of justice, honey. Sexy and a billionaire. Does he have rich relatives?"

They met Sally coming out of the room where Laura planned to put Janet. "It's all ready. Bed is turned down. Towels are under the vanity in the bathroom, and I put out that special soap you like, Laura."

"Thank you, Sally. This is my sister, Janet. We couldn't run this place without Sally. She's an angel," Laura said.

Sally beamed and batted the air with one of her big hands. "Listen to you go on. We're just glad Mr. Colton is happy. Y'all need anything, I'll be back tomorrow and Sunday. Don't usually work on the weekends but Miz

Maudie, she needs extra help this weekend. Ain't every week that we have a big old party on the ranch."

"Double wow!" Janet said when Laura opened the door into her room. "This is all mine?"

"All yours. And mine is right next door," Laura said. "Colton said that I should move into the big house while you are here so we can visit more. We'll have our own space and yet be able to run back and forth without crossing the lawn. Later, you can see my apartment out over the carriage house."

"What does the master suite look like?" Janet asked.

"It's not a lot different than these rooms," she said.

How was she supposed to know what the master suite looked like? Though she'd been invited, she'd never been in Colton's room. She had no idea if it was a suite like they'd had in the hotel or if it really was like the other bedrooms.

"Luggage on the way up," Colton yelled.

"We aren't talkin' about you," Laura yelled back.

"Just makin' sure you know there are men folks in hearing distance," he drawled and then laughed.

"I like him," Janet said.

"I heard that." Colton's head appeared at the top of the staircase and then the rest of his body followed with suitcases tucked under both arms and in his hands.

"Good lord, Janet, did you bring everything you own?"

"Yep, and what you left in the closet, too."

"Why?"

"You might as well have it here as there and I need the room."

"But," Laura started and then clamped her mouth shut.

"And where do these go?" Rusty asked.

Janet pointed to the room next to hers. "If it's not a pink suitcase, it goes in Laura's room."

"How in the devil did you get so many on the plane?" Laura asked.

"Easy. I paid for them, or rather, Andy did," Janet said.

"Janet, this is Rusty. He's my right-hand man on the ranch. I don't even have to tell you that this is Laura's sister because they could be twins," Colton made introductions. "My Aunt Maudie and Roxie are off doing some last-minute shopping. I bet Roxie will join the hen session wherever y'all are having it and you can meet Aunt Maudie tomorrow. We'll get on out of your hair and let you alone now. See you later, darlin'." He gave Laura a pat on the shoulder and it didn't feel as wrong as his attitude on the porch.

"Are you hungry? Want a beer or some iced tea?"

"I'd take a beer, but I stopped and got a burger on the way so I'm not hungry," Janet said.

"Get comfortable and I'll bring some right up."

Colton and Rusty did a workout in the gym then a thirty-minute swim before they came back to the house. He kicked his boots off at the back door, picked up a beer from the refrigerator on his way through the kitchen, and padded up the staircase in his socks.

"I will not!" Laura's voice came through the door.

He stopped and leaned against the wall.

"You've got a sweet setup here, Laura. You'd be a fool to let all this slip through your hands. You can love a rich man as well as a poor one."

He held his breath.

"You are just seeing the money," Laura said.

"Oh, I see the cowboy too. It wouldn't be too tough to crawl into bed with him, and just think of half this ranch on down the road. It's the best opportunity that's ever come your way."

"No, thank you. I respect him and this whole family too much to pull any kind of scam."

He exhaled slowly.

Respect.

It wasn't love but it was a start.

"You're crazy. It's too bad that Andy brought you to work here to pay off my debt instead of me. I'd have already had him wrapped around my finger and then I'd have taken care of both of us for the rest of our lives," Janet said.

"I am a grown woman and I've always taken care of myself. Speaking of which, did you make your meetings this week?"

"One of them. And I did place a two-dollar bet on the ponies but I lost. So I figure I'd best make two meetings next week," Janet said.

Laura's voice shot up. "Dammit! I didn't bail you out of trouble just so you could fall back into it. I'm finished, Janet. I mean it. If you go to those loan sharks again, I'm not paying them off for you."

"With all this, darlin', you wouldn't let me sink, now would you?" Janet's laugh was brittle.

"I could always have you committed," Laura threatened.

"But you won't. I'm the needy, clingy little nobody who makes you feel all good about yourself. You'd better think about your unstable big sister before you walk away from this sweet little deal in the boonies."

He clenched his fists.

"I am thinking about you. I'm not coming back to west Texas when I leave the ranch. I'm going to disappear for a long time and you aren't going to know where I am. As long as I'm enabling you, you'll never stop your gambling and getting into trouble. I love you, Janet. But I'm finished bailing you out. Good night, sister," she said.

"You wouldn't dare," Janet said.

"Consider it already done."

"But I love you and I need you. We can whip the world as long as we are together." Janet laughed.

"I can whip the world all by myself and so can you. You just got to figure that out on your own. We are grown. We aren't little girls anymore. See you in the morning at the games. My team is going to beat your team," Laura said.

"In your wildest dreams you couldn't beat me. You never could," Janet said.

"We'll see."

Colton moved away from the wall quickly when he realized the conversation was over. At that same time, the front door shut and Roxie came up the stairs carrying a thick book.

"What? Laura gave me permission to go to her apartment and pick out any book I wanted to read. There's nothing on television tonight and Dillon has to help his daddy get in the hay or he can't come play tomorrow."

"I thought you'd be bitin' at the bit to get in there with those two women and gossip," Colton said.

"She's here? Laura's sister is here?" Roxie asked.

Laura closed the door to Janet's room behind her.

"She's here and she's tired so I'm going to grab a book and read a while, too. You sure you're all right with this thing tomorrow night, Colton? You've had time to think about it and..."

Colton took Laura's hand in his. "I'm fine with it. Good night, Roxie. See you in the morning."

Roxie went straight to her room and shut the door.

"Come to my room and I'll make you a drink. I can't believe you aren't going to talk to Janet all night. You were so excited all week that you couldn't be still and you've already finished talking? Something must be wrong." He led her to his room and threw open the door. "Welcome to my part of this monster big house."

"I'd like Jack Daniel's, two fingers, neat," she said.

He went to the bar in the corner of the sitting room and poured two drinks, adding a cube of ice to his. She slumped down in the corner of the massive leather sofa and reached for the tumbler when he sat down beside her. She sipped it and sighed.

"Good?" he asked.

"You'll never know how bad I needed this. So you do have a suite."

"Sitting room and you can see the bedroom through the archway. Over on that side is another smaller room with a nice big window." He pointed to the right.

"What's that for?"

"The former owners used it for a nursery. I understand four kids started out their lives in that little room," he said. "You ever think about kids?"

"I'd be a terrible mother, Colton."

"What makes you say that?" He moved close enough that he could toy with her hair.

"Look at what I came from. Would you trust me to have your children?"

"Yes, I would, Laura. I've seen you with Roxie and with Daisy and Donald. You have loving, kind instincts. You'd be a great mother."

"Anyone can love a cat and a duck. You can ban them to the barn. It's kind of hard to do that with a kid," she said.

"I see what I see and I think you'd be a good mother, Laura."

The weight of the conversation with Janet lifted from her heart and she smiled. He trusted her enough to have children with her and Janet wanted her to fleece him? She tossed back the rest of her whiskey and crawled into his lap.

"Please hold me. I don't even want to have sex but I want you to hold me and I want to wake up with you beside me tomorrow morning."

Chapter 16

Roxie stood on the back of a pickup truck and called out the names of the teams. One woman and one man—a total of ten teams. They came forward, some with smiles and some shaking their heads, to stand beside one of the pickup trucks lined up in a row.

"The plan is in the passenger's seat. The name of the game is winning, and Dillon and I plan to do just that. Aunt Maudie has the gun. Leave your window down so you can hear the shot that lets the games begin. Oh, and the winning team will get a five-thousand-dollar check to split between them however they want."

Ten truck engines rumbled like horses snorting to get out of the chute at a race. The envelope had "Colton and Laura" written on the outside and just holding it made her hands shake. She'd wanted to tell Janet in the middle of the argument that she and Colton weren't really dating, that it was a ruse to keep him free from gold-digging women like Janet. She wanted to come clean but she'd promised Andy and the family and she couldn't go back on her word.

"Good lord!" she yelled above the noise of the trucks.

"What?" Colton looked around at her.

"Games, my ass. You are going to get a helluva lot of work out of these folks today."

He grinned. "What's first on the list?"

"Hay, and our field has been marked with the white flags."

"Teamwork, darlin', that's what this is about. And someone is going home with a pretty good paycheck for today's work," Colton said.

Maudie raised the pistol and fired a shot in the air and all ten trucks sped out, leaving nothing but a cloud of dust in their wake and dozens of people cheering them on.

"Read to me. What are the directions for our field?"

"Right there, turn left," she yelled and pointed. "We almost missed it. We're supposed to follow the white flags. But you knew that, Colton, didn't you?"

He crossed his heart with one hand and tapped the brake. "I did not. Since I'm a contestant, I didn't get in on the game plan or the directions. Aunt Maudie, Ina Dean, and Patsy planned it all. She don't abide cheatin' in any form, so I don't know any more than you do. Dammit!"

"What?" She looked around.

"We took off like everyone else without thinking." He turned the truck around and headed back toward the house.

"There are no white flags this way. I'm not forfeiting just because you are the boss. Give me the keys! I'll load this truck myself."

Five thousand dollars was a lot of money in her world and be damned if she'd let it slide through her fingers because he changed his mind about playing—even if playing was really working.

"We need hay hooks and gloves. The time we spend going back to get them will put us ahead in the end. What's next on the game?"

"Fences," she said. "You can get those tools too and save time."

She read the directions and slapped her thigh. "Well, shit!"

"I bet it says that if you are caught with fencing tools in your truck you are disqualified, right?"

She nodded. A bright red truck passed them and Roxie waved from the passenger's window. Colton took off like a rocket and kept right beside them until they slowed down and veered off to the left.

"Why did they do that?" Laura asked.

"Directions, please!" he shouted.

"Equipment is in the barn with the red flag waving from the top. They saw the flag first. It's over there." She pointed.

He whipped the steering wheel in that direction and the big black truck felt as if it was flying. The kids had already grabbed their tow sack full of tools from the table that Maudie, Ina Dean, and Patsy manned.

"I'll get the stuff. You turn this truck around." She unfastened her seat belt and threw the truck door open when he slid to a stop. Maudie handed her a burlap bag with a white ribbon fastened to the front with a safety pin. She sidestepped when she saw Janet coming at her in a dead run. The hussy was planning to trip her so that she'd get a slight advantage.

"You're gettin' smart, sister." Janet laughed.

"I just know you and you aren't going to win by cheating," Laura threw over her shoulder. She tossed the sack in the bed of the truck and off they went for the second time, passing the rest of the trucks coming back for their tools. "Follow the white flags. Right here, turn right, now left, and there it is. The first three bales mark our space and would you look at that? Roxie and Dillon are right beside us."

"They're young and strong but we're experienced. Real quick, run down the list. When is fishin'?"

"Right after dinner."

He smiled. "That's where we will catch up if we get behind."

"Oh, are you a fish whisperer?"

He chuckled. "Damn straight! I could whisper a big old catfish out of a sand pile. You going to drive or load the first time?"

"Load. You can have the next one. Four trips?"

"That's the way I figure it. I bet the rules say if you lose a bale on the way, you have to forfeit that part of the game, right?"

She ran a finger down the list of rules. "It says each team gets one hundred points for each event. Ten points gets deducted for the first bale that falls off; twenty for the second; and fifty for the third. Good lord, we could lose eighty points of our hundred if we aren't careful."

"Twenty-five to the load it is, then. Any more over this rough terrain would be asking for trouble." He jumped out of the truck and dumped the bag of tools in the back of the truck.

"Gloves, hay hooks, and half a dozen bottles of water. No tie-downs. That means we don't stack them very high."

Laura dropped the tailgate, grabbed a pair of gloves, and said, "Drive."

She jogged to the first bale, picked it up by the wire holding it together, and threw it over the side of the truck. When she got five bales she'd ride to the next one and organize them. It wasn't her first rodeo in the hay field and she'd be damned if Janet and Rusty beat the white team.

"Hey, I just read the rules a little more. The one who gets their bales stacked in the barn the quickest gets fifty extra bonus points."

She tossed another bale over the side. They were a lot heavier than they'd been when she was Roxie's age. She glanced over at the red truck and Roxie waved from the driver's seat.

"And," Colton yelled back, "one member of the team is not allowed to drive the whole time. They have to switch off."

"Read the rules," she yelled as loud as she could.

"I am," Colton said.

"I'm talking to Roxie," Laura said.

Colton's laughter echoed across the fields like deep rolling thunder.

On the last load, she and Colton stacked hay with Roxie and Dillon on one side and Janet and Rusty on the other. Sweat stuck Janet's blond hair to her face in limp strands and she panted as if she'd just run a mile.

"I remember now why I'm a hairdresser instead of a rancher." She swiped a gloved hand across her forehead. "But for one day I do remember how to do this stuff and I will beat you."

"You'd better put your hair up in a ponytail and prepare to work hard. I've got the fish whisperer on my team. And I do know how to assemble a wheelbarrow."

"So do I," Rusty said. "I'm the king of wheelbarrows."

"See. Blue team wins," Janet said.

"Only if you whip the white team. Last bale. Time, Maudie!"

Maudie held up a hand. "Too late. Red team gets the bonus points for stacking but several teams get the full one hundred hauling points. Blue team lost two bales so they lost thirty points on that. That puts them ahead by twenty points. Read your directions for the fencing, and good luck, everyone."

They had to drive all the way to the backside of the farm to get what they needed to put in twenty fence posts and string the barbed wire for the next part of the game. Metal fence posts had been set inside the old wooden posts and sagging barbed wire fence on the very back of the ranch. A white flag flew from the last post that Rusty and his crew had reached when they were working the day before. From there to the next post looked like a mile, but it was really only eighty yards, which was less than the length of a football field.

Colton and Laura worked between the blue team, which was Janet and Rusty, and the purple team, which was Preacher Roger and Cynthia. Distance prevented taunting, so that was probably why Maudie planned it that way. Still, Colton couldn't help but keep an eye on the blue team. He didn't really care if he won but he damn sure did not want Janet to beat Laura.

"You take that tape measure and measure twelve feet from right here while I get a post," he said.

She hooked the end of the tape around the post that was already there and walked out twelve feet with it and set her foot where the post should go. He brought the T-post driver and two posts from the back of the truck with him and set the first one where her foot had been. She jerked on her gloves and held the post steady while he began to pound it into the ground with the driver.

"Two feet into the ground and four strands?" she asked.

"That's right. Thank goodness for that last rain. The ground isn't too hard," he said.

"That is good and steady," she said and went running back to the truck.

She hooked the measuring tape to her belt, grabbed two posts from the back of the truck, and jogged toward the end of their section. By the time he was finished, she had measured and laid the posts where they would go, taped off the next one for him to set, and had it ready for him to pound into the ground. When it was steady, she picked up two more posts and carried them down the row.

Colton was amazed at her organizational skills. But what astounded him even more was that working with her felt so right. When the posts were set, he picked up the roll of barbed wire and she got the bag of fencing clips, the wire cutters, and pliers. He stretched the wire. Together they tightened it, cut it with the cutters, and used the pliers to rope it down with the clips. It made for slower progress than setting the posts, but they made it to the end before the blue team got the last of their wire strung.

"Good job," Ina Dean called from inside the truck that she and Maudie used to patrol the fencing test. "White and purple are in a tie which will probably put them in a tie with the red team for the morning's tests. When these others finish up we'll serve dinner back at the ranch."

"Good job." Preacher Roger shook Colton's hand.

Colton threw an arm loosely around Laura's shoulders. "I've got a good helper."

"So do I," Roger said.

"I don't like ranchin' but I can do it," Cynthia said honestly.

"See you back at the ranch," Colton said.

He opened the door for Laura and she settled into the passenger's seat. He whistled as he checked the truck bed to make sure the driver, the rest of the barbed wire, both sets of gloves, and two tape measures were all there. If anything got left behind, points would be deducted. Right now the white team was tied for first place. Rusty would not make a mistake and leave behind so much as one fence clip, so he had to stay on his toes.

"Did you see that?" Laura asked.

"I saw twenty fence posts and a lot of barbed wire. And I saw the most beautiful woman in the world tame them both," he said.

"Well, thank you for that compliment, but it wasn't what I was talking about. Cynthia blushed when Roger said that about her. And when she took her gloves off, her nails were just as beautiful as they were on Sunday. Damn, Colton. She can fence and not even break a nail. And she didn't even have barbed wire bite marks where she let the wire get away from her." She held up her arm to show two long scratches.

He applied the brakes and turned off the engine before he brought her arm to his lips and kissed the scratches. "Why didn't you tell me?"

"I'm going to beat my sister. It will be the first time I've beat her. She always pouted if she lost a game, so I let her win, but this time she's going down. It's only scratches and they'll heal, but I'm jealous that Cynthia can tie me with no bite marks and keep her pretty nails."

"Maybe Roger will be so excited about her that he puts a bite mark on her neck tonight." He unfastened both seat belts and drew her close to his side. He bent and the kiss was hard, hungry, and filled with passion. "I liked waking up to you beside me this morning."

"Me too."

"What happens if we win? What's my reward?" he teased when the kiss ended.

She rolled up on her toes and kissed him again. "Win, lose, or draw don't make a bit of difference in what happens next between us."

~

Laura was amazed at the transformation of the backyard when they arrived. Tables had been set up with chairs around them. Mason jars full of wildflowers with empty pint jars beside them graced the tables. Maudie was standing on the back of a flatbed truck with a microphone and waving at them to join her.

"Y'all have a flat tire? We was about to send out a rescue team to find you."

"No, we stopped for hanky-panky," Colton yelled across the yard.

Everyone applauded except Janet, who smiled and gave Laura the thumbs-up sign.

"Well, I guess that's to be expected," Maudie said. "I just want to introduce Laura to everyone. Some of you folks have already met her. But to those who haven't this is Colton's lady friend, Laura Nelson. And for those of you who might be just now arriving, I'll remind you that the kids had a contest going today too." She motioned toward all the children gathered beside their parents.

"They've picked wildflowers for the table decorations. The empty jars beside their bouquets are for dimes. No pennies, nickels, or quarters. Just dimes. The team who has the most money gets a twenty-five dollar gift card to Hastings over in Sherman. Guess I need to make that clear, twenty-five for each member of the team. The money in the jars goes to the library fund at the Bells Elementary school. So dig into your pockets, folks, and bring out your dimes."

"Don't forget the casserole contest," Ina Dean hollered.

"That's right. The ranch supplied the fried chicken for today's dinner. But the fine ladies of the community brought casseroles. Anyone who wants the recipe for one of their dishes can talk to Patsy Talley. She has copies for one dollar each and the money will be given to the Ladies Auxiliary Scholarship Fund to help pay one Bells High School senior's way to college. Anything else before I ask Preacher Roger to bless this food?"

No one said anything, so Maudie bowed her head and everyone else followed her lead. Before the preacher said three words, Colton's hand engulfed hers. Laura was amazed at how right it felt, but something was wrong, terribly so. She glanced up to see Janet's blue eyes boring into their hands. She had a wicked smile on her face.

Shit! She thinks I'm playing into her scam idea, Laura thought before she quickly shut her eyes.

The preacher said, "Amen."

Colton raised her hand to his lips and kissed her fingertips. "We make a fine team."

"Yes, you do," Rusty said. "Now would you please go start the line so we can eat? We're all hungry."

Chapter 17

At one thirty, Maudie picked up the microphone and informed the teams that it was time for them to enter the next phase of the games that day. They could pick up their equipment at the table in front of the barn where they had stacked hay, and their fishing spots had been marked by team color around the big pond at the back of the property. She and Patsy would be patrolling the area to make sure there was no cheating and that each team brought their fish to the finish line alive and gaping.

Laura and Colton weren't the first to make it to the barn but they came in second behind Rusty and Janet. She expected a bamboo pole and some string, but what she got was a shovel, a tin can, and a long skinny box that had a picture of a fishing rod and reel on the front.

"Some assembly required!" she moaned as she laid the stuff in the back of the truck.

Colton fired up the truck and drove beside Rusty the whole way to the pond. "Which do *you* want to do? Assemble or dig bait? One of us will do each job so that it goes faster."

"First, I'm going to read the rules," she said. "And they say we have to use worms and can't use grasshoppers. Dammit! I can catch a grasshopper faster than I can dig worms. And that it's okay for one person to hold the rod but they both have to carry the fish to the finish line. What does that mean?"

"That we have to hold the fish in both our hands," he said. "Read on."

"You cannot drive in the truck. You have to walk to the finish line and the fish, which must be twelve inches long, has to be in both of your hands."

She frowned. "The finish line is a quarter of a mile back toward the house and if there is dirt or grass on the fish, we get docked points. Maudie is the devil's spawn!"

Colton parked in front of an enormous farm pond. Different colored flags marked out fishing spots and trucks were gathering around the circular pool of water like thirsty cattle.

The white team had a space marked off that was about twenty feet wide with the yellow team, Darcy and Andy, on one side and the blue team, Rusty and Janet, on the other side.

"Y'all might as well go on and play some more hanky-panky because this test belongs to me and Rusty," Janet called out.

"You are going to put your hands in the dirt?" Laura asked.

"No, Rusty is doing that. I'm going to put this rod and reel together. It can't be too difficult, can it?"

"I wouldn't know. I'm diggin' bait."

Janet ripped into the box and laid all the pieces out on the ground. "Good God Almighty! Where did you get this? I thought it would be a simple job of attaching the rod to the reel and stringing the line through the little round holes to the end."

"Never underestimate Maudie."

Andy chuckled as he started fastening pieces together. "She's not one to make it an easy job, but then where would the fun be in that?"

"Y'all don't have to worry about winnin' because me and Andy are going to come in first place this time. I know dirt. I've got the prettiest flower beds in Ambrose," Darcy called out.

"Have you seen my flower beds?" Laura asked.

"Yeah, but your dirt isn't as moist as my dirt. I'm older and I've known dirt longer than you have and this part of the pond is better than your part," Darcy argued.

She sunk her shovel into the ground at the same time Laura did and shouted when she turned it over. "I got three worms right here, Andy."

Andy grinned. "Face it, Laura. She plays dirty!"

Laura giggled. "I got one worm and it only takes one to catch a fish, right?"

"Y'all stop braggin'. Worms ain't worth shit if you ain't got a hook to put them on," Janet called out.

The next shovel full of dirt produced four worms for Laura and five for Darcy. They pulled them free of the dirt and dropped them into their tin cans.

"I bet you Colton gets his rod and reel ready before you do," Laura yelled.

"How much?" Janet asked.

"He finishes first you have to do my hair for the dance and party tonight. You finish first, then Cynthia will do your nails."

"Did I hear my name?" Cynthia asked from the other side of Janet's plot.

"Yes, you did. You will be getting ready for the party with us so I'm volunteering you to do my sister's nails if she beats Colton in getting that rod and reel together," Laura said.

"Be glad to." Cynthia grinned.

"You are on," Janet said.

"Hey, I forgot my rules and left them in the truck. Does it say Roger can't help me with the assembly after he gets the worms?"

"No, it doesn't say that. It says we have to work together as a team and carry the fish back in both our hands," Laura answered.

Janet's head jerked up. "You are shittin' me. Is that true?"

"Yes, it is. I've got a can full of worms. Move over and we'll work together on that project now," Rusty answered.

Laura turned up one more shovel full of dirt, sifted it for worms, and found none. She had several wiggling around in her can and Colton said he was a fish whisperer, so that should be plenty. She carried them carefully to the edge of the pond, sat down in the grass, and took the spool of line from Colton's hand. "I'll hold it like this and you wind it onto the reel. It'll go faster."

Roxie and Dillon caught the first fish but it was only nine inches long when Maudie measured it so they had to throw it back into the pond. Poor Roxie would have to grow a brand-new tongue the next day because she couldn't cuss in front of Maudie or else she'd be disqualified, but the mumbling didn't fool Laura one bit.

Laura watched the red bobble and tried to will it to go under the surface of the water but it floated along as happy as a two-year-old in a wading pool. Janet hadn't kicked the gambling habit at all. Even as a child, she'd bet on anything—if a fly flew off the windowsill in ten seconds then Laura had to do dishes. If it didn't, then Janet would have to mop the kitchen floor. Back then, Laura thought her sister had special powers—that she could will a fly to take wing or a cat to wake up. It was a long time before she figured out that Janet was just very, very good at cheating.

A tension headache started behind her eyes. They'd had the same disagreement minus the scam issue so many times that Laura couldn't remember them all. What she did remember was that when Janet came begging, she found a way to get her out of trouble. Now she was going to have a fantasy engagement and her sister would think that she was in the game with her to fleece Colton because she was engaged to him.

As if he could feel her stress, one of Colton's hands left the fishing rod and came to rest on top of hers. Anxiety left and peace reigned. She looked down at his big paw of a hand on hers and wondered how he did that. When she was tied up in knots so tight that even she couldn't see the end of the problem, one touch and *poof*, they were all gone.

Rusty brought a fourteen-inch bass up out of the pond seconds before Cynthia let out a squeal and hauled in a thirteen-inch catfish. Just a few minutes later Darcy and Andy caught a keeper and then Colton suddenly let go of Laura's hand and brought home a twelve-inch sun perch.

"Just barely big enough but meets the game rules," Maudie declared. "Smaller they are the tougher it is to get them to the finish line, so good luck."

"We got one, Aunt Maudie, and it's a big sucker," Roxie screamed.

Maudie took off toward the other side of the pond.

"Why is it tougher?" Laura looked at Colton for an answer.

"They got to be alive and gaping. And our hands have to be closer together and that means we have to walk in unison," Colton explained.

"Then we'll walk slow. I'll hook a thumb in his gills and you hang on to his tail. What about this equipment? I forgot to read what we have to do with it."

"You have to get it into the truck bed and you can't let go of the fish to do it. You each got a free hand," Darcy called out.

She carried the can of extra worms and the tools they'd been allowed to put the rod and reel together. He carried the box that the thing came in and the rest of the equipment. His stride was twice as long as hers, but after a few steps they adjusted. They tossed the stuff into the pickup bed and very slowly started toward the finish line with Roxie and Dillon coming up behind them in good speed.

Darn little teenagers anyway. She gripped a catfish tail that was at least sixteen inches long and he held on to the mouth end. They swung it between them like a plastic bag of potatoes. But they got too comfortable and too fast. The fish gave a flop and she dropped the tail. It hit the dirt and they both scrambled to pick it back up.

"There goes ten points," Roxie fussed.

"Want to take it back to the pond and wash it off? That's not against the rules, but it'll slow us down," Dillon said.

"We'll take the low score and make it up with the wheelbarrow race. FYI, darlin', I'm pushin'."

"The hell, I mean devil, you are. I ain't intendin' to be the laughin'stock of the whole party. Man pushes. Woman rides," Dillon said.

Laura checked every five seconds to make sure their sun perch was still alive. Rusty and Janet were coming up right behind them and Janet was giggling. Laura had heard that particular high-pitched laughter before and it always meant that Janet was up to no good. She deliberately slowed her step.

"What are you doing?" Colton asked.

"Winning. Just trust me and follow me," she answered.

He didn't argue, but when Rusty and Janet were ahead of them, she whispered softly, "She would have tripped me."

"For real?"

"I know that giggle. When we get to within twenty feet of the finish line, I want to start jogging. We're going to get there with a live fish and leave them in our dust."

Colton pointed with his free hand. "We might come in second that way, but there goes the preacher and Cynthia right up to the line now. They've taken this competition and probably went into first place."

"Don't you drop this fish! I'm at least coming in second," Laura declared.

They tied Janet and Rusty for second, both of them dropping their fish on the table at the same time, with Roxie and Dillon taking third place. Maudie lined all ten teams up when they had checked in, four without a fish at all, and the other members with dirt and grass on theirs.

"Now," she said, "we are ready for the final test of the day. Your wheelbarrows are waiting with your tools on the backside of this barn. We were nice enough to put you all under shade trees. Once the wheelbarrow is put together, the tools go inside it with the lady on the team and the cowboy or preacher in your case," she nodded at Roger and Cynthia, "will push the lady all the way back to the house. I'll be taking pictures for the ranch scrapbook like I have been all day, so don't be thinking you can cheat at this late date. I'm talking to you, Roxie."

"I hear you," Roxie said.

Laura looked at Janet.

"I hear you," she mouthed.

Colton opened the box with the wheelbarrow and Laura heaved a sigh of relief. It was standard issue and not something that Maudie had found with fifty wooden slats. It was a plain old red wheelbarrow with a framework to hold the legs, nuts and bolts to assemble it, and a screwdriver and pair of pliers to do the job.

"This won't take long," Laura said.

"Are you ready for the games to be over?" Colton asked.

"Not really. It's been a fun day. I just want to win so that my sister has to fix my hair. I'd like it to look pretty tonight."

"We really did make a great team, Laura. Would you consider staying on at the end of the month? I really will hire you in any capacity you want to work. You can continue as Andy's assistant. You can be the gardener. You can work on the ranch as a field hand. You name it and your pay rate."

His blunt question caught her by surprise. She thought about it for a while. She liked the ranch. She loved Roxie and she was learning to appreciate Maudie more and more. She was falling in love with Colton.

"Whoa!" she said aloud.

"Just think about it," he said.

"I wasn't pulling up on the reins for that reason," she admitted.

"Then what?"

"Just something else."

In love!

Damn.

She couldn't be in love. She had trust and commitment issues by the bushel basket full. She couldn't stay on the ranch in a permanent position, no matter what it was, because she hadn't even proven that she could tell Janet no. And if she didn't learn how to do that, it would be dangerous to ever have access to the kind of money that Colton had.

"Will you at least think about it?" he whispered.

"I will," she said.

Thinking about walking into a store and buying a five-hundred-dollar pair of cowboy boots was a far different story than really doing it. She'd think about it when she slept beside him, when they had glorious, hot sex, and when they sat at the breakfast table together. But that didn't mean she would actually consent to it.

He kissed her on the cheek and then slid over a few inches further and brushed a hard kiss on her lips—one that set a fire that couldn't be put out for hours and hours.

"Thank you," he whispered.

Roxie let out a piercing yelp when she and Dillon finished their wheelbarrow first and settled into it, holding on to the sides. Dillon pushed her three feet and hit a gopher hole. She went tumbling—ass over ponytail and he stumbled and landed on top of her.

"Maudie is going to ground you," Colton yelled.

High color filled Dillon's cheeks as he rolled to one side, righted the wheelbarrow, and apologized a dozen times to Maudie.

"It's me that got dumped. Don't tell *her* you are sorry. Steady that blasted thing up so I can get in it again," Roxie said.

Meanwhile, Cynthia and Roger got their wheelbarrow finished and Roger took several steps to get a balance. They were five feet in front of Roxie and Dillon when Colton slid an arm under Laura's legs and one around her shoulders. He set her into their wheelbarrow, grabbed both handles, and away they went with Darcy and Andy right behind them.

It was a fight to the finish line with Cynthia and Roger coming in first by the length of the wheelbarrow wheel. Roxie and Dillon hit the line in second place, and Laura and Colton had a third place win.

Maudie tallied up the whole game session and declared Cynthia and Roger the winners of the five-thousand-dollar prize. She handed the envelope with the cash in it to Roger and asked if he had anything to say.

He took the microphone and said, "Of course, I'm a preacher. I've always got something to say."

Everyone in the yard laughed. Even the children stopped playing to see what was so funny.

"Roxie, thank you for pairing me up with Cynthia. She's been a wonderful partner. I couldn't ask for a better one. We've talked about what we might do with this money if we won it today. We could split it and each of us could do something really fun or nice with it but we came up with the idea of leaving it all in one pile and buying a new piano for the church, so that's what this is going for. And Roxie, if you get the job of pairing up the teams next year, I'd love to have Cynthia."

"It'll cost you," Rusty yelled.

"I'd pay," Roger answered and handed the phone back to Maudie.

"Games are officially over. Two hours until supper is served. Then dancing begins at eight thirty and goes until midnight," Maudie announced. "Laura and Colton will start the dancing soon as supper is over."

"You ready to go to the house?" Colton asked.

Laura nodded.

He scooped her up, put her in the wheelbarrow, and before she could wiggle, he took hold of the handles and began to push. "I don't care what the numbers say, I'm the winner."

The applause spooked the crows trying to roost in the trees and they flew off in protest of such noise. When they reached the front porch, he parked the brand-new wheelbarrow and carried her to the porch.

"Nice touch. Ina Dean should be convinced for sure," Laura said.

Nine women piled out of the back of Rusty's truck before Colton could answer. He tipped his hat at them, gave them one of his brilliant smiles, and crawled inside the truck with Rusty.

Laura wished she could go with him.

Chapter 18

BLESS MAUDIE'S HEART!

She thought of everything. The living room was now a beauty parlor with mirrors set up at intervals along two eight-foot folding tables. Beer and soft drinks chilled in a cooler at the end of a table holding a veggie tray, a fruit tray, and finger sandwiches. Half a dozen ladies in black trousers and white shirts in the back waited to do nails and hair.

"We've got two hours, girls," Maudie said. "Let's split it up. Hair for one hour. Nails for an hour."

Roxie raised her hand like she was in the classroom. When Maudie nodded at her, she said, "I want my turn at the hair and I want it to look like Laura's did at the party last week. It's on her phone."

She sat down in a folding chair and pulled her hair down from the ponytail.

The hairdresser picked up a strand of hair. "Sweat, dirt, and mud does not start a lovely hairdo, honey. Go take a shower and wash your hair. Looks like the rest of you might want to do the same."

Laura followed suit and held up a hand. "We've got five showers upstairs. Cynthia, you can come with me. I've got an extra robe you can wear back down. That way we won't get our hair all messed up when we get dressed for the party."

"Robes are over there beside the door," the beautician said.

Cynthia nodded seriously. "Thank goodness. Laura's robe wouldn't cover my butt."

Janet pointed at a lady. "You can shower in my room."

Roxie chose another woman. "Guess that leaves us for the first round. Pick up a robe and follow me. Might as well take your suitcase, garment bag, or whatever you've brought with you because you'll be getting dressed upstairs after our makeover."

"You are in big trouble," Janet whispered behind her. "Have you given any more thought to my idea?"

"It ain't goin' to happen. The only way I'll get married is for love and if I did marry Colton, I'd insist on a prenup saying that I couldn't take anything away from this ranch that I didn't bring with me or buy with my own money."

"You are a fool. I love you because you are my sister, but you are a fool," Janet hissed.

Five bedroom doors were swung open. Laura inhaled deeply to keep from saying another word to Janet. She walked into her room with Cynthia right behind her. "Oh, I hadn't thought of there being ten of us. You two take this room. You others divide up the other two rooms and Cynthia and I'll take over Colton's room for showers and getting ready. He won't mind. Make yourselves at home. See you back down in the ballroom soon."

"And this is where we are going?" Cynthia pointed to the room at the end of the hallway.

"That's right. You can have first shower and get on back down to the ballroom so they can start your hair," Laura answered.

Laura's book was lying on the sofa in plain sight on top of a furry throw. The coffee cup she'd carried upstairs that morning was sitting on the end table, and her nightshirt was thrown on the end of the bed. If there was a doubt that she was Colton's girlfriend, it would be erased as soon as Cynthia could whisper about what she'd seen.

"Sorry about the mess. I guess Sally didn't get around to this room with all the excitement," Laura said.

"I'm not seeing a mess. I'm seeing a gorgeous master suite. Thank you for choosing me, Laura. I've always wanted to see this room," Cynthia said with a sigh.

Laura was really starting to like Cynthia. Roxie had put Cynthia and the preacher together for the games as a joke and it backfired. Now that they'd seen they were good together, they might end up with each other. What a tangled-up affair!

Laura threw herself down on the sofa, kicked her boots off, and propped her feet on the coffee table. Janet was crazy for thinking she'd run a scam on Maudie and Colton. She could barely keep up with the scam the family was running on the whole world. She damn sure didn't have time to set another pot to boiling on the back burner.

In a few minutes, Cynthia came out of the bathroom wearing a long white robe and a white towel around her head. "I feel like a brand-new woman. I'm not an outdoorsy type but neither is Roger. Do you think he meant that about choosing me next year?"

"Oh, yeah, I do," Laura said.

Preachers weren't allowed to lie so she wasn't even stretching the truth.

"Waiting on a woman," Andy said.

"According to Brad Paisley's song by that name, it ain't a bad thing to be doin'," Rusty said.

Roger leaned on the banister. "God put woman on earth to be a helpmeet and to teach a man patience."

"I thought it was to teach a man to run very fast." Rusty chuckled.

One by one they came down the stairs, Cynthia first in a cute little sundress and high-heeled shoes. Roger crooked his arm and she looped hers through it.

"You are stunning, Cynthia," Roger said.

Cynthia beamed.

A couple of minutes later Darcy appeared in jeans, boots, and an army green blouse with ruffles that matched her eyes. Andy followed Roger's lead.

"You look very nice tonight, ma'am."

"Well, every single one of you cowboys look sexy as the devil."

Several cowboy hats tipped in her direction. Shoulders squared up and stomachs sucked in.

Like a gentleman, Rusty was complimentary to Janet—even though he'd told Colton earlier that she was nothing like her sister and not to be getting any ideas about playing matchmaker between the two of them. Besides, he was too old to be thinking about settling down and Janet was too young even if he was.

Colton and Dillon were the last two men standing when Roxie floated down in a cute little pink sundress and matching cowboy boots. Her hair had been styled just like Laura's had been for the Dallas party.

"Feel a little bit like you just fell off a four-wheeler and ate a mouth full of dirt?" Colton whispered.

Dillon nodded. "Yes, sir, I do."

That left Colton as the last man standing. He looked at his watch at least fifty times in the next five minutes and then there she was. When he looked up she was staring right into his eyes and as the distance closed the heat built from a tiny flame into a Texas wildfire.

"My God, you are beautiful," he said.

"Thank you, but I think that's a line from an old movie." She smiled.

"Don't make it any less true. I want to kiss you but I'm afraid I'll mess something up."

"Can't have your cake and eat it too, but I can." She wrapped her arms around his neck and moistened her lips with the tip of her tongue.

In that moment, Colton Nelson realized that he did not want Laura to ever leave the ranch. Not in a month. Never, ever! He might not be willing to give up his heart but he sure didn't want to live without her.

"You were awesome in that white dress, but darlin', you take my breath away in this," he said.

She smiled. "Thank you. Let's forget the party and go to bed."

He groaned. "Can I take a rain check on that? Granny would kill us both."

"Yes, she would," Maudie said from the dining room door. She was decked out in designer jeans, boots, and a bright red Western shirt.

High colored flooded Laura's cheeks, making them almost as red as her dress and Maudie's shirt. "I thought you'd already be at the party."

"I'm going right now. I waited to give you these pearls to wear tonight. Now, y'all give me ten minutes and then you two will arrive and be introduced. Preacher Roger will say grace and dinner will begin with y'all going first. The band will set up while we are eating and you'll have your first dance right after you eat. You have the ring in your pocket, right?" Maudie looked at Colton.

"Yes, ma'am."

Laura could still feel a burn in her cheeks.

"And Laura, I'm glad that you'd give up a party to go to bed with my grandson. See y'all later."

Laura's hands trembled as she and Colton made their grand appearance. Maudie held the microphone and settled the noise in the barn by tapping on the end.

"Colton and Laura have arrived. We are going to ask Preacher Roger to say grace and then they will start the buffet line. Anyone who hasn't met Laura, please feel free to stop and chat with them anytime." She handed the microphone off to the preacher.

All those games must've worked up his appetite because the prayer was brief.

When Laura opened her eyes, Maudie was standing right beside her.

"I'll be right behind you. We want everyone to see a united front from the family in supporting Colton and your relationship," she whispered.

"I feel like a traitor," Laura said.

Maudie patted her arm. "Honey, he's happy right now. No one is causing havoc in his life and for the first time since he got rich he's not stressed out over just going to town to get a tractor part."

"Did you know that Cynthia likes him?" Laura asked.

"Everyone knows that and we all know that she'd never live on a ranch. She might break a nail," Maudie whispered.

Laura and Colton were both seated and had begun to eat when she noticed the place card right beside her and felt guilty. Movement to her right caused Laura to look up. A waiter seated Janet. She unfolded an oversized white napkin and laid it across her lap.

"I thought you were wearing jeans," she whispered.

"So did I but Maudie thought I should wear the dress."

"You listen to her and you've only known her a few weeks, but you won't listen to me and we've stuck together our whole lives?" Janet smiled at Darcy who sat down right beside her.

"She gives me good advice," Laura said.

Darcy leaned backwards and stretched her hand out to touch Janet's shoulder. "This is amazing. The day was so much fun. Andy was a hoot. He's got a tremendous sense of humor and reminds me of my younger brother. And now this dinner and the dance. I'm so glad I moved to Ambrose but what I really want the scoop on is that foreman, Rusty. He's more my age and he's a fine-looking cowboy."

Laura smiled sweetly. "Well, darlin', you just come on out here sometime to talk flowers and I'll be sure to get you some time with him."

Janet poked her with an elbow. "What's on for tomorrow?"

"We sleep as late as we want. Breakfast will be served on the buffet in the dining room just like today. And then we are having a picnic dinner at the pool."

"Where is the pool? I didn't see a swimming pool!" Janet said.

"It's a surprise. And we do have a gym, so eat all you want. You can exercise, spend some time in the sauna, and then the pool if you are really energetic," Laura answered.

"I bet I can get one of these cowboys to take me home with him tonight," Janet whispered.

"I'm not betting against that. I'd lose for sure. You look amazing, sis." Laura hugged her. "And I was proud of you in the games."

"I let the preacher win," Janet whispered. "Rusty and I could have nailed it but I deliberately let her win. She looked like she needed it."

"Really?" Laura's eyebrows drew together.

"Hell, no!" Janet giggled.

Laura air slapped Janet's arm. "You are a rat from hell."

"And you love me, right?"

"Of course I love you."

"And you'd do anything for me, right?"

Laura had her mouth open to say that she would but clamped it shut. "Not this time."

"You ain't no fun anymore." Janet pouted.

"I disagree," Darcy said. "She's great."

Roger and Cynthia were all smiles when they sat down across from Colton and Laura. Roger didn't look a thing like he did the first time Laura met him with a do-rag tied around his forehead, but he sure didn't look like he did on Sunday morning either. He wore jeans—loose fitting instead of cowboy tight—a plaid shirt, buttons not snaps, and cowboy boots, square toes, not pointed. And he was flirting with Cynthia.

Preachers were allowed to do that, weren't they? After all, they were human and the attention was absolutely making Cynthia glow.

"Congratulations again," Colton said.

Roger touched Cynthia on the arm. "We never dreamed we'd win, did we?"

"I didn't even dare hope for it. But Roger is very good at putting things together. We never have to hire repairmen for anything at the church," Cynthia beamed.

Maudie sat down beside Colton. "No hurry, but when you two finish, the band will begin to play and you will dance."

The band was set up on the stage and was just waiting for a signal to start the music. The whole barn buzzed with excitement and conversation. People came by the table to meet Laura and after the first three or four she stopped even trying to put names with faces. It was just impossible.

God was going to strike her stone-cold dead before the night was over. Ina Dean might be fooled, but the Almighty would not think telling such blatant lies and toying with the sanctity of love was one bit amusing.

"I'm getting really nervous about all this," she leaned over and whispered under the ruse of kissing Colton on the cheek.

He shook his head. "If you're going to string someone up, put the rope around Andy's neck, not mine. He started it all by putting us together in church that Sunday morning."

Andy should be banned to the desert to live in a tent with no electricity or even a generator for his computers for the rest of his life. Maybe with only one person to talk to the whole time and that would be Janet, or worse yet, Cynthia. It might be the only place in the world where Janet couldn't gamble and Cynthia couldn't worry about her looks.

Laura frowned.

"Something wrong?" the preacher asked.

"I'm just fighting with the devil's voice in my head," Laura answered.

"You do love me." Janet hugged her.

"Not that much," Laura whispered.

"You two sound like me and my sister. We can't wait to get together and then all we do is bicker, then we cry when we have to be parted," Cynthia said.

"And I always thought I wanted a sister," Colton said.

Roxie piped up from the end of the table. "So did I but all I got was you and I didn't even want a brother."

Colton kissed Laura on the cheek. "I told you. I liked her better before she met you."

"It's time," Maudie said when Laura swallowed her last bite of pecan pie. She raised a hand to the lead singer in the band and he took his place behind the microphone.

Laura stood on shaky legs and let Colton lead her out into the middle of the dance floor. When was all the proposing supposed to take place anyway? After the dance or before it? Dammit! She'd forgotten to ask and now she was jittery with nerves.

"And now, cowboys and cowgirls, Colton and his lady friend, Laura, will start the dancing. Miz Maudie says for those of you who haven't finished eating not to rush. We'll be playing until midnight so there will be lots of time to work some leather off your boots."

The band struck up "I Cross My Heart" by George Strait, and Colton removed his hat and held it with both hands at the small of her back.

She wrapped her arms around his neck and laid her face on his chest. Listening to his heart beating so steady and true settled her nerves. She could do this to be free of the debt that she owed. She kept telling herself that as the singer sang just like George Strait.

"I think Cynthia and Roger are flirting," Colton whispered.

"If they are it's the real deal, not fantasy like our world." She smiled up at him like she was deeply in love.

"This is the real deal, Laura. Maybe not the proposal but the way I feel when we are together. It's not pretend anymore," he said. "Might be that Roger and Cynthia will beat us down the aisle."

The song ended and Laura looked up at Colton with a question on her face.

"Trust me," he said. "This isn't our song."

The singer breathed into the microphone. "Before y'all stampede to the dance floor, Colton has asked us to sing a song just for him and Laura. So this is a Blake Shelton tune, 'God Gave Me You.'"

Colton kept her close to his chest and did a slow two-step around the floor with her. "What was the devil telling you at the table?"

"He was reminding me that my sister will never change if I don't stand my ground and then it's an iffy situation. She might be too old to change."

"Do you want her to change?" Colton asked.

"Yes, I do."

"If she does, she won't be dependent on you to get her out of trouble."

"I'm ready to cut the apron strings."

"Want me to hand you the scissors?"

The song ended and she had forgotten all about the proposal until he settled the hat back on his head and dropped down on one knee in front of her. "Laura Baker, will you marry me?" he said loud and clear.

Gasps were heard all over the barn.

She froze. Absolutely froze, couldn't move or speak.

"Laura, darlin', I'm going to ask you one more time, will you marry me?" He popped the ring box open and the sparkle of the big fake diamond caught her attention.

She nodded.

He put the ring on her finger and stood up, bent her backwards in a Hollywood kiss, and then tossed his hat into the air.

"She said yes," he yelled above the noise.

Dozens of camera flashes going off created a strobe light effect in the barn and her eyes got misty. If only it was real, she would be a happy woman. But it had all started wrong and everyone knew a house built without a foundation could never weather the storms.

"Don't leave my side, promise?" she whispered as he stood her upright.

"Darlin', wild horses couldn't keep us apart." He kissed her again, that time sweeter and not so dramatic.

A drumroll filled the barn and then the lead singer said, "And now it is time for everyone to join the newly engaged couple in a dance. Choose a partner and come on out on the floor."

Roger held out his hand to Cynthia and she walked right into his arms. Janet turned around to find a cowboy grinning at her. He was tall and the word handsome barely covered his description. She pointed and he joined her on the dance floor.

"Who is that?" Laura asked Colton.

"Nothing to worry about, believe me."

"Is he married?"

"He's a widower and not looking for a wife. His name is Mason Harper and he's got a set of twin girls that could scale a glass wall on a rainy day. Don't worry about Janet. She's safe."

"But is he?" Laura asked.

Colton pulled Laura tighter into his arms as the singer started a slow ballad. "Have I told you tonight that you are beautiful?"

She smiled up at him. "Couple of times."

Janet removed her boots and fell back on the pillows piled up on her bed. "Fine party. Best I've ever been to in my life. I'm going back home and tellin' those ranchers how to really throw a party. The games were a hoot and the makeovers were wonderful. And the barn was absolutely fabulous and the cowboy I danced with was very attentive. I might have pressed the issue of going home with him but I found out he's got kids. God, I'd be a horrible mother and so would you, but I'm proud of you for landing a damn billion-dollar cowboy. Surely you weren't serious about a prenup."

"Another round?" Laura pulled off her boots and joined Janet on the bed.

Janet shook her head. "I had champagne and a beer at the party. Better not be trading one vice for another. Let me look at that rock some more. Lord, girl, that thing cost as much as a third-world country, I bet. How many carats is in it?"

Roxie peeked in the open door. "Colton told me five carats in the big stone and three more in the little ones surrounding it. Y'all old ladies aren't tired yet?"

Laura patted her on the shoulder. “Us old ladies know how to pace ourselves. We can run at fifty-five for a couple of days before we crash. You young kids start off at zero and go to ninety in five seconds and never slow down, then you crash at the end of six hours.”

“Well, I’m old as the hills. I danced with a man that is only two years older than me and he’s got eight-year-old twin daughters. I shudder to think of raising kids,” Janet said. “And where is your fiancé? What in the hell are you doing with us? You should be with him tonight.”

Laura finished off the last of her beer. “He’ll be along in a few minutes. My orders are to wait right here in my room until he arrives to sweep me off my feet.”

Roxie propped her bare feet on an extra chair. “He’ll probably lean over the balcony and whistle like he’s callin’ up the heifers.”

Laura gently elbowed Roxie. “Colton is right. You have changed.”

Roxie laughed. “I know it and I like the new me. Rosalee don’t even mess with me no more now that I speak my mind.”

“I’m not calling heifers,” Colton said from the doorway.

His boot heels sounded like drumbeats as he crossed the hardwood floor. He put his Stetson on Laura’s head and gathered her up like a bride in his arms.

“See y’all tomorrow morning,” he said. “We’re going for a midnight walk to look at the stars.”

Laura snuggled into his chest. It had been a perfect day. They’d made a good team and she had memories that no one could ever take from her. But nothing, especially good things, lasted forever.

Chapter 19

THE HOT, DEMANDING KISSES STARTED HALFWAY UP the stairs to her apartment. Laura felt like one of those big lightning balls she'd seen dancing across the Texas flatlands had settled in her lower stomach. The fire was so intense that it would take Colton half the night to get it under control. She couldn't wait for him to drop her on the bed and make wild passionate love to her.

Colton carried her inside, kicked the door shut with his boot heel, and took her to the bathroom. Following another long, lingering steamy kiss, he set her feet on the floor beside the full, bubbling tub. One hand slipped around her back to unzip the red dress; the other went to the nape of her neck to untie the halter strings. He kissed his way down as he pulled the dress an inch at a time toward her feet.

"I've dreamed about this all night long," he said.

She'd removed her boots in Janet's bedroom so all that was left was lacy red underpants. He hooked a thumb under the elastic on each side, brought them to the floor, and tasted his way from the ends of her bright red toenails upward, past her belly button to her breasts, and finally settling on her lips.

She was so ready for the real thing but she didn't want the kisses to end. Her scalp tingled when he began to remove the hairpins, setting her blond curls free. His lips slid to that soft spot right below her ear.

She wasn't sure if she was physically floating through the air or if it just felt that way until he lowered her into the warm bathwater.

"Oh my God," she muttered.

"Too warm?"

"Just right. Join me?"

"I already had a shower. This is just for you. Lay your head back on this towel and shut your eyes," he said.

He hummed the song they'd danced to that night and she smelled vanilla. She peeked and he grinned. "I knew you couldn't keep them closed."

"What are you doing?"

"Giving you a bath."

She glanced at his big hands. "Is there a washcloth under all those bubbles?"

"Now where's the fun in that?"

Rough cowboy hands started at her neck and touched every inch of her body from there to her feet. The soap dissolved too quickly and it took him forever to lather up his hands again. She could not keep her eyes closed. She wanted to see his eyes and bask in the glow when he grinned.

"My hair?" she asked.

"Looks beautiful."

He scooped her up from the water when he was finished and wrapped her in an oversized white towel and patted her dry. She listened to his heart beat as he carried her from bathroom to the bed. He laid her gently on the bed and stripped off his shirt, boots, and jeans.

"Yes," she said.

He was every bit as ready as she was.

"Not yet."

Hell's bells, what was he waiting for? She was about to explode and she could almost feel him pulsating with desire. His face was a study in sexy angles in the candlelight of a dozen candles scattered about in the room and… was that… yes, it was. Velvety soft red rose petals covered the top of the sheets.

He brought her to a sitting position and rubbed vanilla-scented lotion on her back, massaging the tension from her shoulders and neck until she felt like a rag doll.

"Feel good?" he asked.

"Have I died and gone to heaven?"

He chuckled, flipped her over, and in one firm thrust, he was inside her. She wrapped her legs around him and they rocked together in perfect unison.

"Oh, my! I wasn't expecting to float," she groaned.

"Neither was I." His breath came in short gasps against her neck. "I wanted to touch you more and taste you again but I was about to explode."

"I'm not really on earth, am I?"

"No, darlin', we really are floating," he said.

He took her right up to the edge of release, slowed down to let the flames cool, and then did it again and again. When the final thrust brought her to the highest point she could reach and still be on earth, she couldn't even utter his name. All she could do was loosen her leg hold and pant for breath. She touched the top of her head to make sure it was still there and then his cheek, planted firmly on her collarbone.

"Good?" His voice was even deeper.

"No."

He raised his head and looked into her eyes.

"Freakin' amazin'!" she managed to say before his lips closed in on hers for the sweetest yet most passionate kiss they'd ever shared.

"There's dessert," he said.

"Honey, I can't even wiggle."

"Not that kind. Real food and dessert. I noticed that you didn't eat very well at the supper." He rolled to one side, kept her in his arms, and pulled the sheet up over them.

Her stomach growled. Colton was right. She had been a whole lot more at home with the games they'd played and in her flower beds than she was at the Dallas party or the reception.

"Did you put leftovers into my fridge?" she asked.

He propped up on an elbow. Enough moonlight filtered through the lacy curtains on the window and softened his features. She reached up and traced the outline of his jaw. "You are so damn sexy."

"Is that even better than just plain old sexy?"

"A billion times better," she whispered.

Her stomach grumbled again.

"Let's raid the fridge naked," he said.

"I'm going to wrap this sheet around me but you are going to be naked," she said.

"How about both of us being naked while we eat?"

"Good grief, Colton! What if..."

He put his fingers over her mouth. "Watch this."

He swung his legs over the side of the bed. Rose petals stuck to his back and fell to the floor as he padded barefoot across the floor and made sure the apartment door was locked. Rose petals had slid off the slick sheets onto the floor during all the rolling and tumbling around.

She picked one from under her breast and laid it on the end table. Tomorrow morning, she would remember to pick it up to put in her memory box where she kept precious things.

Colton pushed a cart out of the corner behind the recliner and parked it right beside the bed. He moved around it and crawled back into bed with her. "Dinner is served."

"Where did that come from?"

"I brought it up here earlier today. I had an ulterior motive in asking you to stay in the house. I planned tonight and I wanted free access to your apartment so we could have some privacy. I could live in this little place and enjoy it if you were here with me." He opened a door and brought out a huge platter of cold buffalo wings, an assortment of cheese cubes, raw vegetables with spinach dip, and fruit surrounding a small bowl of strawberry dip.

She propped pillows against the headboard of the bed. He brought up a small tray and handed it to her. "You'll have to pop the tray legs up, darlin'. I can't do that and hold the food, too."

"Kind of like diggin' for worms, right?"

"You got it. We're a team."

He dipped a grape in the dip and put it in her mouth. She reached for a buffalo wing and nibbled on it while he removed the caps from two bottles of beer.

"Champagne would be more romantic," he said.

"Depends on who you are talkin' to. Is that really pecan pie over there?"

"It is, but not until we finish off our dinner."

She grinned. "You won't get an argument from me."

"Will I get one if I ask you one more time to stay?"

"Not tonight. But this is a magical night so don't go drawing up the paperwork just yet. I'll think about it, Colton. You might change your mind, so I'm not giving you my word or holding you to your offer. Things might take a sudden turn in a very different direction when one of us crosses the other."

"I don't see that happening," he said.

"See, just like I said. A magical night. Open your mouth."

He did and she fed him an enormous strawberry that had been dipped in white chocolate.

Janet, Maudie, and Roxie were at the table when Laura made it to the dining room the next morning. They'd either finished breakfast or hadn't started yet, because the only thing in front of them was steaming mugs of coffee.

"We've been waiting at least thirty minutes for you to get here," Janet said.

Roxie shook her head and held up two fingers.

Laura hugged Janet tightly. "I love you even when you lie. I smell breakfast burritos and pancakes. And there is Chester bringing a hot batch out of the kitchen."

Janet squirmed free of her sister's arms, pushed back the chair, and headed toward the buffet. "Turn me loose and let me up. You know how much I love pancakes."

Maudie stood up and pointed at Roxie. "I'm going to the church for an early breakfast with the ladies this morning and then we'll have Sunday school and services. Roxie, you behave."

"Yes, ma'am, but it's all right if I spend the day with Janet and Laura, right?"

Maudie looked at Laura.

"I'd love for her to join us."

"Okay then, but no Dillon. This is a girls' day." She picked up her purse from a dining room chair and in a couple of minutes the front door closed.

Roxie giggled. "She's going to church because she wants to hear what the gossip was about the party, and Colton proposing to you, and she wants to see if Cynthia was in hot pursuit of a holy life."

"Roxie!" Laura exclaimed.

"You know I'm right," Roxie said.

Roxie wore a blue halter top that matched her eyes that morning. She was barefoot and her curls had fallen. Like Janet in that respect too. Janet's hair never would hold a curl very long.

Janet stacked pancakes six high on her plate and carried them to the table where melted butter and warm syrup waited. Laura wondered if the white robe would go home with her when she left the next day.

Laura's brightly colored, flowing caftan and flip-flops were a flash of color as she headed toward the buffet. She opted for a stack of pancakes and a breakfast burrito. "So Dillon is really banned from the place on Sunday. I can't believe he's not coming over today."

"Who says he ever left?"

"Roxie! You'd better be glad Maudie didn't hear that," Laura gasped.

Roxie's flippant answer proved that Colton was right. The girl had changed a lot since Laura had arrived at the ranch.

"Gotcha. You ain't as swift as you usually are," Roxie said. "But he's not coming around today at all.

Remember, I get to have a girls' day with y'all at the pool this afternoon."

"I'm still wonderin' where this pool is. We were all over this place for the games yesterday and I didn't see the faintest sign of a swimming pool," Janet said.

Roxie giggled. "You were fishin' in it."

Janet almost choked on a bite of pancake. "You have got to be kidding me!"

"Of course I'm jokin'. Finish your pancakes and we'll ride down to the pool house. You'll want fifteen minutes in the sauna first to get them old bones to workin' before you hit the water. And FYI, the sauna is a two-man pup tent on the side of the pond. We haven't let the cows out of the pasture to get to the water yet, so all the bullshit should be settled to the bottom," Roxie said.

"You," Janet grinned at her, "are a smart-ass."

"Takes one to know one," Roxie shot back.

Janet picked up the burrito and bit into it. "What is that cook doing on a ranch? He could open his own restaurant anywhere in the world."

Chester, a short, round cowboy whose straw hat was his chef's toque, checked the buffet and answered the question, "I'd hate to be cooped up where I couldn't see the stars at night or hear a coyote howling. I like the Circle 6. Y'all will just have to come back often if you want to eat my cookin'."

"Is that an invitation?" Janet looked at Laura.

"As long as I live on this ranch, you are welcome to visit anytime."

"I didn't bring a swimsuit," she said.

"You don't need one," Roxie told her.

"Honey, you are young and gravity has not attacked your perky little cells."

"We got bathing suits in every size and description," Laura said. "You just pick out whatever you are comfortable wearing."

"Wouldn't be no fun skinny-dippin' without boys anyway," Roxie said.

Laura's fork stopped midair. "You should have gone to church with Maudie, girl."

Roxie waved the comment away like a pesky fly. "Hurry up and swallow those pancakes. Aunt Maudie done had Chester set up the food tables at the pool so you won't starve to death."

"Have you seen Colton?" Laura asked.

When she woke that morning, he was gone. He'd left a note on his pillow saying that he'd see her at the supper table and that Granny had invited Roger and Cynthia and it would be served at five so Roger could get back to preach evening services at seven. It was signed with a loosely drawn heart. Did the space at the top of the heart mean that his was open to her?

"He and the guys are helping with the cleanup down at the sale barn. He said he left you a note," Roxie answered.

She'd slipped the note and the rose petal into an envelope to put with her things when she got back to Hereford. But… she wasn't going back, and besides, Janet had packed up her things and brought them to Ambrose. She wondered which suitcase the cigar box was in. That's where she kept her prized possessions: the one picture that she had of her mother and the cheap little heart necklace she'd been wearing the day Aunt

Dotty took her and Janet to Texas. Things like that could never be replaced.

"He did but he didn't tell me what he was doing all day," Laura answered.

"My instructions are to lock the gym doors when we go inside and to not let Dillon in no matter what. And to call Chester if any of y'all want something that's not down at the pool. Oh, and the only way I get to go play with the big girls is if I promise not to even sip a beer." Roxie clicked off her orders by holding up a finger to count each one.

Laura truly wished that she had a camera or at the very least her phone dug out of her purse when she drove the truck up to the barn and parked. Janet's jaw dropped and for a minute or two she was totally speechless.

"No way," Janet said when she could talk. "Is this another Roxie joke?"

"Be prepared for the shock of your life, right, Laura?" Roxie said.

She ushered them into the barn, carefully locked the door behind them, and led the way into the gym. "Anyone like to work out for a few minutes? I'll be your trainer if I can yell at you like coaches do."

"This is my kind of barn. And there is a pool in here?" Janet whispered.

Roxie crooked a finger. "Follow me and I will show it to you. I don't expect you'd like to stop by the sauna on the way?"

Janet shook her head.

"Well, if you change your mind, this is the door and it won't be locked."

"Oh. My. God!" Each word got louder when Janet said it.

Laura threw an arm around her shoulder. "Fascinating, isn't it?"

"Wow! Just plain old wow!"

"I'll take you to the cabana and you can choose a swimsuit. What time do we have to be back at the ranch house, Laura?" Roxie led the way behind the waterfall.

"Better leave here at four because supper is at five and we'll have to clean up. And Maudie has invited Cynthia and Roger," she answered.

Roxie rolled her eyes. "Why, God? Why did you let me put them together?"

"I don't think it was God." Laura laughed.

It didn't take them long to choose bathing suits and dive into the water. Janet swam from one end to the other several times then hopped up to sit beside Laura on the side of the tub.

"You are an idiot," Janet said. "If you don't want to fleece him, then fall in love with him. Just promise me that you won't make him sign a prenup. Hold your hand up and let me see that ring again."

"Money isn't that important," Laura said.

"Honey, it is when you don't have it. Will you just think about the prenup? He's so damned much in love with you that he won't even think of it if you don't mention it."

Laura shrugged. "There is a lot of difference in sex and love."

"You've changed," Janet said.

"I know I have."

"I don't know if I like the new Laura."

Laura shrugged again. "That's your option. Hey, Roxie, let's play a game of pool basketball and then Janet is going to play the winner of that round."

She dived into the pool. Staying would be the easiest thing in the world. Colton had asked her several times and she loved the ranch. But he'd never said that he loved her and until he said the words, she wasn't committing to anything, not even real dating.

"Where are Andy and Rusty?" Maudie asked when Colton slumped down in a dining room chair.

"They'll be along in a minute. Barn is all put back in order. I hope Ina Dean and Patsy are thoroughly convinced."

Maudie smiled. "You enjoyed yesterday more than anyone so stop your bitchin' about doing half a day's worth of cleanup. You ain't gettin' an ounce of my sympathy. Have you talked Laura into staying?"

He fanned his face with his straw hat. "I've asked her and she's thinking about it."

"She's fitting in right well. Andy did good when he hired her."

The fanning stopped. "She deserves more than I can give her."

"Good God, you are a billionaire, Colton! Give her whatever she wants."

"That's not what I'm talking about. Money can't buy love and I'm not so sure I'm willing to trust anyone enough to…" He stopped so fast that the sentence dangled there above them like the wagon wheel chandelier.

"Spit it out," Maudie said.

The fanning started again, this time slower. "I don't know that I can."

"Well, give it a try and I'll fill in the blanks."

"I'm ready to settle down. I realize that and Laura is a good woman and..." He paused.

Maudie folded her arms across her chest and waited.

"Daddy loved Momma but they fought all the time."

Maudie leaned forward and propped her elbows on the table. "Is that what your problem is? Why didn't you talk to me about it before?"

Colton looked absolutely miserable. "I never was good at showing my feelings. Not like my folks. Lord, they showed everything they thought. Sometimes I think that the DNA skipped a generation and I'm more like you than like my dad."

"You are beating around the bush, Colton," Maudie said.

"When I was ten, it was sissy to talk about things like that. It wasn't an issue until now because I didn't want to let a woman into my heart. Cowboys don't go around talking about their hearts and love. I'm rambling. Forget I even mentioned it."

"No, we are not forgetting it. We're going to hash this out and get it out of the way. I'm not so sure that your mom and dad were suited to each other but they were in love from the first time they met. They fought when they dated and broke up like Roxie and Dillon do—every other day. I always feared you'd be like them."

"It's a wonder I'm not, but I hated their fighting," he said.

"They fought about where they were going to college because your dad wanted to go to Oklahoma State

University and she wanted to go to Midwestern over in Gainesville. They loved each other, I'm sure of it, but they could never agree and both of them were so bullheaded it wasn't even funny."

Colton inhaled deeply. "I'm afraid that all marriages will wind up like that. And I'd rather be a bachelor and leave everything I've got to Roxie as take a chance on going through that."

"Didn't you hear me? I said your folks fought when they dated. How many fights have you and Laura had?"

"I don't think we're dating except in a make-believe world."

Maudie frowned. "The night your folks were killed, did you hear the argument?"

"The folks on the far end of the block heard it," Colton answered. "It was about another baby. Daddy wanted more kids. Momma didn't and she was very loudly telling him that all he had to do was make a child but she had to take care of it."

Maudie sighed. "They'd been fighting about that for years. He always wanted a houseful of children but she wanted something more than a bunch of wild kids running around her legs."

"And Momma?" he asked.

"She wanted a career and to live in the city."

"Why'd they ever get married?"

"Honey, they were passionate. They might have fought like banty roosters but they loved just as passionately. Never doubt that they both loved you."

Colton ran his fingers through his dark hair. "Now I'm more confused than ever. If Laura and I don't argue, does that mean we aren't passionate?"

"You think too much. Let go of the past and listen to your heart. And it's not sissy to talk about your feelings. Happiness starts with you, Colton, and to be happy, you've got to open up your heart. Happiness starts down deep in here." Maudie touched her chest with her fist. "When you find someone who truly makes you happy, then hang on for dear life."

"That sounds like experience talking," Colton said.

Maudie nodded. "It is, but that's in the past that I've let go of. I'm happy now with my life."

Andy followed Rusty into the dining room and said, "Y'all leave us any food?"

"We ain't even started yet and it's leftovers from last night," Maudie answered.

"I'd eat raw armadillo right now, I'm so hungry," Rusty said. "Them women left yet?"

"They're having a day to themselves at the pool," Colton answered. "They'll be leaving tomorrow morning. We'll all have supper tonight with the preacher and Cynthia."

Rusty rolled his eyes.

Andy Joe's blue eyes twinkled and a smile covered his face. "We ain't got nothing to worry about from now on. Roxie says that Cynthia has seen the light and is going for the title of preacher's wife."

"Well, praise the lord," Rusty said.

On her way out of the dining room, Maudie bent down and whispered in Colton's ear, "My regrets about the past have nothing to do with you. You are the best part of my life."

Every one of the nine chairs was filled at the table that evening. Laura was seated to Colton's right with Cynthia beside her and Roger next in line beside her. During dessert and coffee, Cynthia leaned over and whispered, "Did it take a long time for you to know you were in love with Colton or did it happen on the first date?"

"Why? Do you think you are in love with Roger?" Laura skirted the question.

"I don't know. That's why I'm asking. I never have believed in love at first sight. But then it wouldn't be first sight since he's been preachin' at our church for a year and I see him every Sunday." Cynthia continued to keep her voice low. "He kissed me good night after the dance."

"And?" Laura asked.

"My toenails curled. He's a preacher, for God's sake, Laura!"

"He's also a man who evidently knows how to kiss."

"He asked me on a real date for tomorrow night. We're going to dinner and seeing a movie over in Sherman."

"Have fun."

"You don't think I'm crazy?"

Laura patted her on the arm. "Honey, you don't ask a crazy person that question."

Cynthia giggled. "Did you know that Colton was rich when you went to work for him?"

"I did and it didn't make bit of difference to me how much money he had or didn't have."

Cynthia nodded. "That's why he fell in love with you. All the rest of the women were chasin' him for his money."

"What are you two whispering about?" Roger asked.

"The future," Laura said quickly.

Janet and Cynthia had both mentioned that Colton was in love with her that very same day. Apparently, he was playing his role better than she was because no one had said that she was head over heels in love with him. And yet, the truth of the matter was that she was no longer pretending.

"And the past," Cynthia came in right behind her.

Roger slipped an arm around the back of Cynthia's chair. "Well, I rather like the present, right here and right now."

"Too bad y'all can't stay around for a game of Monopoly. We're partnering up and Roxie and I are going to whip the newly engaged couple," Janet said.

"Sounds like fun but we've got church at seven. Roger is preaching on the love chapter in Corinthians," Cynthia beamed. "You should come hear it and play Monopoly afterwards."

"Will you two come back and play if we do?" Roxie asked.

Laura bit back a groan. She didn't want to play Monopoly with her cheating sister and she sure didn't want to sit still and listen to any preaching about love. She was having a hard enough time sorting out her own heart and mind without listening to the well-known chapter about love not being selfish.

Besides, that wasn't exactly right. When a person fell in love they were selfish. They wanted the other person to love them more than they wanted anything else in the world and they'd do anything to get and keep that love for themselves. That was selfish served up on a silver platter.

"Sure we will," Roger said. "But only if Cynthia can be my partner."

"Then we'll all be there," Roxie said.

"Since when do you make decisions for us?" Andy asked.

"You going to tell the preacher you don't want to hear his sermon about love?" Roxie asked.

Andy blushed. "I was plannin' on going to church this evening anyway, but you ain't got the right to tell me what to do. Me and Rusty are going to team up and whip your butts at Monopoly."

Roxie's eyes twinkled. "Now we got the four teams to play—me and Janet, Colton and Laura, Rusty and Andy, and Cynthia and Roger."

"What about me?" Maudie asked.

"You are the banker and the ref," Roxie said.

"You've got school tomorrow morning, young lady. If the game isn't over at ten o'clock then you'll bow out and I will be Janet's partner," Maudie said.

"Oh, me and Janet will whip all of you long before ten!" Roxie said.

The Circle 6 crew took up a whole pew that evening and sure enough Roger preached from Corinthians about the qualities that love brought into people's lives. He started off by saying that after the party the day before and watching Laura and Colton work as a team that he'd been inspired to go back and read that chapter before he went to sleep.

Laura wanted to stand to her feet and disagree with him. She and Colton weren't the inspiration for his sermon. He'd read that chapter because he and Cynthia had found each other and love was on his mind. Was that why fate had brought Laura to the Circle 6? Not to find her own true love but to cause Cynthia and Roger to find happiness?

If it was, then Lady Fate really, truly was a first-class bitch.

"Is he talking to us or trying to relay a message to Cynthia?" she whispered to Colton.

He laid his hand on hers and squeezed. "You believe that love is all those things?"

"I believe that love is something that two people work at every day, not something that falls out of the heaven."

Colton squeezed her hand again.

Chapter 20

Janet hugged Laura tightly and whispered, "This is the real thing, sister. Don't blow it. And for your information, I did not cheat last night at Monopoly. Roxie and I won fair and square and it felt damn good."

Then she hugged Colton. "Take good care of her, cowboy. She might be the best thing that God ever put on this earth."

Then she was behind the wheel of her rental car and driving away.

Tears streamed down Laura's face. For the first time in their lives, Janet's pathway was leading in a different direction than Laura's. This had to be the way it felt when a child went away to college. It was long past time for Janet to spread her own wings and learn to take care of herself, but it hurt not to be needed anymore.

You'll always need each other. You are family. You've just stepped up to a higher place—one called adulthood, her conscience said in a rough voice.

Colton hugged Laura close to his side and kissed her on the forehead. "She'll be back. We have the cattle sale in the fall with a party then and there's Christmas. Don't cry."

Before she could remind him that she'd probably be gone long before fall now that her debt was paid, his cell phone rang. He fished it out of his shirt pocket and listened for a few seconds before shoving it back into his pocket.

All Laura heard was, "Hello," and "I'll be right there."

"Problem?" she asked.

"Big one. Roxie's in trouble at school. Evidently Granny is in that area over by Bonham where the cell phone service is spotty and I told them I'd come. The social worker is already there."

Laura's blood ran cold, like ice water shooting through her veins. "What did she do—kill someone?"

Colton started toward the truck. "Guess she tried to. She and Rosalee got into it."

Laura followed. "I'm going too."

"No need. I'll smooth it over and probably barely beat Granny there. Soon as the social worker finds her, she'll stop whatever she's doing and get on over to the school."

Laura opened the passenger door. "I don't care who is there. If the social worker has been called in, it's serious and she'll need all of us. They can't take her away from the ranch for this, can they? That rotten Rosalee has been askin' for this for weeks."

Colton started the truck and headed down the lane. "I told Granny, you don't change a leopard's spots, not even with all the love in the world. Roxie is a sweet kid but she's got her momma's blood and worse yet, her daddy's DNA. We can't knock that out of her even if we want to, and I'll fight the system to my last dollar to keep that kid on the ranch."

The tears dried up instantly. Anger like she'd never known before settled in their place and she stared out the side window at the world speeding past in a blur. She'd known it was too good to be true but she'd think it all through later. Right then Roxie needed her and it didn't matter whose blood or DNA she had, Laura was going to be there for her.

Colton parked in the school parking lot and she was out of the truck before he could turn off the engine. So what if he had to scramble to catch up with her! After that comment he deserved to be left in the dust.

He grabbed for her hand. "What's your hurry?"

She pulled it away and shoved it into the pocket of her jeans.

He opened the door for her and she didn't even break stride as she headed down the hall. When she reached the door marked Principal she swung it open and plowed right in with Colton two steps behind her.

"We are here about Roxie," she said.

"Where's Maudie?" the secretary asked.

"She'll be along but I want to see Roxie now."

"And you are?"

"I'm Laura Nelson."

Colton stepped inside the office and the school secretary looked around Laura at him. "This is your new fiancée, right? Sorry I missed the party on Saturday. We had a family reunion over in Whitewright. Roxie is in the lounge with the social worker. We have to call her when the problem involves fighting, stealing, or such. Roxie might not be in the system but well… you know. You understand, don't you, Colton?"

"Which way is the lounge?" Laura asked.

Colton pointed to a door behind them. "We probably ought to wait for Granny since she's in charge of Roxie."

"I'm not waiting for anyone," Laura declared.

The principal and the social worker were sitting on one side of an eight-foot table with Roxie and another girl across from them. Laura's heart stopped racing when she saw that Roxie wasn't bleeding or holding a broken arm. She had a scratch across her cheek but it was superficial. It looked like the other girl would have a black eye for a week or two. Both of them looked like they'd tried to pull each other's hair out.

"I'm Laura Nelson," she said.

"Colton, where is Maudie?" the principal asked.

"On her way, I'm sure. What happened?"

"She tried to kill me," the other girl whined.

"Oh, shut up, Rosalee! You've been askin' for it ever since you got here," Roxie snapped.

"Roxie," the social worker said.

Laura sat down beside Roxie and put an arm around her shoulders. She leaned forward and looked at Rosalee. "You want to tell them or should I?"

Rosalee shrugged. "I didn't do nothing. She just came at me with her fists and started hittin' on me. I was takin' up for myself when I scratched her and pulled her hair."

"Voodoo doll?" Laura asked.

Rosalee dropped her head and blushed. "That was a joke."

"With a pin shoved through the heart? Don't sound like a joke to me. Cheating in class to try to steal her boyfriend?"

Rosalee glared at Laura. "He don't belong with her. She's white trash. He deserves someone better than that. And I told her so this mornin' when she got off the bus..." She clamped a hand over her mouth.

"So you antagonized Roxie, did you?" the social worker asked. "Why didn't you tell the principal, Roxie?"

"I'm not a tattletale," Roxie answered.

"Well, my work is done. This is your job, Sam." The social worker looked at the principal.

"Then you aren't going to take me away from Aunt Maudie?" Roxie asked nervously.

"No, I am not. But whatever punishment the principal hands out you'd best follow it to the letter, young lady. And Rosalee, next time you taunt her, remember that she's got a mean right hook." The social worker picked up her file and walked out the door.

"You want me to take her home, Sam?" Colton asked.

He shook his head. "School rules say that fighting gets a person in-school suspension for three weeks. That will finish up the summer session for her. She'll be in a cubicle all day every day with her studies in front of her. If she finishes before the day is out, she'd best have a book to read because if she falls asleep, that day doesn't count. Go on back to class, Roxie."

"What about Rosalee?" Laura asked.

"We have a no tolerance rule for bullying. She will get six weeks of in-school suspension. That means when school starts back the first of September, she'll owe us three more weeks before she gets to attend normal classes again. We're waiting on her sister to get here to discuss it and that's all I'm saying. Privacy laws," Sam said.

"Then you don't need us anymore?" Colton asked.

"No, I don't," Sam said.

Colton's phone rang before they reached the truck and he told Maudie what had happened, laughed a couple of times, and put the phone back. He whistled as he opened the passenger door for Laura. He settled into his seat and started the engine.

"What is so funny?" she asked.

"Granny said that she would have decked that kid for Roxie if she'd heard her say that. She also said that Roxie was going to be in trouble when she got home," Colton explained.

"Why would she be in trouble?"

"For throwing the first hit. Granny's rule says that you can't start a fight but you sure better not run from one. Roxie should have waited for Rosalee to start the fight. Now she'll get a lecture or grounded for a week for starting it."

"That's bullshit!"

"What would you do different?" Colton asked.

"Not a thing because..." She stopped and stared out the window.

"Spit it out," Colton said.

"Because I wanted a mother like Maudie. One who loved us like she does Roxie. So I wouldn't do a thing different but, hell, I don't know how to explain it. And if I'm honest, that's not the only reason I'm mad."

"The real reason you want to chew up fence posts is because Janet left, isn't it?"

She glared at him.

He hit the steering wheel with both hands. "What? It wasn't me that started a fight and got in trouble with the principal. And I told you Janet would be back in the middle of the summer."

She jerked her head around to look out the side window and clamped her mouth shut.

Roxie has more on the ball than you do. She will stand up and fight for what she wants. You are planning to run from it, that hateful voice inside her head shouted.

I'm not running. I'm leaving because my bloodline

and DNA would never be good enough for him, she argued silently.

It only took ten minutes to get back to the ranch but it felt like ten hours by the time he parked the truck. She jumped out and stormed to the backyard. She gathered up her gardening tools from the shed and carried them to the first flower bed.

“Dammit!” she swore as she started the tedious job of pruning the crape myrtles from the bottom.

“Coffee?” Colton asked a few minutes later.

She whipped around to find him three feet behind her with two mugs of steaming coffee in his hands. Being careful not to touch his hand, she took one and sipped it.

“Now tell me what is really wrong with you,” he said.

“Nothing is wrong with me. Too bad you don’t see it that way.”

Colton nodded toward a garden bench. “Sit with me, please.”

She laid her pruning shears down and felt like she was in Roxie’s shoes, sitting across the table from the social worker and the principal.

At least Colton had the good sense to sit on the other end of the bench and not crowd her. A monarch butterfly as big as the palm of her hand lit between them, its wings flipping up and down.

“I run from arguments,” he said bluntly. “That’s been part of my commitment issues. I hate to fight.”

“How’d you ever get through school?”

“Not that kind of fighting. I did my share of that and just like Roxie, if I broke the rules, I paid the price.”

She sipped her coffee. She had the same problem. She

was like the butterfly. The minute she smelled emotional danger, she took flight without looking back.

"Why?" she asked.

Colton sighed and looked at the butterfly instead of her. "I was ten when my folks were killed. Granny says that they were passionate in their love as well as their arguments. But the last thing I heard before they dropped me at Aunt Maudie's house while they went out to dinner was another fight."

She wasn't sure that she understood what that had to do with today.

"That night it was over whether to have more children and my mother said that just one kid was enough responsibility for her. My father wanted a house full and she didn't. I'm not so sure I can explain this."

"Keep talking," she said. That's what the therapist had said when she'd said the same words to him on the first visit. Besides, Colton looked absolutely miserable and her heart went out to him as much as it had to Roxie when the girl had looked up at her in the teacher's lounge.

He stretched his long legs out and crossed one boot over the other, raked his fingers through his hair, and finally looked at her. Their eyes locked and she could see pain all the way to the inner parts of his soul.

"Fighting means separation, and since no two people can ever be together without arguments then it stands to reason that commitment will bring nothing but separation. Does that make sense?"

"Perfectly. But why did you ask me to stay if that's the way you feel?"

Colton blinked and looked away.

She understood on a depth that couldn't be explained.

"We've been burned pretty bad, haven't we?" she asked.

His head bobbed up and down. "I don't know what you are mad about, but believe me, I feel it when there's anger in the air. It would be easier if you were vocal, but you retreat into your shell just like I do. That's not a good thing, Laura."

"Well, thank you, Dr. Nelson," she said.

The butterfly spread its wings and flew away.

Colton started to stand but she reached over and put a hand on his leg. "Don't you leave me with all this inside me or I'll explode."

He settled back into his corner of the bench.

The butterfly came back and settled on his knee.

She took a sip of her coffee and said, "I never knew my father and I never heard my mother fight with anyone. To me, any relationship is headed for disaster because there has to come a time when the other party disappears. Why even start something that is only going to end in heartache? If my mother couldn't even love me enough to fight for her life and stop smoking and drinking, then how could anyone else?"

It hit Colton like a class-five tornado.

It wasn't Janet's leaving or Roxie's fight that had set her off but what he'd said about the blood and DNA. If only a person had the means to erase what they'd said like a teacher removing things from a blackboard.

"Guess we make quite the pair," he said.

"I have trust issues because of my past," she said. "You have commitment issues and relate them all to arguments. That doesn't make for much of a relationship outside of the hot bedroom sheets."

"You also have trouble spitting out your problems and keep everything bottled up inside of you," he said.

"And you can't say what you really feel?"

"What you are really upset about is what I said about Roxie not being able to change what she is by birth and nature. You didn't pitch a hissy in the truck about that. You just puffed up like a bullfrog."

"I did not!"

"So what are the rules?"

"It doesn't matter. Like you said, Colton, you can't change what you come from," she said softly.

"No, but if you work at it, you can change what you become."

Was he talking to himself or to her? He wondered.

He leaned across the space and brushed a light kiss across her lips. "I'm leaving now. We both need to think before we talk any more. See you this evening. Rusty and I are going over to Sherman this morning to pick up a load of barbed wire. After supper, maybe we'll take a walk?"

"I'll look forward to it."

The sweetness of the kiss didn't surprise her as much as the fact that the monarch wasn't spooked and stayed on his pant leg halfway across the yard.

Evidently Maudie had gotten the news via phone call from Colton because she was on the phone with the social worker at noon when Laura finished the yard work and went inside for dinner. Maudie held up a finger, said a few more words, and then snapped her phone shut.

She looked at Laura and asked, "Hungry?"

"Starving," Laura answered.

"It's just me and you today. Andy has gone to the bank. Rusty and Colton are still drooling over tractors trying to decide which one to buy. I swear that boy still pinches pennies even though he could buy ten of those tractors and not put a dent in his bank account."

"What about Roxie?" Laura made a sandwich and dipped a bowl of soup from the Crock-Pot on the buffet.

"I got the story from Colton, from the principal, and from the social worker. They were all impressed with you, wanted to know if you had counselor training," Maudie said.

"Not me! I was just trained by the orneriest sister God ever put on the face of the earth. Most of the time it turned out that whatever trouble she was in, she'd brought on herself. But Roxie's put up with enough, Maudie."

"Thanks for stepping in for her. She's come out of her shell since you came to the ranch. It'll mean a lot to her that you took up for her. She'll still have some punishment when she gets home because that's the rules, but I appreciate what you did. Now, let's talk about what's going on the rest of the week. Tomorrow night you've got that dinner in Gainesville."

Laura groaned. "I thought all the party stuff was over."

"Just one more this month. It's the North Texas Angus Association dinner. They have a social evening several times a year for the members and their spouses or girlfriends. It's not like that thing in Dallas. The men folks wear jeans and no ties. The ladies dress in anything from fancy jeans and boots to cute little dresses, depending on how much sag and bag they've got. So don't worry about it."

"Then I don't have to go to Tressa's or shop anymore?" Laura asked.

"You can wear what you had on that first time you went to church and look just fine," Maudie answered. "I hear you and Colton had a fight. Did you talk it out yet?"

"Neither of us are much on talking it out but we're trying. I bottle things up and have trust problems. He bottles things up and has commitment problems. But what does it matter? This is all a farce anyway, isn't it?" Laura asked.

"Is it? From the way he looks at you, I kind of thought you'd moved into reality. But that is y'all's business. The yard is looking very nice. I told Colton when we moved into this big old place that the backyard had potential. Guess you're bringing that out as much as you are Roxie's potential."

"Thank you," Laura tucked her chin down and blushed.

Janet called right after lunch. She'd landed in Amarillo, drove home, unpacked, and gone to a meeting.

"Been a busy girl, haven't you?" Laura laughed.

"I've got something to say and I mean it with my whole heart. And I don't want you to butt in one time while I'm talking or I'll start crying."

There was a long, pregnant pause.

"Well?" Janet snapped.

"You told me not to butt in. I'm listening," Laura said.

"Okay, number one. Don't you dare try to scam Colton. He's in love with you. He might not know it and it might take him a long time to figure it out because he's not a man that loves easily but give him time."

"Number two?" Laura asked.

"I told you not to butt in! Number two. I don't want you to move back here. I want to learn this business of standing on my own two feet and I want to be as strong and as brave as you are. I won't do it if I can run to you with every problem like I have my whole life. And I want your promise if I stumble that you'll make me get back up and try again but that you won't help me financially."

Another pause.

"Well?" Janet said again.

"I'm crying. Give me a minute to blow my nose."

"Do you promise?"

"Yes, I do," Laura said. "Is there a number three? Do I need to bring the box of tissues from the bathroom or is this one going to do?"

"There is a number three. I met a man at the meetings. He's got the same problems I have but he's been clean for two years, three months, and sixteen days now. He's a good man and he's asked me out a dozen times. I didn't have the courage to say yes until I saw you with Colton. We are going to dinner tonight."

Laura gasped.

"His name is James Radford and he's a lawyer. He lives in Amarillo. He lost everything with his addiction problems but he's slowly getting back on his feet. He had a ranch north of Hereford. His wife left him and his two grown kids won't talk to him. He's fifteen years older than I am and that's all I know."

Laura inhaled deeply. "Why this man?"

"Because he looks at me like Colton looks at you and there's a flutter in my heart when he does and if you can overcome our past, so can I. I'm scared out of my mind, sister, but I'm giddy just thinking about going out with him."

More tears flooded Laura's face. "Truth is that I'm scared out of my mind too."

"I didn't hear that. My wings aren't quite ready to fly out of the nest, and until they are I need you to be the strong one just a little longer. I had a wonderful weekend. I even liked that church service that Roxie conned us into. It was all better than any therapy session I've ever been to. I love you, Laura."

"Me too," Laura choked out.

She threw herself back on the bed, grabbed a pillow, and sobbed into it for several minutes. Lord, what a morning!

Laura was sitting on the porch when the school bus pulled up into the front yard and Roxie got out. She walked like her boots were filled with concrete and slumped down in the rocking chair next to Laura as if a full-grown Angus bull rested on her shoulders.

"Does she have the gallows built?" she whispered.

"I didn't see a rope and she left the guillotine in the barn." Laura smiled.

"Thank you for standing up for me," Roxie said. "Rosalee was playing all sweet and innocent until you got there. The social worker didn't believe a word of what I said and everything that Rosalee said."

"Why?"

"You know."

Laura smiled and patted Roxie on the shoulder. "She did look pretty pitiful with that hangdog look and that black eye. What did Dillon say about the whole thing?"

"He said that he should've been the one to take care of it. She's been talkin' smack about me for a whole week and texting everyone all weekend about how she was going to get me sent away so she could have Dillon."

"So tell me what do you and Dillon do when you break up?" Laura asked.

"You know!"

"I really don't."

"We text and we talk on the phone and we say we're sorry and then we kiss a lot," she said. "Isn't that what you did when you broke up with your boyfriends?"

"I didn't have a cell phone," Laura said.

"I knew it! You *are* old!"

Maudie came out on the porch, sat down on the swing, and looked at Roxie. "What have you got to say? Are you aware that if Laura hadn't gotten the straight story things could be very different right now? You promised if you could live with me that you'd stay out of trouble."

"I got tired of her smart mouth. And I did start the fight so I'll take whatever punishment here at home that I have to. I got three weeks in-school suspension for fighting. But at least Rosalee isn't in the room with me. It turned out that she's been living with her older sister because she got in trouble for bullying down in Louisiana. Her sister came to the school and checked her out. She's going back to Louisiana to her momma's house."

"How did you find that out? Weren't you in suspension?" Maudie asked.

"Heard it on the bus on the way home."

"You are grounded for a week. You can't go anywhere next weekend except to church. That includes going out with Dillon. You can keep your cell phone and your computer and I don't care if you text or talk to him, but you can't go out with him. And next time, you block that first hit and then wipe up the school yard with anyone who bullies you. But you do not start a fight. Do you understand me?" Maudie asked.

"Yes, ma'am," Roxie said.

"Good, then that's enough talk about it. Come on upstairs and let me clean up that scratch properly. Never know what a voodoo witch might have under her claws," Maudie said.

Laura didn't know whether to giggle or cry again. Both emotions were so close to the surface that she was afraid to try out either one. So she dug her cell phone from out of her shirt pocket and sent her first text message to Colton.

Talk?

In seconds her phone dinged and she looked down to see: *When and where?*

She typed in: *Snow cones at the school yard after supper.*

The message back said: *Yes!*

Chapter 21

Cool night air blowing through open pickup windows, flashes of lightning, and rolling thunder all blended together for something so amazing that Laura didn't have a sane thought in her head.

"How did we get in the backseat? I don't remember crawling over here," she gasped.

Lightning lit up his sweaty ripped abdomen.

He pulled her lips back to his for another kiss that left them both panting even harder. "Where there is a will there is a way."

"That was amazing," she whispered.

His hands left her back and cupped her bottom tighter to his naked body. "What do you think they put in those snow cones?"

"I don't know but they'd best not put it in teenagers' snow cones or there'll be a raft of new babies next year," she answered.

Lightning split the sky again and hit an oak tree across the street from the school yard with enough force to shear a limb off like a machete slicing through soft butter.

She jumped and covered her eyes.

"Think we'd better put on our clothes and go home?" he asked.

"Not until we talk," she answered.

"We could talk in our apartment, Laura."

Our apartment.

He'd said our, not my, not the, but our.

She wiggled free and reached for her bra hanging on the rearview mirror. When she had it and her underpants on, she climbed over into the front seat and finished dressing.

"Have to be dressed to talk, do you?" he asked. "We have sex naked. Why can't we talk naked?"

"Lightning could strike twice in one place. It's rare that it does but I'm not taking chances that big."

"Why?"

"And I don't want Maudie and Roxie to find us fried and naked."

They'd barely gotten dressed when a police car rolled up beside the truck. An officer got out with a flashlight half the size of a ball bat and shined it inside.

"Colton Nelson, is that you?"

"Howdy, Randall. What are you doing out in this kind of weather?" Colton asked.

Did the man know everyone in the whole northern part of the state? He was on first name terms with the principal at Roxie's school and he'd spoken to everyone at the ranch party like long lost friends.

"Old man Witherly called 911. Said a tree got zapped and he could see a truck in the school yard and the people in it had been killed with lightning. Thought I'd best come take a look." Randall chuckled.

"Laura and I were out for a snow cone when the lightning started," Colton said.

Rain started falling in huge drops that sent dust devils floating up around the truck. Randall grabbed his hat and nodded. "Y'all might ought to go home. Looks like we're in for a toad strangler."

"Hope so. We can use the rain," Colton told him and hurriedly hit the button to roll up the windows. "Guess we'll be talking at home."

An hour later she was curled up beside him in bed. He toyed with her blond hair with one hand. The other had found a place to rest under her nightshirt between her breast and waist.

"I'm sorry," he said.

"About?"

"You know."

She kissed his nipple. "Words, Colton."

"I'm sorry that I said that about Roxie and her background. If that was the truth I'd be in big trouble too. I'd let my temper get away from me and wouldn't be fit to be in a relationship. Is that enough words?" he asked.

"I'm sorry that I fired-up mad about it. I was so worried about Roxie and then there was the issue with Janet. Oh, she called me when she got home."

She went on to tell him what all Janet had said and tears flowed down her cheeks just telling the story.

He wiped them away with his fingertips and kissed both eyelids.

"Not that I want to keep enabling her but it's like the end of an era and I like being needed," she said.

"I need you," he whispered softly.

She propped up on an elbow. "Colton Nelson, you are a rich cowboy. You don't need anything."

He pulled her over on top of his body and wrapped his arms tightly around her. "Want and need are two different things. I can buy anything I want, but there are things I need that evidently are not up for sale and you are one of those things."

He didn't say he loved her, but then she'd heard those words before and they were meaningless without the actions to back them up. She settled her face in the crook of his neck and wondered if need wasn't just as important as love when the dust settled.

Colton laced his fingers in Laura's and opened the door to the banquet room at the Denison Country Club. Tables, covered with white cloths, were set with silver and napkins but no dinnerware. Evidently, the caterers intended to bring the food to the table because she didn't see a buffet anywhere.

"Have I told you that you are beautiful tonight?" he asked.

"Three times since we left home and that was less than twenty minutes ago," she answered.

He'd thought she was drop-dead gorgeous in Dallas, stunning at the ranch party, and downright beautiful in her sundress and boots at church that first Sunday. But that night she wore tight-fitting jeans and a shirt in shades of blue that matched her eyes. Her hair floated on her shoulders and he had the urge to weave it around his fingertips to feel the silky softness. Yes, sir, that night she was a rancher's wife and more beautiful than she'd ever been before.

A tall dark cowboy with a drink in one hand clapped Colton on the shoulder and said, "Great party on Saturday. Man, I never knew an old barn could be transformed like that! I told my girls about it and they whined all day Sunday. Lily said that it wasn't fair that you got a wife when she wants a mother. Gabby said that a mommy was all she wanted for her birthday at the end of summer."

Colton shook hands with him. "Honey, you'll remember Mason Harper. He's the brave soul that danced with your sister."

"Lovely girl," Mason said. "I didn't know she was your sister."

"Don't hog the fiancée. I haven't gotten to meet her yet." Another cowboy joined the group. "I was in Wyoming looking at cattle over the weekend. Just got home this morning. Didn't think I was going to make it to the dinner here for a while. I'm Greg Adams. My ranch is over near Ravenna, not far from Ambrose."

"Pleased to make your acquaintance," Laura said.

"Before the night is over, you'll have to meet my grandmother, Clarice. She's my date tonight. Be thankful that Mason didn't bring those two demon princesses of his to the party," Greg said.

Mason grinned. "Don't look at me, Miz Laura. Greg is being nice. What one of them can't think of to get into trouble, the other one can, and believe me, there is strength in numbers. Right now it's this thing of wanting a mommy for their birthday. Ain't a woman alive who'd take on the job of mothering Lily and Gabby. Those two want a mommy, but there ain't a mommy out there who'd want them."

"Come on now." Laura laughed.

"He's tellin' the truth," Greg said. "I love 'em like nieces but those two could tear up a John Deere tractor with a feather."

"And put it back together with the same feather." Colton chuckled.

"Hey, I thought Lucas would be home by now," Mason changed the subject.

Colton hugged Laura tighter to his side and said, "Greg, Mason, Lucas, and I all joined the Red River Angus Association at the same time. Lucas owns a spread over between Savoy and Ector. He's in the National Guard and his unit got sent to Kuwait," he explained.

"I thought it was supposed to be for only six months," Greg said.

"His foreman Wyatt told Rusty last week at the feed store that they'd extended his time. He'll be there until Christmas."

"Man, that's tough. I'd hate to be away from my ranch that long," Mason said. "Y'all best hit the bar if you want a drink before dinner. They'll be hollerin' for us to find our places in about ten minutes."

"It was good meeting y'all," Laura said.

With a hand on the small of her back, Colton guided Laura to the bar. She ordered a longneck Coors and he nodded that he'd have the same.

"How many are in this club?" she asked.

"You mean the NTAA or the country club?"

"The first one. Are you a member of the country club?"

"Not me. Greg and Mason are, though, and several of the older ranchers keep a membership. I don't play golf and I can't see driving almost twenty miles to go swimming. There are about fifteen of us in the NTAA. Do you want a membership in the country club?"

"Hell, no!" she said without hesitation.

It was too good to be true.

They'd gotten through a blowup, had awesome makeup sex after a long talk, and things had seemed so right when she'd gone to sleep in his arms the night before. But there was a brick in her chest that evening as they left the Angus party and that always meant danger.

The moon hung above the treetops like a beaconing light guiding them home. Stars were diamonds twinkling brightly around it. The night air was warm but not scorching summer hot yet. Everything was perfect and yet nothing was right. Laura Baker did not belong in this world of country clubs and billionaire spa days.

Like Colton said so prophetically, blood cannot be changed.

"When my mother was as quiet as you are, a storm was on the way," Colton said.

"I'm not your mother."

"Do I detect a little anger in those words? We promised to be honest and not keep our feelings inside. What's eating at you?"

"I don't belong in your high-dollar world."

"Neither do I, but it's only a high-dollar world a few days a year. The rest of the time I get to be a rough old cowboy rancher."

He parked in front of the house and turned to face her. "There's the thing in Dallas and the NTAA dinner, the summer party, and the fall cattle sale. Christmas is just family, I promise."

She counted on her fingers. "Four a year and three of them in the summer, right?"

"That's right. Kind of like eating an elephant. You do it a bite at a time and it's not so overwhelming. The

Angus party is one evening, the ranch party a day and evening, and the Dallas affair a weekend. After that it's over until fall, thank God!"

"And the sale?"

"Now that's a big thing. We do have a dance and a dinner after the sale to thank everyone for coming, but believe me, we don't drape the whole barn in that filmy stuff." He laughed.

His laughter set everything back up straight in her world. Could she really, really stay at the ranch and enter into the real world? He had not said that he loved her. Would his need be enough to sustain her through the coming years and would it turn into love someday?

He tipped up her chin and kissed her passionately. "I still feel out of place among so many rich people. But, honey, with you by my side it sure makes it easier. I feel like I've got something none of them can ever have when I walk into those parties with you on my arm. As long as we are together, we'll show all these rich cats how it's done."

As long as we are together.

Janet said that when they were kids. Janet needed her and now she didn't. What happened when Colton didn't need her anymore?

Laura's soul came close to leaving her body when Rusty knocked on the truck window right over Colton's left shoulder.

She jumped straight up off the seat and banged her leg on the dash.

Colton whipped around when Rusty swung the door open. "What?"

"Sorry to interrupt but I've got a cow down and I need Laura," Rusty said.

"Do I have time to change clothes?" Laura asked.

"No, ma'am. If we don't get that calf out pretty soon, we're going to lose her and the baby."

"Hop in the back," Colton said. "I'll drive down to the barn."

"She's not in the barn. She's out by the pond," Rusty said as he crawled into the backseat.

Laura hoped he didn't see the two purple dots on the seat that she'd left behind the night before when she and Colton had stormy sex back there. Colton had licked the snow cone juice from her fingers but two drops had gotten away from him before he could slurp them up.

Wednesday morning she and Colton both overslept and didn't see Roxie before she went to school. Laura missed having breakfast with Roxie and made sure she was sitting on the porch that evening when the school bus pulled up in the yard.

Thursday morning, they awoke early and had wonderful *good morning darlin'* sex before they shared the shower. Laura had never shared a shower with a man before and loved the way their wet, soapy body parts kept bumping into each other.

Friday, Laura opened her eyes, checked the clock to see that she'd awakened thirty minutes early, and rolled over to snuggle up against Colton's back but he wasn't there. She rubbed the sleep out of her eyes and sat up, listening for the noise of the shower. She could hear Sally singing out in the hallway but there was no sound of water running.

She slung her legs over his side of the bed and saw

the note lying on the nightstand. "Breakfast meeting of NTAA in Sherman. Rusty and I'll be back around nine." A heart and the letter *C* followed the words.

Did that mean "love, Colton"? She threw herself backwards on the bed. She loved the sex, loved his family, loved the ranch—hell, if she was honest she loved him—but until he said the words, she had made up her mind that she was not staying one day past her contracted month. They could tell the world whatever the hell they wanted when she was gone. They could make Colton look like the poor billion-dollar cowboy who'd been jilted, or they could say that he figured out she was running a scam on him. She didn't give a damn what news they put out; she wasn't staying without hearing the words spoken right out loud!

She stared at the ring on her finger. It didn't feel so foreign anymore and it had to be a very good imitation because it still sparkled beautifully, especially when the sun rays hit it.

She wanted to replace it with a nice wide gold band. It didn't have to be soon. She wasn't pushing for a marriage, but she wanted the whole nine yards, not just a remnant at the end of the bolt. And after thinking about it all week, need wasn't enough. She needed food to survive. She needed a roof of some kind to protect her from the elements. But it wasn't the same as love and if Colton wasn't willing to give her his whole heart then she'd go on down the road.

Yes, there would be wailing and gnashing of teeth, but she was not settling for need. It made a fine secondary character in the book of love, but only love could have the title of hero.

She was on her way to the bathroom when the ringtone on her cell phone said that Janet was calling. She raced to the jeans she'd tossed beside the bed and answered after the fourth ring.

"Did I interrupt something really nice?" Janet asked.

"Hell, no! He's gone to an Angus meeting. What are you doing up at this hour?"

"I had to call and tell you all about my date. I would've called that night but I've been hugging myself and singing ever since. I don't know if you are aware but in the GA program, I promised not to get involved with anyone for a year and so did James. We're going to be adults and go real slow and honor that promise that we both made but I just know that he is the one," Janet singsonged.

"I'm proud of you for sticking to the rules, but how can you be so sure?"

"It's in my heart just like it's in yours about Colton. I'm not saying that I'm going to rush into anything. We realize we've got to be careful, but it's real, Laura. And I feel good about it and there's something responsible about doing things the right way. You figured out that you were in love with Colton pretty early in your relationship, didn't you? I'm going to be happy, Laura. You be happy too."

Colton sat at the middle of a long table and tried to pay attention to Thomas Corley, president of the NTAA and his former boss. They were discussing whether they should annex Lamar County into their organization. Two ranchers who specialized in Angus cattle had approached them with a desire to join. Colton had never heard of either of them but when the vote was put to the members, he raised his hand to allow that county to merge with them.

He used to look forward to the monthly breakfast meeting at the waffle house with the guys. He loved talking cattle, ranching, hay, fencing, and weather with them, but that morning he wished he was on the Circle 6 having breakfast with Laura.

"Then it is agreed that we will annex Lamar County and any Angus rancher in that area to be a member of the NTAA," Thomas said. "If there is no more new business, we'll adjourn until next month and enjoy our meal."

Colton's phone vibrated in his pocket. He took it out to find a text from Laura that said: *Good morning*.

He held the phone in his lap and sent back: *Me 2*.

Immediately the next one popped up: *Cow on the road. Later*.

He groaned.

Rusty elbowed him. "What's the matter with you?"

"Just heard from Laura. There's a heifer on the road. She must've broke through that old portion of fence we still have to replace. Those posts have been there since the second day of creation," he said.

"Laura will take care of it. She'll have the cow back and the fence fixed before you finish your pancakes." Rusty chuckled.

Colton had no doubt that she'd take care of business. She could probably run the ranch as good as he could. Andy had no idea what a bang-up job he'd done the day he had hired the woman for his assistant. These days, though, since the fiscal year had ended, she spent more and more time on the ranch and less in the office.

Colton had been looking forward to sexy flirting via text messages. Since the argument on Monday, they'd kept the phones hot enough to burst into flames. Their messages had gotten so hot that he was glad for good sturdy zippers on his blue jeans. Now Laura was out dealing with a pesky cow and a busted fence. She wouldn't have time to read his messages much less carry on a hot conversation with him. He turned his attention to Rusty and Mason Harper, who was sitting across the table from him.

"So tell me, now that the ladies aren't around, how did you ever land a woman like Laura? All I hear is good things about her," Mason asked.

"Pure luck. She's my financial advisor and best friend's cousin. He hired her as his assistant. You'll find someone someday," Colton said.

"I don't really want another wife. I had one like Laura, a perfect woman who was a good mother and who could run the ranch standing on her head and cross-eyed. It's the girls who want a mommy and they come with a price tag with wife written on it rather than dollar signs," Mason said.

"Oh, don't let that price tag fool you." Rusty chuckled. "It has dollar signs on it as well as the wife writin'."

That netted them several hearty "Amens" from down the table.

"So how do you know so much about price tags?" Greg asked Rusty.

"Once upon a time I got close enough to see one. Scared me into being a bachelor for the rest of my life," he answered.

Since the big argument Colton had a feeling that

Laura was waiting for him to say that he loved her, but that price tag waving around with those words on it scared him as bad as the one Rusty talked about. The price of giving his whole heart to any woman, including Laura, and promising to love her through the bad times as well as the good times until death parted them… it took a lot of faith and Colton wasn't sure he had nearly enough.

Chapter 22

THE WHOLE CONGREGATION SANG "ROCK OF AGES" and Colton leaned down and whispered softly into Laura's ear, "What color panties are you wearing?"

She almost dropped the hymnbook and high color filled her cheeks. "Maudie will crucify you."

"It's her day to sing in the choir. She can't hear me," he said between the words of the old gospel hymn.

"We're in church," she reminded him.

"So?"

What is good for the goose is good for the gander. They were her Aunt Dotty's words and she most likely stole them right out of Proverbs as much as she read the Bible. Laura didn't care if they'd come from those love story magazines that Aunt Dotty kept hidden under the towels in the bathroom closet. It fit that morning and she was determined to teach Colton Nelson a lesson.

"What color are yours?" she asked.

"You know I go commando," he whispered.

She waited until the last words of the song ended and said, "Me too."

She could feel him tense beside her and heard only the tiniest fragment of a moan.

Roger preached from the book of Ruth, telling the story of Boaz and Ruth. By law he had no right to marry Ruth. There were closer relatives who could claim her after her husband had died, but he did what was required of him and wound up with the love of his life for his efforts.

Roger brought the story to life for Laura. Maybe it was because she was in a strange country just like Ruth. Not physically but emotionally.

"Your gods will be my gods and your people will be my people. That's what Ruth told Naomi and by marrying Boaz, she sealed that promise. That's what all marriages should be sealed with, folks," Roger said in his deep voice.

Laura felt as if someone had poured cold water down her backbone. It had happened—his people were her people. How could she leave them behind? His god—this church where she was sitting in a pew with him—had become her church, even Ina Dean and Patsy. How could she ever leave them behind?

Yet, how could she stay if he didn't love her? Boaz loved Ruth. He was willing to go the length to ask for her hand in marriage, to stand beside her and to be her husband.

Not once had Colton even hinted at love. True, they'd moved to reality and she felt like they were really dating these days, but Laura intended to hold out for it all.

Cynthia pulled Laura aside as soon as the morning services were over. "Do you think he was preaching at me? Was he asking me to leave my people and Ambrose if he got a call to another part of the world to preach?" she whispered frantically. "I need to talk to someone like you who was willing to leave your world behind and fit into the world of the man you loved."

"Invite him to dinner. Hurry. Push your way to the front of the line before someone else invites him first," Laura said.

"But I don't have dinner fixed up," Cynthia said.

"Not at your place. At the ranch with us. That way we can talk," Laura said.

Cynthia scanned the small church and circled around the edge quickly, then cut in line right behind Ina Dean, who was always one of the first people to shake Roger's hand. When it was her turn, she smiled sweetly and said, "We've been invited to dinner at the Circle 6."

"How nice. I'd love to go. Wait for me and we'll ride over together," Roger said.

Cynthia looked over her shoulder and winked.

Maudie tapped Laura on the shoulder. "What was that all about?"

"I invited them to Sunday dinner."

Maudie grinned. "Are you playing matchmaker?"

"Could be but I didn't start it. Roxie did."

"What'd I do?" Roxie perked up when she heard her name. "Aunt Maudie, can Dillon come to dinner?"

"Of course he can. You can't leave the house with him but he can come to Sunday dinner. Rules say that you can visit on the porch or in the living room but you can't go out on the four-wheelers or to the pool. That's too much like a date," Maudie said.

"Fair enough," Roxie said.

"Still worth it?" Laura asked.

"Darn straight," Roxie answered.

"Damn!" Colton mumbled under his breath.

"What did you say?" Laura asked.

"I was looking forward to spending the afternoon

with you, not the preacher," he said. "You and Cynthia and Roxie will disappear and Rusty will make an excuse and I'll be the one stuck."

Laura patted him on the shoulder. "Are you pouting?"

"Damn straight. And I do not mean darn straight."

"Why didn't you tell me before church?" she asked.

"I wanted it to be a surprise."

"Don't pout. They won't stay all afternoon," she said.

"I can pout if I want," he argued.

Colton laid a hand on Roxie's shoulder and whispered in her ear, "If you say one word about us all going to church tonight, I'll ground you for another week."

Roxie stuck her tongue out at him. "You aren't my boss. Aunt Maudie is."

Maudie touched her on the other shoulder. "That's enough arguing in the church house. You say anything about us all going to church tonight, young lady, and I'll ground you for another two weeks. I've got a movie I want to watch this evening. Is that understood?"

Roxie saluted both of them. "Sir, yes sir. Ma'am, yes ma'am!"

Dinner was ham with all the side dishes that accompanies it in the South: candied sweet potatoes, baked beans, cranberry orange salad, hot rolls, and peach cobbler for dessert.

And it lasted two days past eternity. Laura could hardly sit still for worrying about the surprise that she was missing and wondering whether Colton would present it later in the evening. It had been years since she'd had a surprise even for her birthday or Christmas.

Most of the time Janet called and they went to lunch during the week of her birthday but not always. And on Christmas she volunteered at the Amarillo soup kitchen for the homeless.

She was almost giddy when dinner ended. Hopefully when the meal ended Cynthia and Roger would go for a drive, go to the nearest motel, or even go back to the church and make wild passionate love on the front pew. But it did not happen that way.

"I would just love for Roxie to do my nails," Cynthia said.

Roxie smiled sweetly and said, "Of course. Let's go up to my room. Laura, come with us and pick out a color. I'm thinking pale pink would be so pretty for church tonight."

Colton leaned to his right and kissed Laura on the cheek. "Don't take all afternoon," he whispered.

Roxie turned at the door. "Aunt Maudie?"

She held up a palm. "Not me. My nails don't need doing nearly as much as I need a nap. Y'all have a good time."

Roger looked over his shoulder at Cynthia. "If you could get those nails done in half an hour, we could ride over to Savoy. All the young unmarried folks in the area are meeting up for a singing and a social this afternoon. It's an open invitation and there's plenty of room in the church van if any of y'all want to go along."

"No problem," Roxie said. "But I'm grounded, so that leaves me and Dillon out."

"And I've got plans," Rusty said.

Roger looked at Andy Joe.

"Thanks for the invitation but I've got some things

to catch up on this afternoon too. Maybe next time," Andy said.

"What fun," Cynthia beamed. "Don't leave without me."

"Wouldn't dream of it." Roger smiled.

Cynthia was like a sugared up six-year-old that had spent the day at her grandparents' house. She giggled all the way up the staircase and into Roxie's room. She plopped down on the vanity stool and quickly picked out a bright pink polish and looked at the little brass clock on the nightstand.

"That color will cover what's already on my nails just fine so you won't have to take the old polish off. I don't want to keep him waiting," Cynthia said. "If he'd told me we were going somewhere like that I'd have dressed up more. Now talk to me, Laura. I've got to know if you regret moving away from your family and home."

"It wasn't easy at first but I'd never go back," Laura said honestly.

Cynthia splayed her fingers out on the vanity top.

Roxie opened the bottle of polish. "Why are you even asking?"

"Ina Ruth has a cousin in Bokchito, Oklahoma, who told her that they were looking for a pastor for their church. They are sending a committee member down here next Sunday to listen to Roger preach," Cynthia answered. "You are very good at nails, Roxie. You didn't get a drop on my skin."

"It ain't my first time." Roxie grinned.

"How far away is Bokchito?" Laura asked. "And what makes you think that Roger will leave Ambrose? He might be very happy here."

"What kind of name is Bokchito? Sounds like something they'd use in chemical warfare," Roxie said.

Cynthia tucked a strand of brown hair behind her ear. "In Indian language *Bok* means big and *chito* means creek. I looked it up last night after Ina Dean called me. And it's almost forty-seven miles from here. It'd be closer but there's not a bridge across the Red River closer than the one at Hendrix."

Laura swallowed the laughter bubbling up from her chest. "That's not so far from your family."

"Why would anyone want to go to that place?" Roxie asked.

"It's a lot bigger and they've got a high school right there in town. Ambrose is less than a hundred people and Bokchito has almost six hundred," Cynthia said.

"Did he propose?" Roxie asked.

Cynthia shook her head. "Lord, no! We've only been dating a little while."

"Well, I'm sure that God will lead him in the right direction and if he goes to Bokchito, the angels will be sitting beside you every Sunday as you drive across that decrepit old Hendrix bridge to go up there," Roxie said.

Laura had never wanted to hug a kid more in her life.

Cynthia laid her right hand with its shiny new polish over her heart without getting a smidgen of polish on her pink floral dress. "Y'all have both put my heart at peace. Now hurry up with that last fingernail. I don't want to miss another minute with him. I'm just going to be lost when he moves and we get another preacher. Do you suppose the new one will have a wife and kids?"

"Roger hasn't left yet. Could be that God tells him

to stay right here in Ambrose because he's in love with you," Roxie said.

The girl was as full of bullshit as Janet had been at that age. Both of them could sweet-talk an angel right out of her halo.

Colton, Dillon, and Roger lined up in rocking chairs on the front porch in comfortable silence. Cows bawled in the distance. Daisy sprawled out on the bottom step and shut his eyes. Donald quacked a few times, but when he couldn't wake Daisy, he promptly settled in the flower bed and tucked his head under his wing.

Roger finally broke the silence. "There will be strangers in the church next Sunday. A committee from Bokchito, Oklahoma, is coming to hear me preach."

"You leaving?" Colton asked.

"Not unless the good Lord gives me a different sign than he's giving me right now," Roger said. "But they're lookin' for a preacher for their church and they insisted on coming down here and listenin' to a sermon."

"Why?" Dillon asked.

"Ina Dean has a cousin up there who has visited here before."

"No—why ain't you leavin'?" Dillon asked.

"God hasn't told me to go. I've been praying and praying and he hasn't said a word."

"Cynthia?" Dillon asked.

"I've prayed for seven years that God would put the right woman in my life. If this is his answer to my prayer, then I shouldn't run from it. You know what I'm talking about, Colton. You feel like Laura is an answer to your prayer, don't you?"

Colton tipped his straw hat back and wiped sweat from his forehead with a white handkerchief he pulled from his pocket. He had never—not one time—prayed for a wife. He had cussed the women that chased him, gotten really angry at the one who doped him, and wished for a simpler life, but he had never prayed about any of it.

Roger went on, "Of course you feel like she is. I can see the love in your eyes for her. I want a home and a family, but I want it to be as right between us as it is between you and Laura. If I'm right here in Ambrose where Cynthia is, then eventually God will speak and I'll know she's the right one."

"Maybe God is putting her to a test. If she's willing to go like Rebecca was, then she might be the one. If not, then the answer to your prayer might be in Bokchito. That's a funny name," Dillon said.

Roger chuckled. "You were listening to my sermon a few weeks ago."

"Oh, yeah! Maudie asks me and Roxie questions sometimes. If I don't know the answer, I'm afraid she'll tell me I can't stay to Sunday dinner."

Colton's thoughts made a whirring noise in his head when Cynthia led the way out onto the porch with Laura and Roxie right behind her.

Roger held out his hand to Cynthia. "You are early. We might have time for a snow cone on the way. That little place in Savoy opened last week."

"Oh, man!" Dillon slapped his thigh. "We could have gone there today if..."

"But I am still grounded until tomorrow so we'll have to wait," Roxie reminded him. "Ain't no anchor on your butt though if you want to go get one."

He stood up and held out his hand. "Let's take a walk out to the pasture fence. Next Friday night we'll drive over to Savoy and get a snow cone."

Cynthia passed a test by being early.

Roger passed one by saying the right things.

Colton shivered in spite of the summer heat just thinking about the test before him.

"Thank you for a lovely dinner. Y'all sure you don't want to join us?" Cynthia asked.

Dillon and Roxie were both shaking their heads as they disappeared into the house. Wild horses couldn't have drawn Laura away from the ranch that afternoon. Colton had a surprise for her and no amount of singing or even snow cones could be more important than that.

Chapter 23

Colton lost his nerve. Money couldn't buy love and it couldn't buy courage, either.

He'd planned the afternoon for three days and had covered every possible angle, but when it came time to put the surprise into action, he couldn't do it. Not because he didn't want to, because his heart almost stopped when he thought of life without Laura. But suddenly he was tongue-tied when he thought about telling her that he was in love with her and that she owned his heart.

He was downright miserable sitting there in the rocking chair. From the smile on her face and the twinkle in her eyes, she was expecting something and he had nothing.

"Snow cone?" he asked hoarsely.

"I'd rather spend the afternoon in the pool."

Cynthia had ruined the surprise with her worries. Now she'd never know what Colton had planned for that afternoon, but she knew it involved more than a snow cone.

"How about a drive over to Bells to get a snow cone? Afterwards, if you want, we can go swimming."

"Okay," she said slowly.

The snow cone did taste good. She was disappointed when he did not drive up into the school yard but kept driving on south through town. Maybe it was because the temperature gauge at the bank said it was 105 degrees and he was afraid they could slurp up the snow cones before they melted. If that was the real reason, then they wouldn't get to go to the school yard for more than a month because August was even hotter than July and lots of times September didn't always bring relief.

The sign said Savoy was the next place they'd reach if they kept driving, which they did.

They passed a burger joint on the right that wasn't as big as a good-sized storage shed, a snow cone stand on the left that was painted turquoise with hot pink trim, and farther down the highway the school was on the right. She expected him to pull into the school parking lot but he kept driving.

"I really don't want to go to a singing," she said.

"Me either. Besides, the church where it's going on is behind us. If you turn down that gravel road," he nodded off to the right, "you'd run right into Lucas Allen's ranch. His granddad started with a few acres and built on it as he could. Then his dad did the same thing. When his mom died a few years ago, his dad handed over the reins to him and built a little two-bedroom house at the far edge of the ranch, not far from his grandpa's place."

"Lucas is the one who is in Kuwait right now?"

Colton nodded.

"Where are we going?" she asked.

"Just a little bit farther."

"Why?"

Colton smiled but it was a tight grin and that scared her.

He turned right down a gravel road that looked the same as the one he'd pointed out, passed a section line road, and then turned right again into a road that had grass growing up in the middle.

"Please don't throw me out and expect me to walk home." She laughed nervously.

"Lost, are you?"

"Oh, yeah! I'm not sure I could even follow the sun and find my way out of here. Do people actually live in this place?"

"It's ranchin' country and some of the farms cover thousands of acres so it looks more remote than it really is." He made a hard left and parked the car in front of a tiny white building with a steeple on the top and a cross on the door.

"Is that a church?"

The snow cones were gone and he still hadn't regained his courage. He knew exactly what he wanted to say but one word could change his whole world. And fear that she wouldn't say yes terrified him. He didn't like the picture of life looming out ahead of him without Laura.

"Remember when we were talking about Lucas at the Angus party?"

"The friend who is still in Kuwait?"

Colton nodded. He could talk to her about anything but what was really on his mind. "He owns this ranch. His grandpa and grandma bought it years ago and this little church was already here. He preached in it for a long time. It's a nice ride while we had snow cones."

"It's quaint and I've loved it but I miss going to the school yard to eat our snow cones," she said.

Leave it to Laura to be honest. Well, if she wanted

a school yard then she'd get a school yard. He put the truck in reverse and backed out of the church yard and drove straight to the school yard in Bells.

He'd thought that surely if he was sitting in front of a church, God would zap him with all the nerve in the world, but it hadn't happened. Strangely enough, when he turned off the engine in the school yard his bravery returned in full force.

He reached across the seat and put the keys in her hand.

"What's this all about?"

"This truck is yours. I'm giving it to you and releasing you from staying a whole month right now. You can go wherever you want."

She threw the keys with enough force that they bounced off the window and landed in the backseat. "I don't want your truck. And I've got almost another week so I'm not going anywhere. I'm not ready to leave Roxie and Aunt Maudie or the ranch."

"And me?"

Laura stomped her foot so hard that a puff of dust floated all the way to his knees.

"Especially you. Why are you trying to run me off anyway? Did an old flame appear on your doorstep? She did, didn't she?"

Colton stammered and finally spit out, "No!"

"Then why are you trying to run me off?"

Colton unbuckled his seat belt and got out of the truck.

It was plain to Laura that he was going to start walking. He could call Andy and he'd drop everything to come get him. Well, she sure wasn't driving that blasted truck a single mile. If he could walk, she could too.

She bailed out of the truck and met him at the back

tailgate. "I told you I don't want this truck and I'm not leaving. You can stay here and fight with me or go home and puff up like a bullfrog but I'm not leaving the ranch."

"Ever?"

She stopped in her tracks.

"That depends, but I'm sure staying until next Sunday."

"Depends on what?" Colton pushed.

"Whether you fight with me or not. I don't like cowboys who pout."

He laid a hand on her shoulder and she looked up into his green eyes. They slowly slid shut as his lips came closer and closer. She snapped her blue eyes shut a split second before the kiss landed. Passion, peace, and love all mixed together into a roller coaster of emotions in his heart and soul.

He hugged her tightly to his chest. "Laura, I love you. I didn't intend to fall in love with you, but I have. Not only do I love you, I'm hopelessly in love with you. That's a double whammy. I couldn't bear to live through another week knowing every day that you were leaving at the end of it. So I'm setting you free to go or to stay. It's up to you."

She leaned back and stared right into his eyes again. "I love you, Colton. It scares me but I do. You are a good man and you deserve a woman who's confident in her role as a wife and a mother. I'm not but I'll do my best."

He dropped down on one knee in front of her and held out a velvet box. "Laura Baker, will you marry me?"

The ring inside wasn't nearly as big as the fake diamond on her finger but she loved it… almost as much as she loved the cowboy on one knee in front of her.

"The sapphire reminded me of your eyes and there's fifty small diamonds surrounding it, one for each year until our golden anniversary. I chose gold because the band is gold and when you take off the engagement ring to play in the dirt, you can still wear your wedding band. Please say something, Laura. Please say yes."

"Who picked that out?" she asked.

"I went to the jewelry store last week. I promise that Andy didn't. I'm asking again. Laura, will you marry me?"

"Yes, I will." She removed the fake ring from her finger and handed it to him. "As long as we always, always live in a real world from now on, I will marry you. I'm tired of living in a make-believe world."

He stood up and drew her close to his chest.

"You got it, darlin'. When?" he asked.

"Next Sunday, but don't tell anyone. I do not want a paparazzi wedding. I want a real one and I don't want to wait for it. Make arrangements with Roger to take care of it right after church and then we'll go home like always."

"Are you afraid of a long engagement? Are you afraid I'll change my mind? I won't, Laura. It took me a long time to get up the courage to tell you how much I love you. I will never, ever change my mind."

"No, I just want to be married. And tell Andy to draw up a prenup. Without it, I won't ever marry you. It has to be simple. If I ever leave you, then all I take with me is my personal possessions."

Colton frowned. "I trust you, Laura."

"Like I said before, I'm not interested in your money.

I want your heart and I want to give you mine. Neither have a price tag on them."

By the end of the week, Laura wished she'd insisted on a courthouse wedding on Monday morning. She couldn't imagine a six-month engagement when one week made her as nervous as Donald in duck season. What if Colton changed his mind? What if in six months she wished she had waited? No wonder women got crazy during engagements and lost their minds planning a wedding. All she had to do was pick out a dress, go to church, listen to the sermon, and then get married.

No flowers, no ribbons, no pew bows, not even a cake to worry about. Colton assured her that he'd talked privately to Roger, who would be ready to marry them right after Ina Dean delivered the benediction.

She snuggled up against Colton's back and wrapped her arms around his body. Tomorrow she would wake up in the master suite in the big ranch house.

Colton turned over and hugged her close to his chest. "Good morning, Miss Baker. I can't believe that tomorrow morning when we wake up I get to say 'good morning, Mrs. Nelson.' Are you sure, absolutely sure, that you don't mind sharing the house with the family? We can build another house or we can build one for Granny and Roxie."

"Shhh." She laid a finger over his lips. "I love the family and the house is plenty big enough for all of us. Besides, I love all of them. I love having meals with them and we have our privacy when we want it. And," she grinned, "we can always sneak out here if we want."

"It's hard not to kiss you this morning," he moaned.

"I know, but it's our wedding day. I want the first kiss today to be the one when I'm your wife. I can't believe I'm getting married in the hottest month of the whole year. I'm sure glad I don't have to worry with a big white dress. I'd faint dead away in that hot satin," she said.

He picked up her hand and kissed each finger. "I love you, Laura."

"I love you too." She bailed out of bed but it didn't cool her hand or her desire to want an early morning bout of sex that got hotter and more passionate every time she and Colton fell into bed.

He found his shirt on the floor next to the door and his jeans at the foot of the bed. When he was dressed, he hugged her close and said, "I'll get dressed for church and meet you at breakfast?"

"I'll be there."

"I'm terrified that you will change your mind. Promise me you'll marry me?" He held both her hands and looked deep into her eyes.

She didn't blink. "I'll be the one sitting beside you during church. If you still want to marry me when the service is over, then squeeze my hand three times. I'm afraid you'll disappear while Ina Dean is thanking God for everything from tomatoes to Jesus."

"I'm not going anywhere, darlin'." He dropped her hands and was gone before she could answer.

The sun hung above the treetops, promising another hot August day as she crossed the yard from the carriage house to the main ranch house. A sudden burst of indecision hit. Should she go back and change into something fancier? The blue sundress and her best cowboy boots didn't look much like a wedding dress. Lord, she'd be glad when it was over!

She could hear Roxie and Maudie talking about school shopping when she slipped into the office.

Colton stood up. He wore creased jeans stacked up right above his boots and a pale blue shirt. "You are stunning. Please say you've changed your mind and we aren't doing this."

She shook her head.

"Well?" Andy asked.

"I'm not saying a single vow until I sign that prenup."

Andy produced another sheaf of papers. "This is the prenup our group of lawyers has drawn up saying that in the event of a divorce you will leave the ranch with only your personal belongings." He held a pen out to her.

She took it without a minute's hesitation and scrawled her name on the line with a red check beside it. "Colton Nelson, I never plan to divorce you or leave the ranch. If you leave me, all the money in the world wouldn't fix my broken heart. However, if you ever cheat on me, rest assured I will make sure that the buzzards and coyotes do not even know where to hunt for your body. So are you ready for this?"

"That will not happen," Colton told her.

"Okay, kids, let's go to breakfast and then to church," Andy said.

They were lined up on the pew like always. Andy at the far end, Rusty beside him, then Maudie, Roxie, Colton, and Laura. The number for the first hymn was given out when Janet slipped down the aisle and tapped Laura on the shoulder. Everyone on the pew shifted to allow her to sit beside Laura.

"Happy wedding day," she whispered.

"How..."

"Andy can't keep a secret and he was in on the prenup. Good for you!"

It seemed like Roger preached forever, but when he asked Ina Dean to deliver the benediction, Laura looked at her watch and he'd cut his sermon short by fifteen minutes.

Ina Dean finally, after what seemed like an eternity of giving thanks, said, "Amen."

Roger quickly picked up the microphone and said, "If everyone will please remain seated, I have a couple of things to share with you. First, as you all know I've been offered the job of preaching over in Bokchito, Oklahoma. I have prayed and prayed about it and have decided that God isn't finished with the work he wants me to do right here in Ambrose. Second, last night I asked Cynthia to marry me and she said yes. There will be a wedding sometime over the Christmas holiday right here in our church. And Laura has talked to me and joined the church. And, I do love that word and because it means there is more to come, I saved the best until last. Laura and Colton are going to get married right here today. So if you two will come forward, we'll get this ceremony under way."

Colton squeezed her hand three times and they stood up together.

Maudie sniffed into a handkerchief.

"Yes!" Roxie whispered.

"I love you." Janet pulled a gorgeous nosegay of

daisies, roses, and orchids from her oversized purse and handed it to Laura.

"Colton, stand right here," Roger said. "And Miss Laura, you stand here. You two face each other and look at each other, not at me."

In ten minutes she would never be Miss Laura Baker again. Panic clenched her heart into a pretzel.

"Dearly beloved, we are gathered here today in the presence of God and these witnesses," Roger began. "Traditional vows?" he whispered.

Colton nodded.

All the fears, doubts, and worries left Laura when Colton said his vows without stuttering one time and finished with his own words, "All this I vow because I love you and because you own my heart."

Maudie wept loudly into a handkerchief behind her.

Roxie sighed.

Rusty cleared his throat.

"Now repeat after me," Roger said to Laura.

She drew strength from looking deeply into Colton's eyes and blocking everything else out as she repeated her vows, ending with, "All this I promise to do because I love you too, Colton, and my heart is yours for all eternity."

"By the authority invested in me by the state of Texas and by God, I pronounce you man and wife," Roger said. "Now, Colton, you may kiss your bride."

The kiss sealed the vows and Laura knew complete and honest peace in that moment when her husband's lips touched hers.

Roger laid a hand on Laura's shoulder and one on Colton's. "Let me be the very first to introduce to you all in this room, Mr. and Mrs. Colton Nelson. There is a reception out at the ranch with a light lunch, fellowship, and wedding cake for anyone who'd like to follow the new couple out there."

Colton looked at Laura.

She shrugged. "I don't know what he's talking about."

Colton looked at the family pew and Andy winked.

"Andy?" he whispered.

"I might have known." She nodded.

Colton tucked Laura's arm in his and a standing ovation and loud clapping led her out to his truck. He caged her with an arm on each side of her against the truck and kissed her hard, passionately, and with so much heat that she was panting when he stepped back.

Andy was behind Colton when she opened her eyes. "Congratulations! And Laura, I did the reception. Not Colton or even Maudie and Roxie knew about it. Hired a caterer and called Janet. So don't ever be mad at Colton. You both need the memories."

"I'm so happy right now I could never be mad at anyone," she said. "Let's go home."

Colton left a cloud of dust behind the truck the whole way home and skidded to a stop so fast that it scared Donald and Daisy, who'd been sleeping on the front porch. The cat climbed the mimosa tree and Donald flew toward the pond.

"What is the big hurry?" she asked.

"I want to get something done before everyone gets here," he said.

"You ready for this?" Andy asked the minute they were out of the truck.

Colton grabbed Laura's hand and followed Andy into the house.

"Bring it on," Colton said as soon as they were in the office.

Andy pulled a single sheet of paper from the briefcase. "This paper nullifies everything you just signed, Laura. It says that from the moment you became Mrs. Colton Nelson that the ranch is yours as well as his."

"But," she stammered.

"You needed to show me how much you trusted me." Colton signed his name to the bottom of the document. "This is showing you that I trust you."

Tears flowed down her cheeks. "I love you."

He wiped them away with the back of his hand. "Don't cry, darlin'. What's mine is yours and remember what you said about the heart. Well, if you were ever to leave me, I'd die and wouldn't have any need for all this anyway. Now let's go share our wedding day with all our family and friends."

Dear Readers,

A few months ago, four new cowboys showed up in my virtual world and asked, hats in hand, that I tell their stories. I guess word is getting around that I'm a sucker for sexy cowboys with an interesting love story. Colton Nelson wanted to be first and invited me down to Ambrose, Texas, to take a look at the town of less than a hundred people and his ranch, the Circle 6, which was ten times bigger than the whole town. I was hooked from the first line of their story about how they'd even met each other.

Ambrose is at the end of the road, quite literally, since you can't cross the Red River into Oklahoma at that point. The school closed years ago and the kids are bussed six miles over to Bells, Texas. The old school building is now used as a community center. They lost their post office a while back and the mail comes by rural mail delivery. But there is still a church and the folks are a friendly lot who take care of their own.

I fell in love with the small towns in that area as well as the cowboys and their stories. Lucas is from Savoy, not far from Bells. Greg has lived on a ranch in Ravenna his whole life, and Mason lives just outside of Whitewright with his twin daughters.

So begins a brand-new venture in a brand-new area of Texas. Trust me, the cowboys are sexy and the ladies that capture their hearts are very sassy. Here's hoping that you settle in real well with these folks and enjoy reading all about the cowboys from north Texas.

Many thanks to my fabulous editor, Deb Werksman,

and all the staff at Sourcebooks who turn my manuscripts into gorgeous books. I'd like to thank Sourcebooks once again for continuing to publish my books. Also thank you to my agent Erin Niumata and the folks at Folio Literary Management. And Husband, the man who is always ready at the drop of a hat to go with me anywhere I want to go for research. He even drives and takes tons of pictures for me so my hands can be free to take notes. It takes a special person to be the spouse of an author and he has my utmost love and appreciation.

And a very, very big thank you to all you readers! Y'all are truly the wind beneath my wings!

All my best,
Carolyn Brown

Read on for a sneak peek at

Cowboy Seeks Bride

coming August 2013 from Sourcebooks Casablanca

If it was an April Fools' joke, it damn sure wasn't funny.

If it wasn't a joke, it was a disaster.

Those five big horses complete with cowboys didn't look like a joke. Cattle bawling and milling around looked pretty damned real, too. And that little covered wagon, with a bald-headed man the size of a refrigerator sitting on the buckboard holding the reins for two horses in his hands, didn't have a single funny thing about it, either.

Haley's mouth went dry when she realized that the big dapple gray horse was for her and that absolutely nothing in front of her was a practical joke. It was all as real as the smell of the horses and what they'd dropped on the ground.

She slung open the door of her little red sports car. The cowboys were all slack jawed, as if they'd never seen a woman before. Well, they'd best tie a rope around their chins and draw them back up because she was going to be their sidekick for the next thirty days. They could like it or hate it. It didn't really matter to her. All she wanted to do was get the month over with and go home to civilization.

"You lose your way?" The cowboy on a big black

horse looked down at her. His tone was icy and his deep green eyes even colder.

"Not if this is the O'Donnell horse ranch and you're about to take off on the Chisholm Trail reenactment." She looked up into the dark-haired cowboy's green sexy eyes. "Who are you?" She planted her high heels on the ground and got out of the car.

"Dewar O'Donnell, and you are?"

Dammit! With a name like Dewar, she'd pictured a sixty-year-old man with a rim of graying hair circling an otherwise bald head, and a face wrinkled up like the earth after a hard summer complete with a day's growth of gray whiskers. He sure wasn't supposed to look like Timothy Olyphant with Ben Bass's eyes. It was going to be one hell of a month because she wasn't about to get involved with a cowboy. Not even if she had the sudden urge to crawl right up on that horse and see if those eyes were as dreamy up close as they were from ten feet away.

"I'm H. B. Mckay," she answered.

"Well, shit!" Dewar drawled.

"I know. Life's a bitch, isn't it? But I'll be riding along this whole trip taking notes for the reality show to be filmed this summer," she said. "Unless you want to tell me that this is a big silly joke and I can go home to Dallas now."

"Can't do that, ma'am. I was expecting you to be a man, but we're ready to move this herd north, so I guess you'd better saddle up. I was just about to call Carl Levy and ask where you were," Dewar drawled.

"That's the idea most people have. I guess that empty horse is for me and I don't get to drive from point to point and stay in a hotel?"

"That's the plan Carl made," he answered.

She crossed her arms over her chest. "So we are ready to go right now?"

"Unless you want to change clothes," he said.

"Hell, no! I'm wearing what I've got on, and if I get a single snag in this suit, Daddy will be paying for a brand-new one," she said.

Dewar frowned. "Daddy?"

"Carl Levy is my father as well as my boss."

Dewar had always had a liking for redheads, but not the kind that wore high-heeled shoes and business suits. And it seemed like here lately he'd dated every redhead in the whole northern part of Texas. Because both of his brothers and his two sisters had beat him to the altar, now everyone in the family thought they had a PhD in matchmaking and had made it their life mission to get him married off.

He'd rebelled at first, but then he admitted that he really wanted to have a wife and family so he'd started looking around on his own. He hadn't joined one of those online dating services, but he had been dating a lot. Either he was too damn picky or else all the good ones were taken because very few women interested him enough for a second date.

H. B.'s eyes were a soft aqua, somewhere between blue and green like the still deep waters of the ocean. And her lips full, the kind that begged for kisses. He felt a stirring down deep in his heart that he hadn't felt before, but he didn't know if it was anger or desire.

It really didn't matter because the whole damn thing

had to be a joke. It was too ridiculous to be real. Raylen had cooked it up and paid some woman to help him pull it off. He pulled his cell phone from his shirt pocket and quickly punched in the numbers to the office of the Dallas magazine tycoon.

"Carl Levy, please."

Ten long seconds later, "Tell him this is Dewar O'Donnell and this is definitely an emergency."

H.B. shook her head and took her saddlebags from her car. "You are wasting your time, cowboy."

Dewar hooked a leg over the saddle horn and ignored her. "Carl, I've got a red-haired woman who says she's H. B. McKay. You want to verify that?"

He frowned.

"You led me to believe that H. B. was a man, sir. A woman hasn't got any business on a cattle drive."

H. B. yelled over the noise of bawling cattle, snorting horses, and grinning men. "Tell him Momma is going to throw a Cajun fit, and if he's smart he'll walk in the house with roses in one hand and an apology on his lips."

"Yes, sir, that was her," Dewar said.

She held out her hand. "Give me that phone."

Dewar leaned down and put it in her hand.

"You are going to pay for this, Daddy. I'm pissed off worse than I've ever been before in my life. I'm so pissed off that I'm not even going to talk to you about it and you can tell Joel that I know he's behind this shit and I'll get even with him when I get home."

Everything went silent. Even the cows stopped bawling.

"Stop laughing. I'll show you what I can do, but you are going to be sorry. Believe me, you are going to regret it."

She handed the phone back to Dewar. “He says to tell you good luck. You ready?”

He put the phone back in his pocket and nodded toward the dapple gray horse. “Soon as you tie down those bags and mount up. Apache is spirited, but he’s tough. You ever ridden?”

“Once or twice,” she answered.

Cowboy Tough

by Joanne Kennedy

Being a cowboy is all he knows…

Bronc-buster Mack Boyd can ride a wild stallion to a standstill, but he can't say no when his family prevails on him to come home and help run the ranch. The last person he expects to find there is a high-class Easterner like Cat Crandall.

But no cowboy can rein her in…

When Cat Crandall gives up a lucrative advertising job to follow her artistic dreams, she's thinking Paris, Tuscany—not the vast and lonely open country of Wyoming. Her success at Boyd Ranch's artists' retreat could be her ticket to far more exotic places… but the rough and rugged cowboy she meets there is giving Cat a different kind of inspiration.

"Packs a powerful, emotional punch, and when it comes to capturing the appeal and feel of the West and its people, nobody does it better."—*Booklist*

"A truly wonderful cast of characters along with an entertaining story line… a must-read."
—*Book Reviews and More By Kathy*

About the Author

Carolyn Brown is a *New York Times* and *USA Today* bestselling author with more than sixty books published, and credits her eclectic family for her humor and writing ideas. Her books include the cowboy trilogy (*Lucky in Love*, *One Lucky Cowboy*, and *Getting Lucky*), the Honky Tonk series (*I Love This Bar*; *Hell, Yeah*; *Honky Tonk Christmas*; and *My Give a Damn's Busted*), and her bestselling Spikes & Spurs series (*Love Drunk Cowboy*, *Red's Hot Cowboy*, *Darn Good Cowboy Christmas*, *One Hot Cowboy Wedding*, *Mistletoe Cowboy*, and *Just a Cowboy and His Baby*). Carolyn has launched into women's fiction as well with *The Blue-Ribbon Jalapeño Society Jubilee*. She was born in Texas but grew up in southern Oklahoma where she and her husband, Charles, a retired English teacher, make their home. They have three grown children and enough grandchildren to keep them young.

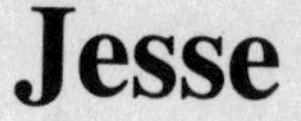

Jesse

by C.H. Admirand

Loneliness will take a man places…

Jesse Garahan has plenty of Irish charm, but having had his heart demolished twice, he's sworn off women forever. Until the fateful day he meets Danielle Brockway and her tiny daughter on their way to their new home in Pleasure, Texas.

But there may be places he doesn't want to go…

Fiercely protective of her little girl, Danielle isn't about to let Jesse get anywhere close enough to hurt either of them, no matter how much longing she sees in his eyes…

Praise for* Dylan*:

"Readers will be left panting."
—*RT Book Reviews*, 4.5 Stars

For more C.H. Admirand, visit:

www.sourcebooks.com